3 0063 00221 5806

Fairmount   Oct 2016

DAVENPORT PUBLIC LIBRARY
321 MAIN STREET
DAVENPORT, IOWA 52801

TRUE-BLUE
COWBOY
Christmas

DISCARD

NICOLE HELM

D1411444

casablanca

Copyright © 2016 by Nicole Helm
Cover and internal design © 2016 by Sourcebooks, Inc.
Cover art by Blake Morrow

Sourcebooks and the colophon are registered trademarks of Sourcebooks,
Inc.

All rights reserved. No part of this book may be reproduced in any form
or by any electronic or mechanical means including information storage
and retrieval systems—except in the case of brief quotations embodied
in critical articles or reviews—without permission in writing from its
publisher, Sourcebooks, Inc.

The characters and events portrayed in this book are fictitious or are
used fictitiously. Any similarity to real persons, living or dead, is
purely coincidental and not intended by the author.

Published by Sourcebooks Casablanca, an imprint of Sourcebooks, Inc.
P.O. Box 4410, Naperville, Illinois 60567-4410
(630) 961-3900
Fax: (630) 961-2168
www.sourcebooks.com

Printed and bound in Canada.
MBP 10 9 8 7 6 5 4 3 2 1

To Mom and Grandma Taylor, who always made Christmas magic.

Chapter 1

FOR SUMMER SHAW, HAPPINESS WAS MADE OF SIMPLE pleasures—a place to call her own, a little patch of land, the big open sky, and food in her stomach. All that was why Shaw Ranch wasn't just happy, it was heaven. Here, she also had family—as evidenced by the tiny week-old niece she held in her arms.

"She's just the most beautiful thing I've ever seen."

"So you've said, approximately three hundred times." Mel sighed, closing her eyes and sinking into the living room couch. "Today alone."

"Why don't you take a nap? I can handle Lissa for an hour or so."

"No, I'm fine." Mel yawned, curling her legs onto the couch. "I'll just close my eyes for a few seconds."

"Of course you will," Summer placated, cradling the baby in one arm while she draped an afghan across Mel with the other. "Your mama needs to learn that she can't do everything," Summer whispered to the bundle in her arms.

"I heard that," Mel mumbled without any heat.

Summer tiptoed out of the room. With any luck, Mel would relax and sleep—at least until Lissa needed to eat again. Mel and Summer's tentative relationship still had its moments of awkwardness, and had since Summer had showed up on the ranch's doorstep over a year ago. But the changes that came with Mel's pregnancy and Lissa's birth had smoothed over those last pockets of distance.

They finally had something to bond them together, so they could get past being so wary of each other.

Summer hummed to the beautiful baby girl, walking her to the den at the end of the house. It was a cluttered, messy room that smelled of old magazines and dirt. Summer liked how it held the distinctive signs of the most recently married Shaw couple: her brother Caleb's ranch magazines and her new sister-in-law Delia's gardening tools stored for the winter.

This space had everything Summer wanted—comfort, the evidence of family, and the big window that looked out over mountains, barns, and so much of the Shaw ranch.

Winter held Montana in its grip, the mountains heavily snow-peaked, the world around her white and glittering. She missed the warmth of summer, but she couldn't bring herself to miss California, even as she entered her second Montana winter. It would be harsh and long, but the upcoming holidays would warm up this interminable season. Her family would gather, and they would celebrate. This was a family who treated her as a person instead of a belonging—albeit a person they didn't know what to do with.

At this point, it was mainly just her father who kept his distance. He had apologized, though, for treating her with silence when she first showed up. And he'd apologized for doing nothing to stop Summer's mother from leaving him even though he had known she'd been pregnant with Summer when she left. He'd explained that he'd had to let her mother go so that he could keep Mel safe with him.

Even so, Summer wasn't one hundred percent sure what to do with that apology, or with the dread that lived in her heart. Because who knew which of her mother's stories were true? She might *not* belong here. Summer winced at the little prick of conscience she felt. She had been at Shaw for almost a year and a half, and she couldn't let that possibility ever take this away.

The Shaws were her family. They never needed to know that there was doubt.

Summer took a deep breath. She'd spent a lifetime—short though twenty-three years might be—learning to soak up life's good moments. She'd learned every deep-breathing, positive-thinking, centered-life meditation and practiced them with every fiber of her being. She breathed day and night, through thick and thin, happy and sad.

That had kept her going, all through the unpredictable prison that had been her life with Mom, and the new freedom she'd found in Montana and at Shaw.

Still, nothing was perfect. Even in moments like this one, holding this newborn—her *niece*—in front of the most beautiful landscape she'd ever seen, the joy could be jarred. A knot formed in the pit of her stomach. Tiny at first. A little pebble. But eventually it would grow until she had a boulder sitting on her chest.

Because a life spent collecting these few-and-far-between perfect moments had taught her one thing: Just when she thought she was on the right track—happy, peaceful, *home*—life would have other plans.

She closed her eyes against the certainty. *Please don't take Shaw away from me. I can handle anything but that.*

Anything but that.

A beat. A breath.

Summer opened her eyes, and her gaze drifted toward the tree line around her little home. An odd structure built onto the back of an old truck, she always referred to it as her caravan. The Shaw land and house had become an extension of home, but the caravan was its heart. It was the thing she'd built. That was something no one could take away. Her home. Her ability to survive. Those were all hers.

Lissa fussed, and Summer began to sing one of the slow country love songs the regulars at Pioneer Spirit tended to drift off to.

At her second glimpse of the caravan way off in the trees, she didn't pay much attention to the little dot of red. The vehicle was a colorful thing as it was. She'd repainted the outside this summer, a vibrant purple and blue to mimic the sky at dusk.

But that red was off. She squinted, noticing the dot of color was moving. It was too big to be a bird, too red to be…well, anything else, but so far away it was impossible to make out clearly.

Her stomach dropped with the sour fear she thought she'd gotten over, except for in her dreams. Surely it wasn't big enough to be her mother. Surely, *surely* Mom wouldn't have followed her here. But that bright, vibrant red had always been one of Mom's favorites.

Run.

Panic bubbled up in Summer's chest, and she backed away from the window. She couldn't let Linda get up here, especially couldn't let her talk to any Shaws. Linda would turn them against Summer and ruin everything Summer's life had become. Who knew what damage she could inflict on the Shaws, on this place Summer was finally beginning to think of as home.

She turned on her heel. She wasn't going to run. She'd promised herself she would never run away again. So, she'd fight.

It was not her mother.

After settling Lissa back with Mel and failing to stay calm or nonchalant, Summer dashed across the snow-packed land that separated the Shaw house from her caravan. She arrived breathless and near tears, only to find a little girl. A little girl dressed in red. Red coat, red boots, even her pants were red. She had a shock of unruly, curly blond hair, and she stared at Summer with big, blue eyes.

Summer wasn't great at guessing ages, but the girl had to be old enough for elementary school, though probably not much older than that.

"Hello," Summer offered once she could breathe almost normally. "Are you lost?"

The girl continued her wide-eyed staring.

"Are you okay?" Summer pressed, taking a few uncertain steps toward her. She didn't know of any neighbor children. A few families around the ranch made sure not to associate with any of the Shaws. There was a lot of not-so-pleasant history there, mainly involving Caleb being a bit of a ne'er-do-well as an adolescent.

"Are you a fairy?" the little girl whispered.

Summer's eyebrows shot up. Maybe the girl was really lost—days lost and delirious. "No, sweetheart. Are you cold? Hungry?"

"Are you an angel?"

"No, just a human."

Summer carefully knelt in front of the girl. She knew what it was like for strangers to approach you, touch you, speak to you, and leave you uncomfortable.

Summer swallowed a lump in her throat, swallowed away old, bad memories, and resisted the urge to touch the girl to see if she was shivering. It was far too cold for a little girl to be left wandering around.

"Is that yours?" The little girl nodded toward the caravan.

"Yes."

"It looks like a fairy palace."

Summer smiled. *Fairy palace* might not have been the aesthetic she was going for, but *colorful* and *free* meant different things to different people. Maybe that description was about right.

"It's a little cold to be walking around alone. Can I help you get back to your house?"

"I got a little lost." She bit her bottom lip, the downy, pale slashes of her eyebrows drawing together. "Daddy will be mad." The little girl's big, blue eyes filled with tears.

The chill in the air was no match for the chill in Summer's heart. Angry fathers weren't something she had any experience with, but angry parents or adults who scared children… She knew them, and the memory was disturbing.

She felt immediately protective of this lost and scared little girl. Poor thing. She needed a friend.

"I'm Summer. What's your name?" She held out her hand. An offer, if the girl felt so inclined to take it.

The girl opened her mouth, but before any sound came out, a man's voice bellowed through the trees. "*Kate!*"

Instinctively, Summer stepped between the trees and the girl. The little thing didn't need an angry man yelling at her when she was lost, teary, and scared, whether he was her father or not. Parentage wasn't a get-out-of-being-a-monster-free card for anyone. "If you want to hide—"

But the dot of red darted around her.

"Daddy! I'm here!" Kate waved her red mittens and jumped up and down, then got distracted by the snow puffing up in drifts as she jumped. She giggled, kicking the snow in powdery arcs, any threat of tears gone.

"Katherine." The man burst through the tree line. He was obviously furious and frustrated, but the predominant emotion on his face was neither of those things.

He was *terrified*.

Summer knew she should soften. A man who felt terror as he searched for his missing daughter was more than likely not the kind of man who would hurt her as well.

Or so one would hope.

But Mom had been loving and thoughtful one minute, quick to raise her hand the next. Everything inside Summer coiled into a tight, tense ball. It took a great feat of strength not to reach out and grab the bundle of red away from the man. A lot of people were very, *very* good actors, after all. She had found people who were honest and good as well. She just had no idea which one he was.

The father sank to his knees in front of the girl, grabbing her shoulders. "What are you doing? You can't keep doing this to me." He ran his gloved hands down her arms and over her face, as though he was checking for an injury. Once he was satisfied, he pulled the bundle of red against his chest. For a few quiet minutes, he simply held her there, his eyes closed, some of the tension in his shoulders draining away, clearly moved and relieved that she was unharmed.

"I'm sorry, Daddy. But look." She pointed at Summer, a bright smile showing off two missing front teeth. "I found a fairy palace."

For the first time, he looked at Summer. He got to his feet, his mouth tightening into a frown. He was a tall man, a broad man, and neither the puffy work jacket nor the cowboy hat that now shadowed his face could do anything to hide the obvious—that he would be far stronger and more powerful than her.

"Who are you?" he said. No, that was too kind—his tone was all demand as he stepped in front of Kate as if he could shield her from Summer.

Summer wanted to shrink away or hide, but she'd learned something about standing up even when it was the scariest thing imaginable. "Maybe I should be asking *you* that."

"Why are you talking to my dau—" Kate grabbed the hem of his coat and he stopped.

"Daddy," she whispered, tugging on his coat. She grinned up at Summer. "She's a fairy *queen*. Just like in the bedtime book."

"We're going home." He moved his daughter by the shoulder, steering her toward the trees that separated Summer's clearing from a fence she'd never crossed. She'd never even given a thought to what lay beyond it, because Shaw had been enough. Shaw felt safe.

For some reason, nothing beyond that fence ever had.

Chapter 2

THACK DIDN'T SPEAK AS HE MARCHED KATE BACK TO THE ranch. All he did was hold on to her hand and text Dad with his free one.

Found. Okay.

He didn't trust himself to say much of anything. Yelling wasn't the answer. Blubbering all over her *certainly* wasn't the answer, even though that's all he'd wanted to do after he'd spent a good half an hour searching the property for her. Finding no sign of her.

The problem was that he had no idea what the answer was anymore. If he couldn't trust Dad to keep an eye on her, and he couldn't trust her to follow the rules, would he have to trust someone else?

Not an option. Not if Kate was going to run away and talk to strangers. A woman he'd *never* seen before, and Kate had been all but curled up in her lap. She could be anyone. She could pose any danger. She could have kidnapped Kate easy as you please.

Thack took a deep breath and let it out. Kate was safe. *For now*.

The ranch came into view. The house he'd grown up in. The house he was busting his butt to keep up with. From the outside, covered in snow, it looked picture perfect, if a little dull, with sun-bleached logs and roof. But as winter settled in and work with the cattle became mainly feeds and ice breaks and keeping the herd alive, Thack's attention had to shift to fixing everything that had been ignored during the hectic spring and summer months.

The barn needed a new roof and door. The back porch on the house needed a new joist, which would be a pain to replace in all the snow, but the floor was currently a danger to his rebellious daughter.

"Daddy…"

"You know you're not supposed to wander off like that," he said, exhausted. Wrung out. "It's dangerous. Not to mention you left the property. That is absolutely one hundred percent against the rules." The things that could have happened to her while he was looking the other way…

Kate huffed out a breath. "But I saw a fairy palace! And I knew just where I was." She tugged her hand out of his grasp. "Kinda."

"You're not supposed to wander alone. You're not supposed to cross the fence. You're not supposed to…" He trailed off. This had been a constant refrain for how long? She just didn't listen, and Dad didn't listen either.

Kate ran across the yard and up to the porch where Dad was standing and flung her arms around his waist. He patted her back and said something Thack couldn't hear. Thack took his time crossing the yard, hoping to rein in some of his frustration before he spoke to his father.

When he reached them, he looked at Kate instead of Dad. "I'm very disappointed in you. You did something you knew very well you were not supposed to do. Go to your room, and do not come out until I come talk to you."

"But I'm hungry." Big, blue eyes looked imploringly up at him. Because she was too smart a kid not to know how to hit him where he couldn't deny her.

"Up to your room. I'll bring you something to eat once I talk to your grandfather."

She grumbled something under her breath that sounded a lot like "mean Dad," and then ran inside. The sound of her crying echoed out the door, in his ears, and down into his chest. Everything *hurt*, and every time he thought they'd outgrown the hard part, more hard parts cropped up.

You are doing this all wrong.

He finally met his father's gaze. Why couldn't he get this man to listen? Dad had his own way of doing things, and it didn't matter how much Thack begged for coopation. Dad still did what he'd always done—whatever the hell *he* thought was right.

"We can't keep doing this," Thack said, irritated that his voice was hoarse instead of harsh.

"Now, Son, I know you had a bit of a scare." Dad turned away, as if this wasn't important. As if Kate being safe in the end made everything okay.

"She wasn't even on the property."

"But Shaw's right next door."

"She crossed the property line. If she had wandered onto Parker land, she could have fallen into their pond. She could have come across a wild animal." All the promises he'd given Michaela would have been broken, and he could have lost Kate, his most precious gift. The thought was unbearable. "She could have been ab—"

"Boy, she isn't an infant. She's seven. Your mother and I let you—"

"I don't care. I do not care. There is nothing about what you and Mom did that pertains to my daughter."

"My granddaughter. You can't lock her up. You can't magically keep her from the dangers of the world."

"She's *seven*! That is my job." But he couldn't do it and run the ranch at the same time. Not without someone he could count on. If he couldn't even leave Kate with his own father, who the hell *was* he supposed to trust? "She was with a stranger, Dad. A complete and utter stranger, and I have no idea for how long. I don't know what was said or done. That woman could have given her drugs or told her to—"

"On Shaw property? You sure it wasn't the Shaw boy's wife? He got married last month, was it?"

"No, it wasn't her."

"Oh, was it the mystery sister? You know, talk over town is that she—"

"It doesn't matter who it was. It matters that it could have been anyone. It matters that Kate is too young to be wandering the property alone."

"That's how you learn to be a man. A Lane. You explore—"

"She's not a man. She is a little girl."

"Now, isn't that the sexism they're always talking about?"

Thack shook his head. He couldn't do this and keep his anger under control, and as much as he'd love to lay into his father, lay into anybody or anything really, he'd made a promise to himself ever since they'd lost Michaela.

He would never be the kind of man his daughter would fear. He would be even-tempered and fair. She would always know she was loved and safe. They had sacrificed so much to bring her into the world, and he wouldn't let anything, *anything* happen to her.

Lord knew life had tested every last inch of that promise, but he wasn't about to let it go. That promise was the only thing keeping them all sane. He hoped.

So he walked inside instead. His first stop had to be the kitchen, since Dad had probably let her eat pickles and ketchup and juice for lunch. That was all Kate ever wanted. Well, this time she was getting a sandwich. He'd make sure she ate real food, even if that made him the bad guy again.

He kept thinking things would let up, but Halloween was bearing down on him, and Thanksgiving would be here before he knew it, before he got half his repairs done, and then it would be Christmas and a brand-new year. He kept putting little Band-Aids on things, only to have them fall off altogether.

Thack paused with the sandwich half made, closing his eyes against a fresh wave of helplessness and hope-lessness. Would he ever get to the other side? The side where things went smoothly? Where he didn't have to worry and micromanage and just...be petrified every second she wasn't in his sight?

"You need help."

He didn't spare his father a glance, because he would lose his shaky battle with emotion if he did. "You're supposed to be my help."

"We need a woman around here. It's been—"

"Do *not* go there. Mom's been gone how long?"

"Not the same."

"Exactly the same. Fifteen years. You haven't even looked at another woman."

"I wouldn't go that far. I just didn't let you know about it."

"It doesn't matter. Kate is all I have room for." Dear God, how could he possibly add another relationship to his life when every spare minute was stretched as thin as possible? And he was supposed to add a woman? For *help*. Right, because relationships like that didn't take any time at all.

"Well, at the very least you could make room for a housekeeper. Or a nanny. I know you don't like the idea of trusting anyone else, but we do need help. Even if I did everything the way you want me to with that girl—which I won't, because you can't cage her up like an animal—we can't do it alone anymore."

"Why? We got through the hard years. The baby years and the toddler years. She's in school now. She—"

"She needs more than just us, Thackery. The sooner you accept that, the happier we'll all be." Dad left without giving him a chance to respond.

Not that Thack had anything to say. He wanted to be everything his daughter needed. He was trying so hard. She deserved everything he could give her, and yet it all seemed to come up short.

But what could a stranger offer? Bringing in a *nanny*. It was like paying someone to love Kate, paying someone to give her their time and false affection until they moved on to the next job and left Kate behind. She didn't need any more loss. The problem with people was they always left. Whether willingly or not, they left.

Kate had already had enough of that to last a lifetime. Why would he willingly add more?

Frustrated with himself, with *life*, Thack trudged upstairs with a sandwich and a juice box.

When he opened Kate's door, she was sprawled on her bed, looking at one of her books. Michaela had loved to read, so her parents had shipped all her childhood books to them when they'd found out Kate was a girl.

Memories like that, so out of the blue, could gut Thack a million different ways. If only Michaela had been able to see this: their daughter so perfect and happy, enjoying what Michaela had enjoyed as a little girl.

"Daddy. Look." She waved him over to the book she was inspecting so closely. "See! It looks just like it."

Thack crossed the room, taking a seat on the floor next to her bed. The book she handed him was one he'd read to her a million times at least. He looked at the fairy castle illustration on the page Kate held open.

"That's green and pink. Hers was blue. And this is surrounded by flowers. That place was surrounded by snow. But it had trees just like this." Kate pointed at the illustration animatedly. "And she looked just like the fairy queen. See? She had brown hair tied with a ribbon, and a big skirt like that, and—"

"You know she's not a fairy, Katherine Marie."

Kate sighed. "I know, but it's fun to pretend." She closed the book and grabbed for the juice box, but he held it back.

"Five bites."

"Ugh." She took the sandwich, putting the bread just barely to her lips, taking a bite so minuscule he was certain she got nothing but air.

"No juice box until you take five *real* bites."

"What about five fairy bites?" she asked hopefully, even though they had this same conversation and struggle at almost every meal.

"No, ma'am."

She rolled her eyes, and he saw a glimpse into her teenage years. His heart all but stopped beating. How would he ever survive this?

You just will.

They were Dad's words, after they'd buried Michaela. Dad had promised, so somehow Thack had made it through.

For her. For Kate. For the daughter who could be lost to him just as easily as his wife had been. "I know it's hard sometimes, but you have to follow the rules, Kate. You have to. The rules will keep you safe."

"It's so boring when no one will explore with me," she whined, taking an air bite as if he wouldn't notice.

"You're always welcome to come riding with me."

She wrinkled her nose. "It's boring. You just fix fences and stuff."

Just fix fences and stuff. A seven-year-old's description of his life's work was not exactly flattering. "I thought you liked the horses."

"I like to watch them run. Grandpa read me this story about Pocahontas, and she got up on the horse and it flew, and can I—"

"No."

Kate flopped on her bed. "Why is everything so *boring*?"

Thack looked up at the ceiling. The only time he'd been bored as a kid had been when he was trapped in the house on blizzard days or in English class. He was doing a disservice to Kate by letting her be bored, but why did everything she want to do have to be so damn dangerous?

"Would it help if…we had someone come watch you in the afternoons?"

"Like a babysitter?"

"Well, more like…someone to play with."

"But Grandpa plays with me."

Thack didn't say what he wanted to. That he didn't trust *Grandpa* or anyone else. That she was the most precious thing in his life, and no one seemed to take that nearly as seriously as they should. But he was going to have to make an effort to trust, just a little, for her.

"Can it be a girl?"

"I don't know yet, Katie Pie. Would you listen and follow the rules?"

Kate looked at him slyly. "Could it be the fairy queen?"

"Absolutely not." The *fairy queen* was some stranger at the center of the town's gossip. She would not be the answer to his needs. And she didn't look anything like a fairy. A hippie, maybe. Trouble, definitely. Beautiful and fierce together were always trouble. Just like the girl on her bed taking fairy bites, reading fairy stories, and wanting to ride flying horses.

"Did that lady say anything to you?"

"No. She was just trying to help."

Yeah, she probably was.

"Well, whoever it is will at least have to know *some* fairy stories. And know how to make that stuff I had at Grandma and Grandpa Jenks's house that one time we visited. What was that stuff?"

"Pot roast." He had a seven-year-old who thought a pot roast was magic.

"Do you know how to make pot roast, Daddy? Can we have it for Christmas this year?"

"I'll see what I can do." He couldn't ignore the situation any longer, not with Christmas less than three months away. Not with a daughter whose imagination was bigger than the ivory tower he was so desperate to keep her safe and sound inside.

Dad was right. They needed help.

Chapter 3

SUMMER STALKED BACK TO THE SHAW RANCH. SHE WAS going to make sure that girl was safe. Mel and Caleb would have more info on the guy, probably. Hopefully. They'd be able to reassure her, or help the little girl, or do whatever needed to be done.

Because in her experience, little girls didn't attempt to run away from home unless their lives were isolated and unhappy. Her experience wasn't exactly normal, of course, but that didn't matter.

She couldn't push that little niggle of fear away. Not when she knew exactly what could happen.

She burst into the Shaw house to find Delia and Caleb in the mudroom, bundled up in boots and coats. Mel stood in the hall just outside, bouncing Lissa.

"There you are. We were about to send a search party. What's going on?" Mel demanded.

"I..." It hit her with a force she didn't expect. Three people were demanding to know where she'd been, not because they were angry or inconvenienced, but because they were worried about her. She wanted to hug them all tight, maybe cry a little, but the Shaws were not the demonstrative type. There were times when she was scared to let them know how much it meant—to belong, to feel loved.

She had to clear her throat to talk, and everyone exchanged glances. They were *Summer's being emotional again* looks, but she didn't mind. It was nice that they had looks that meant something about her.

"I thought I saw someone down at the caravan, and when I got there, there was a little girl."

"A little girl?" Caleb repeated. "How little?"

"Probably elementary-school age. I guess she was lost. Her father found her, but…"

"That was probably the Lane girl. The fence on the east side of your caravan is on the line between our ranch and the Lane property. She'd be about that age," Mel offered.

"And you know them?"

"Well, sort of. I mean, when I was running Shaw, Thack and Merle and I would talk on occasion. Good ranchers."

"But are they good *people*? Do you think that girl is safe?"

"Safe?" Mel exchanged a look with Caleb, but it was one of their unreadable sibling looks that didn't make Summer smile. That kind made her feel set apart, left out. She might be their sister, but she hadn't grown up with them. She was still an outsider.

"I've never had any reason to believe the Lanes are anything but good people."

"It's just that he was angry with her. And…I don't know. I got a weird vibe." She turned to her sister-in-law, because unfortunately she knew Delia was her best target on this.

"It's not really your business, Summer," Mel said.

If someone had *made* it their business when she was a little girl, she wouldn't have been used like a prop, like a doll, having to fend off inappropriate advances for most of her childhood. Dodging the volatile whims of a woman Summer didn't understand to this day.

"Look, Summer, I know Thack Lane too. He isn't

the type," Delia offered, as an attempt to appease, Summer supposed.

"Because there's only one type?" It wasn't like her to lash out at Delia. Considering Delia would know all about what an actual abusive father looked like, Summer knew she shouldn't have. "I'm sorry. I just got a feeling and wanted to make sure I was overreacting."

"I think you are," Mel said firmly. "The Lanes have been through a lot. I know you mean well—of course you do. But if his daughter was lost, Thack was probably worried sick. Wandering off in these parts can have real consequences for kids."

Mel seemed to hold her bundle a little tighter, and Summer blew out a breath. She should trust these people, people who actually knew the family.

"He glared at me like I'd been the one to let his child wander off his property."

"I'll have a talk with him."

Summer looked balefully at her brother. The note of protectiveness in his voice warmed her heart, but it wasn't what she wanted. "I don't need to be protected from the big, bad wolf. I just need to know that no one should be stepping in on the little girl's behalf."

"I'd be very surprised, Summer."

Which didn't tell her much of anything. That little girl had been alone on Summer's property, cold and *alone*. Scared…before her father had arrived.

But even if her siblings didn't see a problem, that didn't mean Summer shouldn't listen to her gut. She could make sure the little girl was okay on her own.

How, she had no idea, but she'd think on it until she thought of something.

———∿∿∿———

"I'm not going to put fliers up, for Christ's sake," Thack said to his father while cleaning up Midnight after a full day of ranch maintenance. Kate was making a snowman just outside the barn in the fading twilight, and Thack looked at her so often that it was taking twice as long as usual to get the horse bedded for the evening.

"How else are you going to find someone?"

"I'll ask her teacher when I drop her off at school Monday. Maybe she'll know someone trustworthy. Or I'll ask Garrett." Surely between a police officer and a school employee who had to have background checks, he could find *someone* he could trust his daughter with. His girl, the seven-year-old who was his entire life, whom he'd promised to protect from everything.

Sure, there was someone out there he could trust. *And Midnight could grow wings and fly.*

"I called up Cal."

"Cal Shaw?" Dad had been good friends with Cal Shaw years ago, but ever since Cal's paralysis and both men losing their wives to different things—cancer, divorce—Cal had been something of a hermit.

"I was asking about that daughter of his. The mystery one. He said she's a nice girl. Does a bit of housekeeping for him and Caleb, though not as much now that Caleb's gotten married."

"This better not be going where I think it's going."

"I know it's a bit silly, but Kate wants the fairy queen, so why not—"

"No."

"Yes! The fairy queen. Da-a-addy."

Somehow Kate was in between them in a flash, jumping up and down and clapping her gloved hands together. "Please, Daddy. Please, please, please—"

"You don't even know her." He raised his gaze to his father. "And as much as I always liked Cal, I'm not sure I trust his judgment these days. Not with Caleb running things."

"Married now."

"To as big of a screwup as he was."

"Well, we ain't asking those two. We'd be asking the younger one."

"On Cal's word? We don't know anything about her—where she came from, why she's a mystery, where the hell she's been."

"Cal said his wife was pregnant when she left for California. So, that's where she's been."

"And that's that?"

"I'm not saying that's that. I'm saying it's what your little girl wants. You might as well look into it."

"Did you talk to Mel?"

"She wasn't there. Living over at the old Paulle place with that hockey-player husband of hers. They have a baby and—"

"Yes, I know." Thack didn't understand his dad's love of knowing what was going on with everyone in Blue Valley. Didn't they have enough on their own plate without knowing everyone else's business?

"Daddy. She's in the book! It's like a sign. Like… like…Mary Poppins or something. I dreamed her, and she appeared."

"That isn't it at all, honey."

"Oh, let the girl have her daydreams."

Thack pressed his lips together so he wouldn't respond. He didn't like arguing with Dad in front of Kate, especially since it always made him look like the bad guy. He loved his daughter's imagination, but he didn't think he needed to encourage her real-life application of it.

"I'm going to talk to a few people and see if they know of anyone. We have to find someone we can *all* trust, and someone who's…going to be a good role model." Thack rolled his eyes at himself because Kate certainly did not care about having a good role model.

But *he* cared. He wanted someone who was going to take the job, and Kate, and his wishes seriously. Someone who wasn't going to leave if they got a better job or decided to move. Kate needed a solid core. She'd lost enough without ever really knowing it.

Life might have a way of taking people from him, from her, but that didn't mean he had to willingly expose Kate to more hurt.

"Son."

Thack hated when Dad used that soft, concerned tone of voice on him. The sympathetic one. Because for all Dad's faults, he'd always been here, trying to make the best out of being one parent, the only parent.

Thack had been a teenager when his mother died, but he knew it wouldn't matter if Kate were older. He'd still worry, and he still wouldn't measure up.

"It's not going to be perfect."

"It'll be as close as I can get," Thack returned, finishing up with Midnight. "Ready for dinner, Katie Pie?"

"I was reading this book where they had dessert first, and—"

"No."

Although his seven-year-old argued with him the whole walk back to the house, her red-mittened hand tucked in his, and even with the weight of the world on his shoulders, Thack could only be damn grateful for moments that seemed just about right.

Chapter 4

THE NEXT MORNING, SUMMER WOKE TO THE STRANGEST sound. Her caravan door bumped with a series of little thumps, barely audible over the furiously tinkling wind chimes. Summer sat up on her mattress and drew the curtain away from her window to find the world mostly dark.

There was a glow on the horizon toward the Shaw ranch, but the sky was covered in thick clouds that made the light faint at best. She scrubbed a hand over her face, trying to wake herself fully.

The odd thumping persisted. Maybe a board or some part of the roof was loose outside. With all the wind and the threatening winter storms, it would make sense.

Summer ignored the odd sense of foreboding that rippled from that sound. She rolled out of bed and pulled on her winter yoga clothes, layer after layer, to ward off the subzero temperatures. Come rain or shine, snow or blizzard gale, she took her fifteen minutes to reflect on where she had been and where she was now in order to wake up enough to engage with the day.

This time to herself was why she didn't live at the big house, even though she'd been invited. For the first time in her life, she had privacy and solace. Sure, it was a little lonely, but sometimes being with the Shaws was lonely too.

She loved them, she did. But even after over a

year, they treated her like a bit of a museum artifact. Sometimes they seemed reluctant to touch her or to fold her into things too easily. Maybe they were afraid of being reminded of the ways their lives had diverged or that Summer was hiding something about their mother.

Mel and Caleb were two of the strongest people she'd ever met. And that wasn't even counting all they'd done to keep the ranch afloat on their own after their father's accident. Information about their mother had been too much to put on their shoulders after Cal's paralysis and withdrawal from the world.

Summer blew out a breath, got the wood-burning stove going for her morning tea, and then grabbed the detachable stairs she had to put on the ground to step down from the caravan.

But when she unlatched and opened her door, she gasped. The odd thumping sound hadn't been from any storm.

It was the little girl, dressed in red, clutching a book under her arm.

"Hi," she offered above the whirling wind.

"Hi." Summer had to swallow so her heart would stop pounding in her throat. "Are you lost again?"

The girl shook her head. "No. I wanted to show you something."

"Does your father know you're here?"

The girl smiled, a guilty smile that showed off a dimple and way too much charm for anyone's good. "Here. Look at page twenty-eight." She thrust the book at Summer, completely ignoring the question.

Summer had to fight back a return smile. Little Kate was adorable. Formidable, really, and Summer was almost jealous. She couldn't resist stepping down the stairs and opening the book to page twenty-eight. It was a well-loved book about a fairy kingdom, illustrated in a whimsical, almost old-fashioned way.

On the designated page was a painting of a fairy queen with Summer's hair and eye colors, standing next to her palace. Summer smiled. She didn't look exactly like the fairy queen, but based on the conversation yesterday, she knew where the girl was going.

"Sadly, I don't have wings."

"But wouldn't it be amazing if you did? I used to wish for wings every night."

It made Summer a little sad that Kate had already outgrown wishing for something. Even if the girl had new, just as fantastical wishes, she'd already given up on one. "It would be. I think I'd fly to the top of that mountain and watch the sun rise above the clouds."

The girl's face split into a grin so sweet and beautiful that it seemed to light the air around them. "And you could turn the snowcaps into gold and make glitter come out of the sky instead of snow." Round blue eyes met hers. "Don't you think that'd be pretty? Gold glitter snow. And then there'd be gold-capped mountains instead. Right? Wouldn't that be magic?"

Magic. Oh, it was hard to resist anyone who believed in magic and gold-capped mountains.

"Thank you for showing me." Summer held the book back to the girl. "That seems like a really important book. We should probably get you home before it snows. Do you know the way back to your house?"

"Yup."

Even so, Summer wouldn't feel right letting the little girl go on her way alone. "All right, sweetheart. I'm going to walk with you, but first I need you to promise me that…everything is okay there. Because if it's not, I will help. I promise."

Kate cocked her head. "So, if I said it's not okay…"

Summer's heart beat hard in her chest, and she knelt until she was eye level with Kate. Carefully, gently, she touched the girl's shoulder. "I'd help you get away. I *promise*."

Kate frowned. "Oh, I don't want to get *away*."

"Oh." Summer couldn't figure this out. Kate really didn't seem scared or desperate to escape. But then why did she keep showing up?

"I just get bored. Grandpa can't play the games I want to play, and Daddy has to work, and I want to explore." She flung her arms wide. "Like in all my books. I want to hike in the woods and build tents and catch fairies and…" She blew out a frustrated breath. "Daddy doesn't let me do *anything*." She mumbled something after that, but Summer didn't catch it.

Summer got back to her feet. She really did need to get Kate home.

"Let me grab a wrap." She reached inside the door and pulled out the first piece of fabric her hand landed on—a crocheted shawl she'd picked up at some thrift store along the way. It wouldn't do much to ward off the cold, but combined with what she was already wearing, it should do for what was hopefully a short walk there and back.

She locked the caravan door and studied the little girl looking up at the dark, swirling sky with a gap-toothed grin.

So no immediate danger, and the girl didn't want

to escape, but that didn't mean everything was good. Especially if her father wasn't letting her do anything, and she was somehow sneaking out at the crack of dawn.

Something wasn't right. Summer couldn't get over that feeling, and she'd learned to trust her gut. It had gotten her this far in her new life, and she couldn't stop trusting it now.

"All right, lead the way."

"You know, Daddy is going to get somebody to come watch me in the afternoons." Kate slanted Summer a very adult look as they walked through the trees.

"What does your daddy do?" She helped Kate through the fence, then managed to get over it herself.

"Oh, Daddy is like a real-life cowboy. He doesn't like when I say that, though. He says, 'Katherine, I am a rancher. There is a big difference between a cowboy and a rancher.'" She had adopted a low voice and a different posture, and Summer couldn't keep herself from smiling.

Summer wanted to ask about the girl's mother, but she held her tongue. She knew what it was like to be asked about a missing parent when you didn't know how to answer. The girl's mother didn't seem to be in the picture, one way or another. Maybe her father was trying his best, and he was simply overwhelmed. Although, honestly, wasn't it awfully irresponsible to allow the girl to keep escaping like she did?

A house came into view, and Summer's steps slowed. It was…amazing. A vision of what the Shaw ranch could have been if everything at Shaw hadn't been beaten down by age and bad luck. It was a little colorless, maybe, but the cabin was made of gleaming wood that was clearly taken care of year in and year out. There were two peaked windows on the second floor, a stone chimney, and a wraparound porch with a swing that looked like it might need a few repairs, but which somehow added homeyness to the picture.

With craggy mountains in the background, the house was absolutely beautiful, even in the murky dark of a stormy morning. Summer could just imagine it lit up for Christmas, colorful lights wreathed against the pristine snow…

"Daddy is doing chores in the stables. And Grandpa does his secret chores until—"

"Secret chores?" Summer followed Kate around the house toward a stable, also gleaming and sturdy and so different from what they had at Shaw that it was almost jarring. She'd never really considered that there would be parts of Blue Valley without that aura of years of struggle, of being beaten down and out.

No wonder Kate believed in magic. This place *looked* like magic.

"Grandpa has a hard time breathing sometimes, and Daddy said there's certain things he can't do. So Grandpa does his secret chores when Daddy's busy. I can't tell Daddy, but I think he knows."

Summer blinked and tried to wrap her mind around all of that—what it might mean, and what it told her about this place. Kate only talked about two men. Dad and Grandpa. There seemed to be a lot of secrets between all three of them.

Kate stopped a few feet away from the stable and offered that charming smile up to Summer. "We don't *have* to tell Daddy I came to your fairy palace. We could just say…"

"I think it's really important we tell your dad the truth." Summer paused, resisting the urge to touch the girl's arm again. She clutched the shawl closer to her chest instead. "Unless you're afraid."

Kate seemed to consider this, and Summer held her breath. It had nothing to do with her, but she just…she had to step in if the girl needed it. Maybe she'd found this place for a reason and—

"But if you tell, I lose TV privileges for a *week*."

Summer blew out a breath. TV privileges. For heaven's sake. "Well."

"And Grandpa's TV shows are stupid. So, so stupid. It's always people yelling. And then *he* yells at them. And I can't read when he's yelling '*You greedy bastards*.'"

Summer had to press her lips together not to laugh. The girl certainly had her impressions down. "No, that doesn't sound very fun. But, you can't keep coming over if you're not supposed to."

Her whole face lit up. "But I can come over if I have permission?"

"Well, sure. I'm not always home, but I'd be happy to have some company."

Kate clapped her hands together, then grabbed Summer's. "Come on. You just have to make Daddy say yes."

"I don't know—" But Kate was pulling, and Summer couldn't bring herself not to follow. It sounded like the girl did need some fun time, if all she had were a working father and a yelling-at-the-TV grandfather. Summer had to wonder if Kate had friends at school, or if that was against the rules too. Would she have friends to trick-or-treat with or spend Christmas break making snowmen with?

Kate pulled Summer to the door of the stables and then inside. The ground was covered with hay, and there were rows of stalls. Where Shaw only had two horses, this place had at least eight, in a range of different colors. Their sleek heads stuck out over the gates of their stalls.

Kate's father stepped out of one stall, carrying a shovel full of horse poop. He had in earbuds, apparently listening to music as he worked.

The stable was warm, so Summer let the shawl fall to the crook of her elbows. She supposed she should be the one to say something first, but he disappeared into a corner.

Kate marched toward him undeterred, but Summer felt suddenly wary. When he came back into view, he was hefting a bag of feed from a back corner, a low humming sound coming from his mouth.

His back was three-quarters of the way toward them, broad and strong and…um. Wow. He was…*strong*.

The glow of overhead lights glinted against his dark hair and what looked to be a day or two of whisker growth.

Summer tried to swallow or look away or something, but her eyes were glued to the outline of his arm underneath the heavy fabric of his work shirt.

She didn't like this man, so there was certainly no way she could be attracted to him. Besides, he…he…

Muscles.

He happened to glance to the side, then swore, dropping the feed as he turned. He tugged the earbuds free.

"You scared the…" He pressed his mouth into a firm line, arms crossed over his impressive chest as he glared daggers at her.

No, it was not an impressive chest. She'd met lots of cowboys—er—ranchers since she'd moved to Blue Valley, and a lot of them were in decent shape and…

Old.

And plenty were attractive and…

Old.

He wasn't old. He wasn't family either. He was…hot.

She squeezed her eyes shut for a second, trying to draw in a cleansing breath. So what if he was hot? So what if his eyes were a kind of unearthly green? She shook her head. He was a jerk, and his poor little girl needed a friend. So she opened her eyes.

"What did you do, Kate?" he demanded of the girl standing next to her, her shoulders back, charming smile in place.

"Well, Daddy…um. I wanted to ask you if I could…" Kate tugged on Summer's shirt until Summer somehow, with way more effort than should be necessary, looked away from the imposing, angry, *hot*—no—

Kate motioned her close, and Summer bent down so her ear was close to Kate's mouth.

"What's your name?" she whispered.

"Oh, um." Summer glanced at Kate's father, who looked like he was about to charge across the room, toss her over his shoulder, and…

Oh, wow, no. That was not a turn-on. It was menacing and scary. Or so she was going to tell herself.

"Summer. My name is Summer," she replied, forgetting to whisper.

"Go inside, Katherine."

"But, Daddy, Summer said I can go over to her house if I have permission. And I think it'd be really fun to—"

"Inside. Now."

Kate turned and looked at Summer, rolling her eyes in a gesture so teen-like that Summer had to fight a smile. But then looking at Kate's furious father, the urge vanished completely as Kate trudged away.

Maybe that little girl wasn't in express danger, but she needed something. Or someone. Summer knew all too well what feeling alone and stuck was like. She raised her chin, because she was not going to be intimidated. She'd had her fair share of that, too. "Your daughter seems like she needs a friend."

He took a few steps toward her, his hands curling into fists. For the first time, Summer realized they were alone. Isolated. He could do…anything. This was not good. She should be afraid. She should run.

"Stay away from my daughter," he said in a low voice.

His daughter. Who wanted to dream about gold glitter rain and explore and… For that little girl's sake, Summer had to pretend like she wasn't scared. And maybe for herself too. "Your smart and charming daughter showed up at my place. Twice. *Twice* completely unsupervised. Do not try to blame this on me. Maybe she's trying to get away from *you*."

~~~

It was only when the woman took a few steps back that Thack realized he'd been advancing on her like some kind of bully. It was when she said those last four words—*get away from you*—that the Shaw woman gutted him completely.

She likely had no idea what she'd done, and he hoped to keep it that way, but she might as well have taken his heart out of his chest and stomped on it a few times for good measure.

"I would appreciate it if you didn't encourage her," he managed to force out. He attempted not to sound like he wanted to throttle something, but he doubted he succeeded.

"And *I'd* appreciate it if I wasn't blamed for your lack of supervision. How safe is it to leave a little girl to her own devices?"

"Where do you get off, coming onto my property and lecturing me about my parenting skills?" He'd beat himself over being a dick later, but for now it felt pretty damn good to talk to someone who didn't treat him with kid gloves and tut-tut over how hard he must have it.

Six-plus years after the fact, he was still the poor widower who needed help and sympathy. This Summer Shaw woman either didn't know or didn't care, and he was quite happy with either situation.

"I walked her back home because she showed up at my place. What would you have had me do? Send her back without making sure she got here safely? Or perhaps I should have called the police."

"You don't get how Blue Valley works, do you?"

She frowned at that, dark eyebrows drawing together. Then she closed her eyes, took a dramatic deep breath in, and then an equally dramatic one out. She opened her eyes, mouth curving into a pretty smile like they were suddenly on friendly terms.

"She's a little girl who wants to explore and feel free. I'm sure we've somehow gotten off on the wrong foot, but she's a sweet girl. She's welcome to come over. I'm home most mornings, and—"

"You honestly expect me to let my only child go to a stranger's weird-butt caravan in the woods?"

"Did you just say weird…butt?"

"No. I… Weird-ass. I meant ass."

She pressed her lips together like she was trying not to laugh, which frustrated him even more, because it *was* ridiculous. It was just… He'd made a conscientious effort not to swear in front of Kate, and sometimes that spread to other conversations. And that was *so* not the point.

"The fact you'd even suggest I let my daughter spend time with a woman I don't know, a woman all and sundry in Blue Valley have theories about, proves how little you understand about children."

Her dark eyes widened. "There are theories about me?"

"Yes, there are theories about the mysterious Shaw daughter. Did you think you were invisible?"

The scowl was back. "You are not a very nice person."

He looked at her for a moment because she seemed dead serious. Her return insult when he was being a total asshole to her was that he was not a very nice person. He tried not to feel guilty.

"And you are a strange girl, Summer Shaw. Now, I have work to do. Stay away from my daughter. I'd hate to have to call the police myself."

"She deserves better than you." She seemed so sure about that, and again this stranger was stomping all over his heart. Because she was right. Of course Kate deserved better than a stressed father and a sick grandfather. She deserved fairies and glitter and exploration and a mother who was alive and a grandmother who didn't cry at the sight of her.

She deserved the world, and he couldn't give it to her. The only consolation was the fact no father could give the world to his daughter, no much how much he might want to.

"And I am not a *girl*," Summer added, hands on her hips.

Thack raised an eyebrow at her, giving her a look up and down, and not at all comfortable with the odd jump in his gut. It wasn't... No, he just hadn't had breakfast yet, and she'd screwed up his schedule.

The hips she had her hands fisted on weren't girlish, and the tight red sweatshirt and equally tight orange yoga pants accentuated a very...womanlike figure. There were plenty of women he wasn't attracted to. The ones he was interested in—which did not include *her*—he didn't have the time for.

"I'm almost twenty-four. I've probably been more places in my life than you'll ever hope to see. I have been through plenty. Besides"—she waved a hand at him, kind of a sweep from his boots to his hat as she readjusted the weird knitted wrap thing she had around her shoulders—"you can't be *that* much older than me."

"Life made me older."

She snorted. "You know nothing about me."

"Ditto."

They regarded each other, and something passed

between them in the moment, as though they were sharing the same thought.

You know nothing about me. Not what's happened. Not my flaws or fears or sad sack of a past.

He was imagining things. Pretty, smiling women—especially ones who made Kate think of fairy queens—weren't bogged down with the kind of baggage he was.

"I'm not a bad person," she said into the heavy silence, her voice hushed, almost reverent. Like being a good person was all she had.

Luckily, it helped snap him out of the moment. She wasn't the enemy any more than anything else was, but that didn't mean she wasn't a threat. "Kate is my *everything*. I make every choice in my life with the thought of keeping her safe. Your word that you're not bad isn't good enough. It never could be. That isn't personal."

When she didn't respond and didn't move, he strode past her. Because he didn't have time for all this. He had a daughter to feed and lecture and hug and protect—and make a damn fairy Halloween costume for.

So, he left Summer behind in the stables, because he didn't have any interest in spending any more time with the strange, irritating, *beautiful*—nope—woman who was currently nothing but a thorn in his side.

Chapter 5

SUMMER KNEW SHE SHOULD GO. KATE'S FATHER HAD MADE a few decent points—she *was* a stranger, and wouldn't her life have been different if her mother had cared about letting strangers into their lives?

On the other hand, the little blond girl who'd shown up at her caravan wanted to explore and dream of adventure, and Summer also understood how vital that could be.

But the bottom line was that Summer had no claim on Kate and was nothing to Kate's father, who...

She didn't know. She couldn't quite figure out what her conflicted feelings meant. Nothing, really. Probably nothing. He was just a man, one she didn't know. She couldn't even remember his first name. Hank? Tack?

Like Mel and Caleb and Delia had all warned her, she shouldn't be pushing herself into Kate's world. This didn't have anything to do with her, and after talking to that man both in front of Kate and alone, she didn't get the sense that anything sinister was happening here.

But that girl and this place tugged at something else inside her, and she'd made it to Montana by listening to those kinds of feelings. She'd opened up to the universe, and it had brought her the life she'd dreamed of.

So she couldn't make herself leave, but she would need a better explanation for... Darn it, what was his name? Calling him "Mr. Lane" seemed so weird. He might have a daughter in elementary school and obviously a lot on his plate, but he didn't look *that* much older than her.

Not that these conflicting feelings had anything at all to do with how he looked. Or the weird crackling energy between them that she might have called attraction with just about anyone else. He'd been vaguely threatening toward her, and bullying was *not* attractive.

All that didn't matter, though. What mattered was following her intuition, because it hadn't steered her wrong before. So, how to convince Mr. Grumpy Cowboy Pants his daughter would be perfectly safe with her?

She took a step toward the outside, just as someone else stepped into the stable. It was an older man, tall if a little paunchy. He had dark hair sprinkled with silver and an almost pure-white mustache. He looked at her, then to where Grumpy Cowboy Dad had gone, then back at her. His lips twitched into a smile. "Ah," he said in a gravelly voice that sounded a lot older than he looked. "You must be the Shaw girl."

Summer smiled—she couldn't help it in the face of some kindness. "And you must be the grandpa with the yelling TV shows."

"Ah, yes, that would be me."

He didn't say anything else, just kept…studying her. It was unnerving, but it didn't register on what she tended to call her creep-meter. Which was odd. Most extended staring landed on the meter at least a little.

"I was just bringing Kate back," she offered. "She was at my door this morning."

The older man sighed. "Poor thing wants to roam and explore. She's got magic on her mind." Unlike the younger Lane man, the grandfather seemed to admire those attributes in his granddaughter.

He cocked his head. "You know, I talked to your dad the other day."

Summer straightened. She couldn't help it. Any mention of her father made her unsure and uncomfortable.

"Said you were a nice girl. Try real hard, always a kind word for anybody who crosses your path."

"He said all that?"

"Was he lying?"

"No, I just didn't know he noticed." Or that he'd bother to tell anyone if he had.

"He's a different man than he used to be."

"So I hear," she muttered before she could stop herself. She tried to soften it with a bright smile, but truth be told, she was tired of hearing that her father had changed. All that seemed to mean was she'd missed the years where he'd been…present…involved.

You mean, if *he's your father*. She shook her head. Of course he was. The math added up, and she looked so much like Mel. Surely that wasn't *all* Mom's genes.

"You know," the man said, shaking a finger at her. "I have a good feeling about you, girl."

"Do you?"

This time he jabbed his finger into his chest. "And I *always* trust my gut feeling. Always. Do you?"

"I've been trying to."

"All right, then. You'll come with me."

"I…will?"

He was already striding out of the stables, but he looked over his shoulder at her. "You like our Kate, don't you?"

"She seems like a sweet, imaginative girl." Summer started following him, having no idea what she was getting herself into.

"She's a wild stallion. Analogy might be a little odd, but the girl wants to roam, and locking her up isn't going to change that, no matter what my son thinks. You might be just what we need."

"Oh. But…" *Need*. She missed it, that sense of having a purpose, the feeling you could do something for someone. Ever since Delia moved into the Shaw main house, Summer had felt less and less like they *needed* her. Sure, they liked her. Every once in a while she was almost knocked flat by a feeling that had eluded her for her whole previous life. *Belonging*. But she missed that feeling of someone needing her. Even if that need had been warped and wrong, her mother's dependence and manipulation had at least been a comfort when Mom wasn't in one of her violent moods.

Oh, you are one messed-up little girl.

The grandfather strode right up to the pretty, gleaming house, taking the stairs with hard, authoritative strides. Summer couldn't quite bring herself to mount the stairs. As much as she wanted to follow her intuition, she knew what lay on the other side of that door.

Mr. Lane looked back at her as she stood still at the bottom of the stairs. He arched an eyebrow. "You coming, girl?"

Summer paused, the internal debate not easily won or lost. "He's not going to like this."

The man grinned, turning the knob and pushing the door open. "I know. That's half the fun."

—~~—

The minute Thack had gone inside, he'd made quick work of serving Kate breakfast, then settled into a chair with her Halloween costume and his damn needle and thread. He wasn't going to think about where Dad had disappeared to, and he definitely wasn't going to think about Summer Shaw.

He tried not to swear as he attempted to attach wings he'd bought off the Internet onto one of Kate's sparkly pajama shirts. Normally making her Halloween costume was his evening chore, but he was running out of time. If only he hadn't put it off till the last minute, he might have been able to order a fully made fairy queen costume, but he'd been so wrapped up in organizing roofing repairs…

Thack rubbed the back of his neck. He'd tried Velcro that he could just stick onto either side of the fabric, but the wings still drooped. They looked like they still would even after his current sewing efforts.

He sighed. "I'm sorry, Katie Pie. I don't know if this is quite what you had in mind."

Kate hopped away from the table where she'd taken not one bite of the bagel he'd slathered in cream cheese for her. "Can I try it on?"

Thack squatted to eye level, fitting the button-up shirt over the long-sleeved T-shirt she already had on.

He buttoned it up, frowning at the way the wings still drooped. But Kate squealed and hopped before he'd even buttoned up the entire shirt.

"I have wings, Daddy! Sparkly wings." She threw her arms around his neck and squeezed, planting a loud kiss on his cheek.

Though she wiggled in an effort to make her wings flap, Thack held her close. His little bundle of glittery sunshine. She wanted wings to fly, and he didn't know how to give that to her without *losing* her the way he'd lost so much.

"When I say trick-or-treat, can I throw glitter at people who open the door?"

Thack dropped his forehead to her narrow shoulder. "I think we might have to save the glitter throwing for home."

Kate wriggled out of his grasp and pranced around, jumping to make the wings move. They weren't perfect, but they were staying on the shirt, and Kate was happy, which was the most important thing.

When he heard the door open and Dad's heavy footsteps in the hall, he didn't think much of it...until he heard conversation. Dad's raspy voice, followed by a soft female one.

He frowned. He'd thought Dad was off doing the woodworking they both pretended Thack didn't know about because the old work shed triggered Dad's emphysema.

But apparently he'd been somewhere collecting a woman? Leaving Kate completely unsupervised this morning long enough that she could run off to Summer's—

Wait.

He was about to cut them off at the pass before Kate saw anything, but they entered and Kate squealed.

"Summer's here!"

"You are a bad penny," Thack muttered.

"What's that mean?" Kate demanded.

"It means your father has forgotten any kind of manners," Dad said, the boom in his voice completely undercut by the hoarseness of his emphysema. And yet, Thack practically winced because he knew what that tone meant.

"Apologize, Thackery."

He was twenty-eight damn years old, and his father had just scolded him and called him by his full first name. Worst of all? He had to apologize because Kate was watching him with wide, impressionable eyes.

"I apologize for my rude greeting," he managed through gritted teeth.

"Um."

"Now, come on in, Ms. Shaw." Dad led Summer closer to the counter at the center of the kitchen, and Thack had to breathe through the desire to order this woman out of his house and lecture his father for the millionth time. Because Kate had taken a seat at the table and was eating her bagel *finally*, and he was worried enough about her eating habits.

If she was eating, he would suck it up. And yell at his father in private. Tomorrow. When Kate was at school. As for Summer... He didn't have the last clue what to do about Summer Shaw.

"Why don't you explain to the rest of us what you're up to?" Thack managed to get out the words in a tone he hoped passed for something not as near "undeniably exasperated" as he felt.

"Summer has agreed to work for us."

Summer's eyes widened, but she didn't say anything or react in any other way. Mostly she just stood there, looking like an oddly colorful statue.

Thack felt *nothing* like a statue. He felt like...one of those geysers. He was Old Faithful-ing all over his damn kitchen. He met his father's gaze. "You have crossed a line."

"My house," Dad replied, as easygoing and unaffected as ever.

Dad's house. Dad's ranch. Oh, Thack could argue it was *theirs*. Could argue family and legacy and all that, but he didn't care. None of that mattered. What mattered was that Dad bringing a stranger in here affected *his* daughter, and *that* he did not have to sit back and take.

"No, I'm sorry. You can't strong-arm me by announcing this in front of Kate." Thack was downright furious with his father for trying, but he wouldn't be manipulated. Not on this. "We do not know this woman."

"Who said anything about Kate? I'm hiring her as a housekeeper."

Summer blinked. "You...are?"

Thack almost, *almost* felt bad for the woman. She'd just gotten swept up in one of Dad's grand plans where he listened to absolutely no one. He paid no mind to what was right or prudent, and just did whatever he wanted.

Because he had that kind of luxury. Thack did not.

"Sure, gotta iron out a schedule, and wages, of course. But if Thack won't hire help for what he needs help with"—Dad looked pointedly at Kate—"then I'll hire you for the other stuff."

"Well, honestly, it's kept very clean." Summer gestured around the kitchen. "I'm not sure you—"

"That boy works like a dog to keep this place sparkling. Oh, we have a cleaning lady for the particulars, but I'm more talking about cooking, running errands. You know, I make these little figurines and I sell some at the Old Town Emporium. In fact, we'll just think of you as *my* assistant. How's that?"

Dad smiled at Summer, then at Thack.

"Katherine—"

Kate blew out a sigh, pushing her plate back. Only a small chunk of bagel left, thank Christ. "I know. I know. Go to my room." She slid off her chair and trudged toward the living room, but Thack didn't miss the sly little smile she sent Summer. Because she and Dad were so sure they were going to get what they wanted, even if it was the worst possible thing for all of them.

Not this time. Thack was not going to be steamrolled. Kate was getting older, pushing more boundaries every day, and if he didn't stand his ground, he was going to get trampled. Someone had to keep her safe, and considering the sad state Dad had been in during Thack's teenage years, Thack shouldn't be surprised at having to be the responsible one now. Ever since Mom had died, Thack had been in charge—of himself, of the ranch— and every time he'd wandered, every time *he'd* ignored a responsibility, a grave consequence had been waiting for him.

Thack would do everything in his power to make sure Kate did not suffer one of *his* grave consequences. If it meant constantly butting heads with Dad, if it meant being not particularly nice to this woman, well…Kate's safety was more than worth all that.

Dad had gotten out a pen and paper while Thack watched to make sure Kate really did go up to her room. When he turned back to Dad and Summer, they were hunched over the table talking about money and days of the week.

"On the weekends I play music at Pioneer Spirit," she was saying.

Thack closed his eyes and sank into the seat Kate had vacated. Sweet pickles. No, *sweet Jesus*. It was really irritating that he couldn't even swear in his own head half the time. But what was *really* irritating was his dad hiring this woman as an *assistant*, which the poor woman didn't seem to understand meant *tool for making his son miserable*.

And she worked at Pioneer Spirit. They wanted him to let her be around Kate when she worked at a rough-and-tumble bar as well known for its fights and police calls as it was for a quick drink with a buddy. "You work at Pioneer Spirit."

"She *plays music* at Pioneer Spirit," Dad offered, as if that changed everything. Oh, she didn't *pour* the drinks and break up the fights, she *sang*. Like there was a difference.

"A *bar*," Thack repeated. He knew that once Dad got an idea in his head, he couldn't let it go, but this was getting out of control. This woman came in contact with the worst Blue Valley had to offer every weekend, and he was supposed to be okay with her being around Kate?

"Like you've never stepped into Pioneer Spirit," Dad scoffed. "You know, one of the Rogers girls runs that place now, the one who was Michaela's friend. Oh, what was her na—"

"Enough." Thack didn't yell. He didn't slam his fist into the table like he wanted to. He sat perfectly still and said it in a perfectly reasonable tone.

Maybe that's why Dad stopped so abruptly. Maybe he finally recognized that Thack was at his breaking

point, and this didn't help. Mentioning Michaela helped
even less.

Thack didn't stand. He didn't move. He didn't say
anything else. He didn't trust himself to. Kate had probably snuck back down to witness the fireworks, and he
wouldn't do that to her or to his father.

He was calm. He'd keep it contained because he
had to.

"I'll go check on Kate," Dad said gruffly. "Summer,
I'll show you out."

"I can find the way," she said, heading for the door
they'd come in. Dad nodded and went the opposite route
to the living room and the stairs.

Thack still didn't move. He was afraid if he did,
everything shuffling for space inside him would pour
out into this empty kitchen and drown him.

"I'm…sorry."

He startled at the female voice and lifted his head to
see Summer still standing in the opening between the
kitchen and the hallway. "You are?" he asked, because
he couldn't quite bring himself to believe *she* was apologizing to *him*.

"Yes, I am." She took a tentative step back into the
kitchen. Toward him. "I didn't quite know what he had
planned, and that was a bit of an ambush. I feel…bad."

"So, you won't do it? You won't be his assistant or
whatever nonsense he's spouting."

She was silent, dropping her eyes and wringing
her hands in the edge of the blanket thing she still had
wrapped around her shoulders. "Well, truth be told, I
kind of need a job. They don't need me at Shaw house
much anymore now that Delia's there, and my job at

Pioneer Spirit is only a few evenings a week. I've been looking around, but Mel just had her baby and—"

"You work at a bar." Why didn't anyone else see a problem with that? She was going to be around his seven-year-old, and she worked in a rough bar in a rough town. She might look all fairy queen-ish, but looks were darn deceiving. *Damn deceiving. Damn, damn it.*

Her eyes zeroed in on his again, and there was that… thing. Like a catch in his gut, something inside him not settling right. What *was* that?

"I *sing* at a bar," she said resolutely.

"My daughter is seven. Impressionable. She…"

"Look, you can ask Rose. Rose Rogers, she runs the—"

"She runs the bar."

"Right. Your dad mentioned…" She trailed off, clearly pained at the history she didn't know. "You know her. You can ask her about me. They're good people."

"Maybe. Maybe not." They hadn't been *friends* or *good people* when Michaela had died and he was left picking up the pieces. Why should that be any different now?

"What about Mel?" Summer demanded.

"What *about* Mel?" God, he was tired.

"Everyone trusts Mel. Ask her about me. You know she wouldn't lie."

"Actually I don't know that, seeing as she's your sister." Thack pushed away from the table. He had the breakfast dishes to clean and the morning chores to finish. But instead of leaving, Summer followed him as he gathered dishes and stepped to the sink.

"Right, but she just had a baby. Who she lets me watch, by the way. Surely you could trust someone like Mel, who's also a parent of a little girl."

"Who you're related to." He flipped on the tap.

Summer reached across him and slapped it off, the fringe edges of whatever the hell thing she was wearing drifting across his hands, an odd floral scent invading his space. She stared up at him, her dark brown eyes with just a hint of green imploring.

"Give me a chance. Please. You won't be sorry."

His heart was doing an odd thick-beating thing in his chest, but he had to ignore it. He needed to ignore how close she stood, and the way she smelled like nothing in his life had smelled in a long time. Now was *not* the time for attraction. He was not attracted to *her*.

"It's not enough," he said, refusing to meet her gaze any longer, having to clear his throat to keep talking. "Not when it comes to my daughter."

She didn't say anything for a few humming seconds, still too close. This was not normal. Strangers didn't stand quietly this close together, not when all this air around them shouldn't be this thick or this fragrant.

Finally, she stepped away, which gave him leave to move and grab the skillet off the stove, but not because he needed space. He was a rock. An island.

Hard.

Sweet pickles. *Christ.*

"Your father is the one who hired me," she said primly.

"He's free to do whatever the hell he wants. I'm free to make sure Kate is nowhere near you when you're around." He dropped the skillet into the sink. "And that is that."

It was his final word, and he was going to stick to it. No matter what.

Chapter 6

Summer hiked back to her caravan, her whole day out of whack. Her entire *body* felt out of whack and *humming* with something.

Irritation probably. Yeah, it had to be irritation. Because it just…simmered along her skin like a rash.

She puffed out a breath, unlocking her caravan and collecting her yoga mat. Caleb had built her a little platform for her birthday so she could do yoga outside even if the snow was on the ground. He'd told her she was nuts, but he'd built it of his own accord. Every morning when she shoveled the snow off the platform and set up her makeshift yoga mat, she remembered his sweet gesture, and she smiled.

Because she had a brother who would do things like that, and what a gift that was. Even with the Thacks of the world trying to mess with her joy.

She went through her daily routine, failing to find any kind of center, which made her even more irritated.

At this point, she usually laced up her running shoes, Rose's birthday gift to her. Her entire life here was made up of stitched-together thrift finds and the gifts of her family and friends. She had never been happier, even in the days Mom had been particularly flush and they'd had a nice place to live.

It hadn't been worth the cost—a sunny smile followed by a cold threat.

Summer shook her head. She was messed up today, all dark thoughts and jumbled feelings. Running might help pound them away, but music soothed the soul. Besides, running in the snow wasn't exactly comforting. Practicing her set would be a better way of working through her irritability.

She climbed into her caravan and set up everything so that she could enjoy the warmth of inside but still look outside her door and see mountains and trees. That was better—she needed to focus on something away from Shaw, and definitely away from the Lane place. Just her, the mountains, and music.

She went through the softer folky songs that she preferred and Rose frowned upon before shifting into the country and the raucous songs that got the late-night crowd buying beer after beer. She played those more because Rose wanted her to than because she enjoyed them.

This morning? She let the anger and frustration course through her, riding on the howls of the cold, whipping wind and the threatening skies.

She finished the loudest, most full-of-swearing song she knew, and as she strummed her last chord, someone started clapping.

"That was quite a show."

Summer let out a screech of surprise, tripping over her little stool and dropping her guitar so it clattered onto the floor. "Shit, Delia, you scared me."

"Shit? Awfully early for you to be saying *shit*. You must be having a bad day."

Summer moved her stool and guitar so Delia could enter the caravan. "Just…off-kilter." She looked down at her sister-and-law and frowned. "What's wrong with you?"

"Who said something is wrong with me?"

But Delia had her fingers twisted together and her whole bearing was slumped, when usually she went everywhere with a kind of shoulders-back, screw-the-world stance. She climbed into the caravan with a reticence that wasn't at all usual for her.

Summer was still in awe of Delia. The woman had been through so much and never lost her strength or sense of fight. Summer had spent a lot of time in the past few months trying to emulate some of that.

"Tell me what's wrong," she said, trying for authoritative. When Delia took a seat on the little bench connected to the caravan wall and rested her chin on her hands as though she was going to do just that, Summer scooted the stool closer.

This was serious.

"I think…maybe…possibly…I might be…" Delia looked around, as if people were lurking in the nonexistent nooks and crannies of Summer's home and trying to hear their conversation.

Apparently weird days were going around. "Might be what?"

"I think I might be…"

"Oh my God." Summer clapped her hands over her mouth as it dawned on her, and then dropped them with a squeal. "You're pregnant!"

"Shh," Delia said, waving her hands in front of Summer.

"Shh? We're inside."

"You left the door open, and sound carries around here." Delia blew out a breath. "I'm not sure. I need to get a test, but it's…possible. I mean, we weren't trying, but there was a night where—"

"La-la-la, no details."

Delia smiled at that, but it quickly melted into a groan. "Oh shit, I don't know what to do. Do I wait it out? Do I get a test? Do I tell Caleb?"

"You haven't told Caleb?" Summer screeched.

"No, I haven't told Caleb. What if I'm wrong? And we haven't talked about this at all. And…what if I'm wrong?"

"Then, I'm guessing, you try, try again."

Delia groaned and flopped forward, her chest now resting on her knees. "I'm not prepared for this, Summer. I'm still figuring out this whole 'being someone's wife' thing I'm…so not ready."

"You know what part of that whole wife thing you seem to be missing?"

Delia glanced up. "What?"

"Talking to the other person, duh!"

Delia groaned again. "Don't duh me, little girl."

"Then don't be stupid, Delia Shaw."

Delia sat completely upright at that. "You know I hate it when people accuse me of being stupid."

"I do, but I also know you're a big softy, and I am not afraid of you *or* your husband." Summer reached across the distance between them, squeezing Delia's hand. "It doesn't matter if you are or aren't. You still have to tell Caleb. You know that, or you wouldn't be here telling me. You'd be hiding it or getting a test."

"But…" Delia swallowed, a nervous gesture so unlike her. "What if he's disappointed?" she whispered, the apples of her cheeks going pink with a blush.

Delia was blushing. Summer couldn't help but smile. She'd always believed in love, especially the true, lasting kind that made people partners in life, the kind that shared hopes and dreams and children. She'd needed to believe that was possible in the utter absence of it.

So, she squeezed Delia's hand tighter. It was nice to be the sounding board for this. To be someone's friend. Someone's...sister. "Disappointed by what?" she asked gently.

Delia shook her head, looking to the roof. "That I am," she mumbled. Then her head drooped. "Or if I turn out not to be."

"He loves you, Delia."

"Well, I know *that*. Don't get all mushy Summer on me."

"It's not mushy. It's the bottom line. It doesn't matter which one disappoints him or which doesn't, because he loves you, and as with a lot of the bigger challenges you two have overcome, you'll figure out a way to navigate whatever this is."

"I *hate* when you're all smart and reasonable beyond your years."

Summer grinned. "And yet here you are."

"Here I am. And...thanks." She squeezed Summer's hand back and tried to tug it away, but Summer held on a little tighter.

These moments of feeling like she really did belong here, that she'd built a forever-from-this-point family, were when she got so scared she'd lose it all and had to hold on tighter. "You need me, right?"

Delia cocked her head. "Do you want me to need you?"

Summer blew out a breath. That was the thing with

people—everyone seemed to be holding something back. Some secret. Some insecurity. A hope, a dream, a fear. Everyone had all of these emotions brimming under the surface that they didn't or wouldn't let anyone see. Including herself.

She couldn't seem to completely trust herself to let all her feelings go, or that her family would accept them. But if someone could need her, really *need* her to be here, then those hidden things wouldn't matter. She released Delia's hand and forced herself to smile. "I guess it's just nice to be needed sometimes."

Delia contemplated her in one of those moments where it felt like they had more in common than either of them realized or wanted to expose. "It is. But you'll come to find at some point that people needing you isn't the same as... You have to come to need something yourself, and not be afraid of letting people see what that need is."

Summer smiled and nodded, pretending that made perfect sense, even though it didn't make any at all. She'd survived by not needing anything from anyone and being whatever she could be to others.

How could she let that approach go when it had gotten her this far?

Thack couldn't believe he was wasting his afternoon doing this. He should be making sure he had Kate's Halloween costume perfect. He should be lining up some-one to fix the porch before the snow got impossible to work through. Hell, if he had half a brain at his disposal, he should be doing some early Christmas shopping.

He should go to the grocery store or run his weekly errands in Bozeman. He should be doing anything but knocking on Mel Shaw's door.

And yet that's exactly what he was doing.

Mel opened the door. In every interaction Thack had had with her in running neighboring ranches, she'd seemed poised, put together, in charge of everything. Today she looked tired, her hair sticking half out of a ponytail, and she held a wriggling bundle of tiny baby in her arms.

He barely remembered Kate as a baby, but the pang of those days, the ones so mired in grief, hit him with a force he didn't know what to do with.

"Thack. Hi. Um. Can I…help you?"

He had to take a deep breath to find some calm amid all the pain and fight to remember why he was here. "I would like you to tell me about your sister."

"My sis… Oh, you mean Summer?"

"Do you have another one?"

She gave him one of those *This is not the Thack Lane that Blue Valley knows* looks, quickly followed by something worse. Pity.

Because anyone who got the tail end of Thack's temper was surprised, but then they remembered. Widower. Tragic. Poor Thack Lane. But it predated that. Really, it had started with Mom's battle with cancer throughout high school, followed so quickly by everything else.

So, since he'd been fourteen, everyone in town responded to him with surprise, then pity. The chorus of *been through a lot* followed him wherever he went, however much he smiled or didn't.

"For some insane reason, my dad has seen fit to hire Summer as some kind of housekeeper-slash-assistant, and I need to know with absolute certainty that she will not pose a threat or be a bad influence on my daughter."

"Oh. You're worried about Summer?" When the baby in her arms began to fuss, Mel offered her a pacifier. She stepped back, gesturing Thack inside the kitchen with a nod of her head. "I wouldn't be. I'm not sure I've ever encountered a girl more desperate to…" She stopped short as if reconsidering her words. "Summer has a really good heart. I'm not sure there's a bad bone in that girl's body."

"That's it?"

"Did you want more?"

"To trust her to be around my daughter? Yeah, I want a lot more."

"Well, she'd be able to tell you more about her experience than I would. I only know she takes care of the Shaw house without ever complaining, even though Dad and Caleb are obnoxious people to live with. She's a great cook. Tidy. She'll do what's asked of her, and I can't imagine her being anything but adoring to your little girl."

"How do you know all that?"

The baby began to fuss in earnest, and Mel glanced at the clock. "I don't know what you want from me, Thack. She's a good kid. If you're looking for an endorsement, I'm giving it."

"No offense, but you defended Caleb for a lot of years. Why should I trust you?"

Everything about Mel's exhausted posture straightened. "Oh, because he's running Shaw—"

"Into the ground."

"Not anymore. Look, you don't want to trust me? Don't. It doesn't matter to me. *You* came *here* to ask me my thoughts. There they are. You want to worry about someone, why don't you worry about keeping your daughter under control so she's not showing up at Summer's place?"

Thack glanced at the bundle in Mel's arms. Tiny and vulnerable, but the thing about babies was that you could keep them in their cribs. You could hold them and keep them completely safe.

Then they grew up, and you didn't have any control anymore. Safety was an illusion, and there were threats around every dang corner. "Thanks for your time," he muttered, all at once needing to get out of there.

He turned on a heel and left the old Paulle place, now some kind of weird llama ranch. Why *was* he asking Mel's opinion? She'd left Shaw and married some ex-hockey player who raised llamas. *Llamas*.

Summer was her sister. What had he been thinking? That he'd get a legitimate reason to tell Dad no? Or worse, a legitimate reason not to worry about Summer coming into their lives?

He climbed into his truck, determined to drive home. He was responsible for Kate's happiness, and Dad was just going to have to live with that. And so was Summer. So why he slowed down in front of Pioneer Spirit, why he parked in the lot in the back, why he walked toward the entrance he'd never quite understand.

Thack took a deep breath. Even with the chorus of *What are you doing?* running through his head, he couldn't turn away. He had to open this door, because the questions would eat at him until he found an answer.

He stepped into the dark of the bar. He'd been

twenty-one when Kate was born, so he'd never spent much time in the place. Back when they were an on-again, off-again thing, Michaela had snuck in, under age, with all her ne'er-do-well friends.

Any time he'd tried to join that group, something bad had happened at the ranch. They'd lost two cows to an ice storm, or Dad had accidentally started a fire in his old woodshed.

Thack had finally gotten the picture. He was not one of those people who could get away with bending or breaking the rules.

So, he'd broken up with Michaela, determined to save her the trouble of being with some stick-in-the-mud who couldn't step a toe out of line.

A few weeks later, she'd told him she was pregnant. They'd married quickly and quietly, and not too many months after that, they'd found the cancer that she would refuse treatment for until Kate's chance of survival was better than her own. All during that hard, lonely time, not a single one of those ne'er-do-well friends had stopped in to wish them well.

They'd been too busy living their lives fast and loose here, night after night. He wasn't sure he had it in him to forgive that.

So, whether it was fair or not, places like this seemed a symbol of all he'd never have, and all that had been taken away. People like Rose Rogers, who had enjoyed Michaela at her fun-loving best, just reminded him of everything he'd lost.

He forced himself to take steps toward the mostly empty bar and the woman working behind it. A woman he had no interest in talking to at all.

Her eyes met his, and if she was surprised, she didn't show it. But then, Rose Rogers wouldn't show much of anything if it didn't suit her. "Howdy, sailor."

Rose acting like she didn't know him was weird, but just about as weird as seeing anyone who'd been close to Michaela before. Six years didn't make it less weird.

"That any way to greet an old friend?" The last word may have held a touch too much bitterness.

Rose's gaze sharpened. "Prefer Mr. Lane? Or Thackery? As I recall, we were never much in the way of friends."

No. He'd only ever joined that group to moon over Michaela. He rubbed at the ache in the chest, wishing he'd never had a reason to face pieces of his past. But he was here, so…

"My father wants to hire Summer Shaw a few days a week to do some work for him. What do you know about her?"

Rose's eyebrows rose. "Summer?"

"Yeah, she said she works here."

Rose studied him for a long minute. "Summer sings here on the days I can pay her to do it. She is…surprising."

"Like felon surprising? Like can't control herself around alcohol or drugs or…" He wasn't sure why he couldn't say *men*. He needed to be certain Summer was the kind of woman she seemed. Why would he trip over any insinuation?

He didn't want to think about it.

"Summer is surprising because she looks like this little ball of sunshine. She sings like an angel. And yet, when someone's an ass, she doesn't dissolve into a mess of tears. She doesn't get offended. She manages to put the drunk asshole in his place, all with a smile. The girl is magic, and I wouldn't expect it of someone so annoyingly cheerful."

Thack frowned. He wasn't sure that told him what he needed to know. But it was interesting.

"What exactly do you want to know?"

"That I can trust her around…" He stumbled because Rose *had* been Michaela's friend. But he didn't know if she knew Kate's name, or… He didn't know.

He hated this. Why had he come here?

"How's…" Rose looked away, brushing a hand over her long fringe of bangs.

He had to clear his throat because they'd traveled into territory he'd become an expert at avoiding. "She's…a great little girl," he managed lamely.

Rose nodded. "Well, anyway, Summer's a good egg. Never had a bad word for her, never heard a bad word about her. I can't tell you what to do about…kid stuff, but I'd trust her with my bar. I trust her with my cash register, and that puts her on a very, very short list of people. As a businesswoman, I can't say a bad thing about her. As a person? I'd just as soon laser off all my tattoos as party with her."

A weird ringing endorsement, but an endorsement nonetheless. What excuse did he have now?

"So, want a drink? On the house."

An olive branch of sorts. "Thank you. Really. But I have to get back."

"Right. Hardworking Mr. Lane."

Thack managed his best approximation of a smile. "That's me." Had to be. He walked toward the door, but Rose cleared her throat.

"Listen, uh…" She fiddled with a row of glasses. "She was lucky to have you."

He had to rub that ache in his chest again. Amazing that an emotional pain could hurt so damn physically. "You sure about that?"

Rose's dark eyes met his, and she gave him a nod. "Yeah. Definitely. And think of that kid—she got the best of both worlds, right?"

The best of both worlds. Thack tried to absorb that friendly offer, although it landed like a blow. He hadn't been giving Kate any of Michaela lately. Not her joy or her fun. He'd been so wrapped up in his promise *to* Michaela, keeping Kate safe, that he'd forgotten all about giving her *fun* and laughter.

He tipped his hat at Rose and then escaped the dimly lit bar. The late-afternoon sunlight was jarring after the dark of Pioneer Spirit, and the brisk winter air was quite a contrast to the hot burn of grief in his chest.

He hadn't found what he'd been looking for. He'd hoped to hear a clear-cut reason to get this odd woman out of his life, not reminders of Michaela and his past. Not a painful memory of what he'd been forgetting.

But he couldn't get over the feeling that Summer was… Trouble wasn't the right word. But he wasn't sure what *was*. Cheerful, colorful, loved-by-everyone Summer Shaw was something like a threat.

He got into his truck and laughed. Everyone thought this girl was unthreatening. Everyone spoke the world of her. Everyone was willing to trust her and bring her into their homes, their businesses. And he thought she was a threat.

Maybe *he* was the problem. Wouldn't that be… well, fitting.

Chapter 7

SUMMER RETURNED TO HER CARAVAN AFTER AN AFTERNOON of working with Caleb and Delia at Shaw.

Eventually she'd left them to sort out Delia's...concerns. While she was happy—happy for them and happy, period—something about seeing both Mel and Caleb happily married, settled, and stumbling toward families of their own left her with an odd sense of longing.

Summer didn't know what to do about that, any more than she knew what to do about the dot of red sitting next to the caravan on her yoga platform.

Oh, Kate.

She didn't want to be in the middle of this. This... whatever it was with the Lanes. She'd pressed this morning, but secrets and lies ran through Shaw and her place there. Why would she want to enter another house just like it?

But when Kate saw her, her whole face lighting up as she jumped off the platform like Summer was the answer to all her problems, that little niggling emptiness disappeared. It was replaced by something Summer wasn't sure she understood, or would ever be able to.

She remembered what it had been like to squeeze Delia's hand and give her advice and make a difference, and she so wanted to do the same for this little girl.

Maybe secrets and hidden selves were just a part of life.

"If you're down here without permission again, I have a feeling you're in for a pretty serious punishment."

Kate's smile didn't fade, but something in her expression changed.

"Kate, you can't keep doing this." She walked to the girl, trying to find the right words. "It isn't because I don't like you, I hope you know. But your father is concerned about—"

"Daddy is concerned about *everything*."

"I suppose he has his reasons." Summer thought about reaching out and touching the girl's flyaway hair, but...well, boundaries. There had to be some boundaries. As much as she thought this girl's father was far too controlling for *anyone's* good, she couldn't help but wonder if it was a different kind of controlling than her mother's.

Mom had made a good show of making everything about Summer's future, or *their* hopes and dreams, but it had become abundantly clear in those last weeks that her mother's behavior had been a lie. Mom didn't care at all. Not about *Summer*. Not her well-being, not her hopes or dreams, not about much of anything except what Summer could do for *her*. And if Summer wouldn't do that, the consequences would be *dire*.

While Summer sometimes wondered whether she had the ability to discern honest feeling from manipulation, she had learned to trust her gut. As much as Thack Lane irritated her, her gut feeling was that his controlling came from caring.

"I just wanted to make sure you were going to come back to the ranch. Grandpa said you were, and Daddy said you weren't. *I* want you to come back."

Oh, this little girl. Summer had once *been* this little girl, desperate for someone to open up her life. For a few years, she'd latched on to anyone Mom brought wherever they were, hoping that person would be the key to making things different.

They never were, and then Summer had gotten old enough to be of interest to those strangers, and everything had changed. Mom had started to use that interest, and that's when Summer had run.

"We're caught a little bit between a rock and hard place, Kate." Instead of touching the girl, Summer held out a hand. An invitation. She had come to greatly appreciate the freedom of an invitation.

Kate happily took it. Summer couldn't possibly fight the wave of protectiveness that swept over her. Even if Thack did care, even if Kate's grandfather did care, they weren't enough for this little girl with stars in her eyes and glitter snow in her imagination.

Summer gave her hand a little squeeze. "How about this? I promise to keep trying to convince your father that I'm safe for you to be around. But you need to promise me you won't disobey him." Summer couldn't quite settle into that black-and-white ultimatum. "Unless it's absolutely gravely important."

Kate hopped. "I so super promise."

Summer nodded. "All right. Then we need to get you back home."

"But—"

"No buts. No arguing. We have to work together, and we have to play by the rules. The rules are very, *very* important. They can keep you safe."

Again Summer chafed at the black and white of that

statement, but she began pulling Kate toward the Lane property. "And if you ever feel like a rule is wrong…" Summer searched for the right words for a seven-year-old. "There are ways to…" This was so not her place, but she couldn't step out of the situation anyway. She just couldn't. "You don't just disobey them. You try to change them." And if you can't—you run far, far, far away.

But that was an answer for another day.

Kate kept squeezing Summer's hand as they walked toward the trees. She gave a test swing and grinned when Summer went along with it, their joined arms swinging cheerfully.

"Do you know how to ride a horse?" Kate asked.

"I've been learning. They still make me a little nervous."

Kate wrinkled her nose. "Why? Horses are great. Daddy still won't let me ride without a helmet or without him right next to me." She sighed gustily. "I can't do *anything* by myself."

Summer felt bad for asking, considering she knew what it was like to grow up without a parent, and how the question rarely had an easy, happy answer. At the same time, though, she thought she should know, if for no other reason than to better understand what was going on.

"Kate…" She took a deep breath, trying to walk the line between being helpful and…whatever it was that meant keeping her nose out of another family's private matters. "Is it just your dad and your grandpa at your house?"

"Yeah. We have ranch hands for part of the year, but I'm supposed to stay away from them, too."

"And your…mother?" Summer closed her eyes. She

didn't want to see Kate's face as she answered that question. She wouldn't be able to handle it if she caused the
girl grief or sadness or—

"She's gone."

Summer blew out a breath, finally looking at Kate's
face. Her answer hadn't told Summer anything useful, and
her expression wasn't all that haunted or hurt. *How* was
Kate's mother gone? Had she left, like Summer's own
mother had left this place? Or had something terrible happened that was the cause of Thack's overprotectiveness?

But then wouldn't Kate's grandfather be overprotec-
tive too?

Torn between pressing further and leaving it be,
Summer hiked her long skirt up to her knees to prepare
for climbing the fence. "Gone… How—"

"Katherine."

They both came up short as the low, male voice
seemed to boom out of nowhere, but while Summer had
to swallow down a screech, Kate just sighed.

"Uh-oh," she muttered under her breath before mus-
tering a smile for her father. "Hi, Daddy."

Thack stood on the other side of the fence and held out
a hand, but it wasn't much like the invitation Summer
had offered Kate. No, this was more of a demand. *You
will take my hand* now. For a second Summer thought
Kate wouldn't release her. Summer was completely
frozen both by the initial shock, and the area between a
rock and a hard place Kate kept thrusting her into. But
after a few seconds of Summer's inner panicking, Kate
released Summer's hand and took her father's.

She stepped with him to the fence, and he helped her
over it. Summer watched them, openmouthed, trying to

force some words out, but she didn't know what to say. Not even a little.

How much had he seen or heard? What was he thinking?

He glanced back at her, and something about his dark green gaze made her heart hammer against her chest. It felt like fear and not like fear, both wrapped up in one weird, heart-pounding moment.

"Follow us," he ordered, and whether because of the look on her face or common sense, he offered a half-hearted "please" afterward.

"Follow…you."

He gave a curt nod, and this time when he held out a hand, it was for her. Like he was going to help *her* over the fence.

Oh.

Well.

She wanted to refuse. After all, she could get over the fence without any help, and she wasn't all that sure she wanted to obey his order. But Kate was watching her expectantly. So.

With a completely fake smile, Summer took his offered hand. It was big and callused, roughened by work. Hers felt small and soft compared to his, despite all of the damage they'd taken over the years. Playing the guitar tended to do a number on her fingers, and learning how to ride had beaten up her once soft, delicate hands.

But compared to Thack's? No contest.

She had to use her free hand to pull the edge of her long skirt more firmly around herself. She stepped onto the bottom rung and swung her leg over, Thack's free hand resting on her waist for balance. But the shirt under her cardigan didn't go all the way down to the waistband of her skirt, and with her arms elevated, the bottom of her coat had hitched up to belly-button level.

His hand was touching the skin of her waist, which was the kind of intimate touch that strangers helping each other over fences shouldn't dwell on. Or lean into.

So, she hopped over quickly with a short, sharp inhale and let go of his hand, moving out of his reach. Something about him touching her, no matter how innocently, had a lot of not-so-innocent thoughts trying to run through her brain.

Summer had learned a lot more than she'd wanted to know and much too early about men—about, well, lust, she supposed—from way too much exposure, but she'd never *experienced* much of anything. She'd seen things, heard things, but her mother had kept her "pure" for what turned out to be a rather nefarious reason.

And so, Summer had never been overly interested in exploring those things. She'd kissed a few guys of her choosing before she'd left Mom, but since she'd come here, men had been something of a nonissue.

Now? It seemed like maybe something of an issue. Kate's father's big, rough hand on her waist was something she seriously wished she knew how to handle.

Get a hold of yourself.

She was torn about whether to look at him or not. Torn between a million things. What was she getting herself into here?

She looked at Kate instead, the instigator of all this and the reason Summer had "obeyed" Thack's command to come with them. Because she knew what it was like to be a little girl who needed a friend. *That* was why she was here, so the other stuff was probably all in her head. But when she looked at Kate, the girl was looking at her father.

"Are you coming, Daddy?"

As Summer glanced back at him, he cleared his throat, but then he easily hopped the fence. Summer had no idea what to attribute his pause to.

But she would wonder. Curling the fingers of the hand he'd held into her palm, she would definitely wonder.

Thack strode through the trees at the edge of his property and then the yard around the house. He didn't know what to say, so he left things silent. Silence was best, even if he had invited Summer to come along.

Invitation was probably an overly kind way of describing it. *Order*, more like. He was used to giving orders. Granted, only the ranch hands listened to him with any sort of regularity, but still. He'd forgotten how to interact with people who weren't working for him or those he wasn't trying to protect.

Summer very well could be working for him. Dad was adamant and Kate was adamant. Thack could find no outside reason *not* to hire the woman. Still, his uneasiness about her persisted. Which was why he'd kept an eagle eye on the house this afternoon, probably screwing his chores up, but that was repairable.

His daughter's safety was not.

He'd followed Kate this time when she slipped out the front door. He'd stayed far enough behind that she wouldn't notice, because he needed a reason to bar

Summer from their lives. He didn't know why he felt so certain, but no matter how many people gave glowing reports about her, no matter how clean Garrett said her background check had been, he just had a feeling he couldn't let this woman into their lives.

But here she was, and after listening to her talk to Kate about following the rules and him only caring about her safety…

He couldn't fight it. He couldn't fight someone who might *agree* with him. Because he knew he was on an edge. He kept hoping things would get better and easier, that he could trust Kate more as she got older, but it hadn't worked out that way.

Not when Dad wouldn't lay down the law, not when Michaela's parents couldn't help, so drowned in grief they'd had to move away.

He had no one on his side, no one to trust. He'd never be able to *trust* Summer wholly, not with his child, but maybe…

He didn't know, and the uncertainty was weighing him down more than he already was. "Kate, go inside."

"But—"

"Now."

She sighed, grumbling something under her breath and stomping up the porch so hard the jack-o'-lanterns trembled.

"She…" Summer stopped herself, rocking back onto her heels. She was all…flowy this afternoon, wearing a long skirt with miles of fabric and a puffy, bright yellow coat. She was covered in bangles and necklaces, all jangling, colorful…woman.

She was a woman, and Kate would probably need

one of those around, no matter how Thack tried to be everything to her. "She what?" he asked, hoping to distract himself from thinking about *how* much of a woman Summer was, how her hand had felt in his, her waist under his palm.

That had not been a good moment. It could not be repeated, and even as he told himself that, his eyes dropped to the tiny strip of pale skin. It was the smallest of gaps between jacket and skirt—how the hell had his hand landed there?

Warm. Soft. *Shoot.* "I talked to Mel. And Rose," he announced with no finesse whatsoever before Summer could answer.

Her eyes widened. "You did?"

"Yes." Thack cleared his throat, trying to find some sense of balance. Of authority. He was in charge here. "I also heard most of what you said to her back there. You told her to follow the rules."

"Well, of course I did." Summer clasped her hands in front of her, something like a nervous gesture, only her expression radiated nothing but a calm kind of peace.

God, he could use some peace.

"I happen to agree with you on a lot of things when it comes to Kate. I don't think she should be crossing property lines alone. Though she does know the way, and she wants to explore. I can't help but think there's a happy medium somewhere."

Ah, not peace at all, because people always seemed to discount his worry without thinking things all the way through. "What if it had gotten dark?" he demanded. "Would she still know the way? Would she know what to do if she came across a wild animal?"

Summer's eyebrows drew together, and she seemed to think about his words, considering them far more than his father ever did. "Maybe you should teach her," she finally offered.

"Give her the skills to disobey me?"

"Give her the skills to survive," she replied without even pausing. "Everyone deserves those." She said it quietly but firmly, passionately. As though survival was something she'd ever had to worry about. Looking at this colorful, jewelry-bedecked woman, he had a hard time imagining her needing to know how to *survive*.

"That's why I'm here. A parent's job is to keep their children safe. She's seven. Needing the skills to survive—"

"She escapes."

Thack opened his mouth to argue, to tell her she was wrong, but given the simple way she offered the truth, he couldn't argue. He couldn't fume that she wasn't listening. He couldn't pull out any of the arguments he used with his father.

Because Summer was right.

He was supposed to protect his daughter. He had promised Michaela, but he couldn't do it. Not when Kate escaped at every turn, determined to be wild and free. She didn't understand the potential consequences of that. She didn't have nightmares about all the things that could happen, but he didn't want to give her those either. She deserved a few years to think of the world as it was in her books, full of fairies and princesses and happy endings.

She would learn soon enough that happy endings didn't exist, that the world was harsh and unforgiving too much of the time. She could live without that knowledge for a few more years.

"I do think you're trying to do what's best for her," Summer offered quietly into the twilight.

"But you think I'm failing?"

Silence stretched out between them, and he looked toward the setting sun. The orange ball burned brightly, but would soon be gone and the world would be dark.

"Does it matter what I think?"

It did and it didn't. He didn't know how to explain that. By itself, her opinion didn't particularly matter because he didn't know her enough to value it, but…

He knew. He knew he was failing whether she agreed or not. He just didn't know what to do about it.

"If you're sure you want to accept my father's job offer, I won't stand in your way. You can be here and you can work for him. You can even be around Kate, but not alone."

She frowned, but he couldn't let her argue with him. This had to be ultimatum time, and then he would walk away. He didn't have the fortitude for more arguments.

"I don't know you well enough to let you be alone with her yet. If she's there, my father or I need to be there. End of story. And if you do anything to jeopardize my daughter or the environment I am trying to raise her in, I can fire you without my father's permission. The house is his, but most of the land is mine. I am in charge, and my daughter is my number one priority. You can take it or leave it."

Odd how he somehow hoped for both. Parts of him wanted her to take it, wanted to believe that some amount of the weight he hefted could be lessened by this woman's help. Most of him wanted her to leave it because he couldn't shake the feeling she would only be another burden.

"I'll take it," she said resolutely.

"I'll let Dad know," he replied. Only his mother's voice in his head kept him from leaving it at that. "Would you like me to drive you back to your place?"

She shook her head, eyes on the sky to the east where things were already dark. "No, thank you. I'll be all right."

Wasn't she the lucky one?

Chapter 8

SUMMER WOKE UP TO THE TELLTALE HUSH OF FRESH snow. The last week had held on to the slightest hints of fall, and she'd been hopeful it would hold out.

She should have known better. Maybe someday she would. Winter in Montana meant the icy grips of snow and below-freezing temperatures could show up at any time and stay as late as they wished.

She peeked out the window, and sure enough, a few more inches of white snow had fallen overnight. Even though she was disappointed, she had to smile at learning her guess had been right. She was getting to know Montana. She was getting to know her life.

She went through her normal morning ritual: tea and stoking the woodstove that kept the caravan warm. Bundling up to do her yoga outside with the sunrise. Scraping the snow off her platform took a few minutes, but she didn't mind. There was a newness to this morning and a freshness to the week.

She was starting to work for the Lanes today, and along with nervousness was an odd giddiness she didn't know what to do with. She'd felt this way when she'd started singing at Pioneer Spirit too.

And yet...

There was something different at play this time, but she wouldn't dwell on that. As she stretched and greeted the sun, she did *not* think about Thack Lane. Or his hands. Or the green of his eyes. Or the way he held his jaw so tightly that she thought no one must ever run their palm along it and tell him to relax.

She wasn't new to inappropriate crushes, but she had at least thought she'd left them behind in California. Apparently she hadn't mastered keeping her heart and imagination out of things yet.

But she would. She would take an example from Mel and Delia. She could learn from the way they held themselves, believed in themselves, followed their goals. They didn't moon over inappropriate people. They didn't let others walk all over them.

They were strong women who'd paved their own ways, rather than manipulating someone else to pave it for them. That was the type of woman she wanted to be. Good and kind, but also a little formidable. Not scary like her mother could be, but confident.

She'd found that there was a whole world of things she *could* do, if she only put her mind to it.

The job was only part-time and wouldn't interfere with her gigs in the evenings. While she knew her existence didn't cost the Shaws *much* money, and she paid them back with meals and cleaning, this would ease her conscience as well as keep her busy.

Mornings would be for exercise and doing her work up at Shaw house. Afternoons, she'd work for Mr. Lane, and evenings would either be for quiet meditation or singing.

She was building a life she had not dared to dream of two years ago. A life with family and filled with activities *she* enjoyed.

It was heaven.

She soaked in the weak rays of the sun, stretching her muscles, taking strength and center from the familiar movements, breathing in the fresh crispness of snow and the blue-skied winter morning.

No, she didn't miss California at all.

Once through her quick yoga routine, she grabbed her bag and hiked up to the Shaw house. Though it was bitterly cold, she never tired of the scenery or the way Shaw house would warm her up. She'd have a shower and breakfast, put a few things together for lunch and dinner for the Shaws, and then go off to the Lanes.

She ignored the jitter of nerves and focused on routine. It was a pleasure to have a routine of her own making, where no one could tell her what to do or who to spend time with. No one could monitor her eating, what she wore, or what she said.

She got to be *herself*.

With a smile on her face, she reached Shaw house. Caleb and Delia would already be out with the herd, feeding, breaking ice on water troughs, or checking on the heaters.

But when Summer stepped inside, there wasn't silence, or even the blaring of the TV. All she heard were Caleb and Delia, voices raised.

"No."

"You can't… Are you…" Summer heard a bang and rushed into the living room. Delia and Caleb were squaring off, which wasn't all that unusual. They fought. A lot. Even though Summer could see the love that wound its way through their battles, she still wasn't comfortable with the way they went after each other when they were mad.

She stepped into the fray because her heart couldn't

take the thought that people she cared about were hurting. Not if she could do something about it.

"Good. We have a second opinion," Caleb said, gesturing toward her. Both Caleb and Delia had their work gear and coats on. Their cheeks were flushed and their fists clenched as they faced off.

"I don't need Summer's fucking opinion." Delia glanced back at her briefly. "You know I don't mean that in the way it sounds."

"Well, su—"

Caleb glowered. "Until you go to the doctor—"

"Until you bite me—"

"You could be—"

"I know very well what I could be and what that means and what I'm capable of, you self-righteous jackass," Delia returned. "You do not get to boss me around just because you put a ring on my finger or because you may have knocked me up."

"Funny, I thought that meant I had some say in—"

"Funny, you're wrong." Delia gave his chest a shove and then stomped past Summer and into the mudroom.

Caleb glared after her, but he stayed where he was in the kitchen.

"What's going on?" Summer asked, schooling her voice to sound calm and sympathetic.

He shook his head. "Someone needs to talk some sense into that woman. She…" He shoved a hand into his hair, knocking his hat to the floor. He didn't seem to notice. "I don't know what the hell happened."

"I'm going to take a guess," Summer offered, picking his hat up off the floor and handing it to him. "You're both scared."

Caleb scowled at her. "I don't want to be psychoanalyzed by you."

"You never do." Still, he tended to listen. He tended to act like she might have something to say. Oh, he blustered a good deal about it, but he cared.

"Instead of poking back, why don't you try to talk calmly and—"

"That's not the way we work, Summer."

"Maybe you should."

He tossed his hat on the couch, shaking his head again. "No. Listen. Do you have time to check the water and break any ice?"

"Of course, but I think—"

"I think you need to mind your own business." Caleb forced a cheerless smile. "I'm not trying to be a dick, I'm just... I know you don't like discord, but this is how we work."

"But, that's—" She stopped talking because he was already going up the stairs after his wife. Still, she couldn't get over the idea he was wrong. How could yelling at each other be good? If she was ever going to find someone she wanted to marry, she'd want them to be sweet and good and nice. No yelling. No anger. It would be pleasant. It would be calm and comfortable.

The telltale squeak of a wheelchair sounded behind her and she turned. She never knew what to call...*him*. She'd been here a year and a half, and she couldn't muster up a "Dad" any more than she could call him by his first name.

But he didn't wheel away, which was his norm about ninety-nine percent of the time. He seemed poised to say something, but then he gave a little shake of his head.

His hand moved to the wheel of his chair, but she took a step toward him.

"Is there…anything I can do for you?"

Summer didn't know why, after all this time, she was still nervous. She shouldn't be. He didn't care. He probably wouldn't care if she turned out not to really be his daughter. To him, most of the world meant nothing. He barely engaged with the children he'd raised, and he'd been in a wheelchair for seven years now.

He'd refused to hold Lissa, had refused any and all attempts to get him to visit Mel in the hospital or at her ranch.

Summer wished she had the courage to shake him, to yell at him. She wished she could muster Delia's condescension or Mel's force, but mainly she felt…

Like a fraud.

But he was a fraud too, because whether she was his or not, he'd known about her, thought she was his. Unless he was keeping even deeper secrets than he'd admitted to last year—that he'd known Mom was pregnant when she'd left him. That he'd let Mom leave with his child inside her in order to keep his other child. That he'd sacrificed Summer for Mel, even if it had been an unfair deal Mom had insisted upon.

"No," he finally said, his voice gruff from disuse. He turned his wheelchair so his back was to her, and Summer exhaled. She always seemed to hold her breath around him, like she was waiting for him to see through her.

"Sometimes the worst thing is someone you can't trust with your anger."

She stared at his retreating back, trying to make sense

of the words. Or why he'd spoken them…or even why he'd spoken them to *her*.

But his comment didn't make sense. He didn't make sense, and she had work to do.

~~~

Thack tried to concentrate on inventory. He really did. It was important to gauge how much feed he had, to note if he would need to make adjustments to his normal order. November and December were hard months to get in to Bozeman and unpredictable weather-wise.

He needed to concentrate, but all he could think about was Summer inside his house with his little girl. Who had spent almost all of Halloween night talking about Summer. About her caravan, about how she looked like the fairy queen and how she hoped Summer would teach her how to braid her hair.

Thack knew Kate needed that. The hair braiding. Kate loved things that were so beyond his realm of experience. Thack *knew* he had to unclench.

But knowing and doing were two separate things.

Thack gave up concentrating. It'd make more sense to eat lunch, then check on everything. Then he could concentrate. Of course, with his luck, he'd discover that Dad had taken off for Bermuda or some such, and Summer and Kate would be in the kitchen dancing with knives over hot coals. Or something.

Okay, he was probably nuts, but that didn't stop the worry from clutching his mind like some kind of robot claw. He forced himself up the stairs of the porch and in through the front door—and then immediately froze.

What on earth was that noise?

A guitar. Singing. Had he fallen into some bizarre rendition of *The Sound of Music*? Of course, he didn't have six kids, Summer wasn't a nun, and there was no way he was that… They were…

Okay, his stalling had officially taken a ridiculous turn, so it was time to force himself to move into the kitchen. He would eat his lunch, then go back to work and somehow not worry that everything had taken a turn for the *different*.

He stepped into the kitchen, hoping the visual check would calm the constant whirring of his brain. There were just so many things to worry about, so many things he couldn't seem to let go of.

Summer was sitting on one of the counter stools. Dad had his harmonica out and was playing and tapping his foot while Summer accompanied him on a guitar. Kate sat at the kitchen table, clapping along.

His gaze dropped to Kate's lunch plate. Half a hot dog, two nibbled-on strawberries, a couple half-eaten carrots. Cracker crumbs. A glass of milk, half drunk. If she'd honest to goodness eaten what was missing off that plate, he was almost ready to call Summer a miracle worker.

"Daddy, listen to Summer. She sounds like an angel when she sings."

Thack glanced at the woman sitting next to his father, the fair skin of her cheeks going pink. "Oh. Well. Let your dad eat lunch, sweetheart." Summer popped off the seat, heading for the fridge. She was wearing another one of those long, colorful skirts that swished around her like fairy mist.

Kate's books were apparently getting to him.

Summer glanced back at him, catching him looking at her.

Why was he staring? He was just getting used to her in his space. It didn't mean anything. But she caught him anyway and inclined her head, as if she wanted him to come stand next to her.

Stiffly, he walked over to the fridge. She handed him a plate made up of a big sandwich and fruit and celery filled with peanut butter. It was such an odd meal, all in all, something he never could get Kate to eat.

"Do you push?" she whispered, leaning her head toward his as she handed off the plate.

She was wearing some kind of flowery scent, a feminine perfume that mingled with the smell of the peanut butter, and he felt like a child. For a flickering instant he was entirely at the mercy of this woman—Summer, who was supposedly five years his junior but somehow felt like the only adult in the room.

"Push?" he repeated dumbly.

Summer's eyes slanted to Kate behind them, but she was busy making designs out of her half-eaten strawberries and not paying them any mind. "Do you push on the food? Would you want me to push her to eat more, or is that okay? Or do you want me to mind my own business?"

Her questions were so deferential that he was caught by surprise, somehow forgetting that he'd been the one to set all the strict ground rules. "That's a lot more than she usually eats."

"Oh." Summer looked down at the counter, gathering up plates and things that must have been left over from lunch prep, but he couldn't miss the way her mouth curled into a smile, or how gorgeous her profile was.

Which was just... She was beautiful. He couldn't argue himself out of that. But it really, truly, one hundred percent didn't matter either way.

"Well, I tried to give her a little bit of a lot of things. I hope that's okay."

Thack opened his mouth to tell Summer she didn't have to ask if things were okay, but that was the whole point. He didn't know her, didn't trust her, so she *should* ask regarding anything that involved Kate.

"It's a good strategy."

"Great." She began loading the dishwasher, then nodded at the plate still in his hands. "You should sit and eat."

"Right." He should sit and eat and remove himself from whatever weirdness was swirling around them. No, it wasn't weird. He was just getting used to having someone else underfoot, that was all. Someone who made music with his father, while his daughter ate more for lunch than she usually did in a day.

He sat down at the table, and when Kate got up on her knees and opened her mouth, he handed over the pickles on his sandwich without a second thought.

Dad chuckled and Thack glared at him. "What are you laughing at?" he muttered.

"Nothin'." Dad brought the harmonica to his lips and played a few notes, something Thack thought he recognized, but he wasn't sure he wanted to try to figure it out. When Dad grinned, Thack knew for a fact he didn't want to know. Whatever that song was, the answer was only going to piss him off.

"Play more, Grandpa! Daddy, can we watch *The Little Mermaid* tonight? You said for the three-day weekend we could stay up late."

Thack all but choked on the bite of sandwich he'd taken, finally recognizing the snatch of the tune.

"Kiss the Girl."

He forced himself to stare at the sandwich. He would not look at Summer. He would not let on he'd recognized the song.

"Sure," he muttered to Kate, choking down the rest of his sandwich. Best to get out of here before things got weirder. "Make sure Grandpa gets out the VCR this afternoon."

"You barely took a breath between bites, boy. In that big of a hurry?" Dad clouded the question with concern, but Thack could hear his father's laughter underneath the question.

"Busy day. Gotta finish inventory and do a ride around." It was an unnecessary explanation. Dad knew exactly what needed to be done. "I'll be back for dinner."

He just needed some space. To recalibrate. Change always required a little adjustment period.

Chapter 9

SUMMER HAD DINNER IN THE OVEN HALF AN HOUR LATER than she'd planned. The living room was a mess of feathers and glitter because she'd thought a little craft project would be quick and easy to do with Kate. Mr. Lane had suggested it before he started napping in a chair in the living room.

He'd tried to be sly, but Summer didn't miss the little oxygen tank he was trying to hide behind the recliner. When she had her head down with Kate, he'd place the mask over his face and breathe into it—but the minute she moved even an inch, he'd shove the mask back out of view.

Summer had been so distracted by *that*, and by keeping Kate occupied while still being around Mr. Lane, and not letting Kate out of her sight, and trying to keep things tidy, that dinner had completely gone out of her mind until nearly five.

What had started so easily, so *perfectly* was falling apart. *She* was falling apart. But she had to keep it together because Kate and Mr. Lane were sitting at the kitchen table doing a puzzle while she frantically shoved her carefully planned chicken dish into the oven.

Mr. Lane had said Thack always came in for dinner between five fifteen and five thirty, unless there was cow trouble, and Summer prayed fervently for that kind of delay.

She set the timer and winced when the front door creaked open. Neither Kate nor Mr. Lane seemed to notice, but they probably hadn't been listening for the footsteps of doom.

He'd been so...shocked and impressed at lunch. She'd felt like a queen. On top of the world. Now...

She closed her eyes and tried to breathe through the fresh wave of embarrassment and disappointment. She was being so foolish. He could hardly blame her for a little mess and a late dinner, especially when she'd been entertaining two people all afternoon.

And yet, his surprise and awe this afternoon had been wonderful. She'd felt like she'd won some kind of lottery.

And you liked the way he stared at you.

Summer scoffed at the unbidden inner thought. He had not. Sure, she'd felt a little skitter across her skin, that rash-like feeling from the other day. Only without irritation behind it, the tickle on her arms hadn't felt so much like a rash.

It felt like a caress. The kind you actually wanted.

"Well, the living room is full of feathers and glitter. Let me guess—you've been building fairies?"

Thack stepped into the kitchen, and she *knew* she was being foolish. She knew she was letting her imagination and silly notions of romance take over reason and sense, things she had promised herself she wouldn't do anymore. But the air changed when he came in the room. He was handsome. Kate was always talking about how Summer looked like that picture of a fairy queen, but Thack looked like a cowboy out of an old movie. He was broad and strong, with a smile for his daughter that made jittering sensations cartwheel through Summer's chest.

Do not be stupid, Summer. How could she have gone so quickly from not liking him at all to gooey-brained attraction?

He touched Kate's flyaway hair almost reverently, and that tenderness was the key to Summer's undoing. For as irritating and off-putting as Thack had been in the beginning, his dedication to his daughter had melted so many of the defenses Summer had mustered.

What must it be like to grow up knowing you were safe and loved?

His gaze lifted to her, and something in her chest shifted awkwardly.

"Everything okay?"

Okay? Ha. Not by a long shot. But she had it under control. She was strong. She was resilient. Right? Right. "Dinner's a little late, I'm afraid."

"That's all right."

"When the timer goes off, it's ready. No fuss, really." But that wasn't what Mr. Lane had asked of her. Two meals a day, snacks for Kate. She hadn't had a chance to help him with his woodworking shop today, but he hadn't been feeling well, so she'd had to keep her eye on Kate.

"You're going to eat with us, aren't you? And watch the movie! Oh, and spend the night."

Summer's heart stuttered over saying no to Kate's exuberant offer, but as much as she wanted to shower the motherless little girl with whatever she asked, she knew Thack wanted boundaries.

It would be best if she gave herself some boundaries

and calmed down. Typical first-day jitters—typical putting too much pressure on herself. She wasn't going to fall back into that habit, that old Summer. Trying to please a volatile and unpredictable woman.

So, she smiled at Kate. "I would love to, of course, but I have to go have dinner with my family."

Kate pouted but went back to her puzzle without making too much of a fuss.

"I'll just go tidy up the living room." She'd put in a little overtime, and then Thack couldn't find her lacking.

She grabbed a rag and slipped out of the kitchen and went to the craft-table mess. She'd simply set this to rights, then—

"You were supposed to be done a half hour ago. You don't have to clean this up."

She turned to face Thack. He was as tense as always, but she thought he was trying, probably very hard, not to appear so…foreboding. He had his hands tucked into the pockets of his jeans instead of tensed at his sides, and his mouth wasn't that firm, disapproving line.

It wasn't a smile either, but she wasn't about to expect *smiles* from Thack Lane. Not yet anyway. Maybe that was a goal to aspire to.

"That's what your father's paying me for though, right? Housekeeping."

"From eleven thirty until five thirty. You don't need to put in any overtime on cleaning. You made lunch and dinner, and Kate didn't escape. That's pretty much what he's paying you for, and we *have* been surviving without you."

"I'm here to make that surviving easier. I don't mind putting in a few extra minutes to clean up a mess I initiated."

"All right. I…I'll help." He walked haltingly toward the table as Summer collected the feathers and stuffed them back into the craft box. Thack used the rag she'd set down to wipe up the glitter, and Summer picked at the little glue spots.

It was weird to work side by side with him, silently cleaning. He was so…big and…hot.

Come on, Summer. Be an adult. "You have quite the artist on your hands," she quipped, probably far too cheerfully as she tried not to notice the easy, almost relaxed way he cleaned up the glitter. As though this was just part of his day. It probably was, but it was hard to reconcile this rough, strong *cowboy* with a man who read his daughter bedtime stories and, according to Kate, hand made her a fairy queen costume.

"Yes, I keep hoping if she focuses all that imagination into *art*, she'll stop taking off on me and scaring years off my life." When Summer didn't say anything, he sighed. "It's okay. You can tell me I'm too uptight. It isn't exactly news to me."

"I-I mean, I understand. You want to keep her safe. I think that's admirable."

His eyebrows lifted. "You do?"

"Well, I mean, I might go about it a *little* differently. But I'm me, and you're…you."

He cocked his head. "Thanks. I think?"

She chuckled and shook her head, handing him the box of feathers. "Anyway, I should head out." Because if she stayed, she might be tempted to give him more compliments. Which wouldn't be such a bad thing, but she had a feeling she might be a little transparent, and she didn't want to make things weird.

"Would you like a ride back to Shaw?"

"No, thank you. It's a short walk." And she needed to get her head together. Somewhere away from this different side of Thack she was seeing.

"It's cold and getting dark."

"I don't mind it." Which was true, but more, tonight she needed it. Some time in the dark cold would give her space to get her thoughts together, to figure out what to do with a complicated attraction to a very, very complicated man.

———

Thack couldn't stop himself from watching Summer as she walked away from the house. It was probably creepy, but the idea of her walking in the dark woods bothered him. She should be more careful.

But that wasn't any of his business. Summer Shaw was no concern of his outside his home. Where she'd spent the day somehow making his life... *Easier* wasn't the right word. *Lighter*, maybe?

More colorful, certainly. Not just because she dressed like a rainbow, but in the way the air... He really needed to stop reading Kate so many fairy stories. He was starting to believe Summer might be a little bit fairy herself.

The front door squeaked open, and Dad stepped out onto the porch.

"Dinner ready? I'll—"

Dad blocked the door. "Few minutes yet."

"Okay, so what's Kate do—"

"Put in the movie. Told her we could eat on TV trays." He folded his arms over his chest. "We need to talk."

"About?"

"You."

Thack turned away, back to the railing and the view of trees and the flash of Summer's colorful clothes disappearing deeper and deeper into the dusk-heavy woods between their properties.

Dad took a step next to him. "She's a pretty girl."

"Too young for you."

Dad snorted. "You'd be surprised."

Before Thack could lose his lunch over *that* comment, Dad clapped him on the shoulder. "Sweet girl. Good to your daughter."

"And, thanks to you, an employee."

Dad shrugged. "So what?"

He wasn't going to argue with Dad about whatever he was trying to suggest. So Summer was young and pretty and good with Kate? He didn't have time in his life for a woman. He most especially didn't have time in his life for *that* woman. He might not know her well, but it didn't take much knowing to suspect that she'd bring all kinds of complications into his life.

Not to mention Kate was already attached, which meant he couldn't allow himself to be. Someone had to keep their head out of the clouds.

"You need something outside these fences, Thackery."

"I don't have time for—"

"You need to make some time. Hire a full-time ranch hand. We can afford it. Your life can't be this ranch and that girl alone."

"I love this ranch and that girl alone." What was wrong with that? Most of his old friends from high school didn't have *half* what he had. "I don't need anything else."

"Yes, you do, because if this is all you have, it's going to give you a heart attack before you walk that girl down the aisle."

Thack shuddered, though he wasn't sure which idea bothered him more—Kate walking down the aisle to some jerkwad who could never be good enough for her, or the idea of him not living to see it. How would she cope with neither of her parents being there when she was an adult and trying to tread water through all life's cruelties?

"You need something. Maybe it's a woman. Maybe it's a hobby. A vacation."

No time. Not now. Besides, he did love the ranch—working it, running it. Sure, it was more of a burden than he was always comfortable with, but welcome to his life. "I'm fine."

"I want you to be more than fine. I want you to be happy."

Happy. Thack wasn't sure when he'd lost that.

It wasn't that he was unhappy. It was just…things had started seeming more and more insurmountable. Ever since Kate started kindergarten, and he'd had to unclench for hours at a time, the time he did have with her had gotten…harder. The worries seemed to multiply in those hours. But the more he worried, the less control he seemed to have. The problem was, he didn't know how to fight his reaction. Even after identifying it and acknowledging it, how did he get rid of it?

"I know I was not the best role model when your mother died."

"I don't want to talk about Mom." Or those dark years after she'd died and Dad had utterly fallen apart.

They'd gotten through them. That was the important thing.

"Maybe we should. Things were bad, and you had to take on a lot of responsibility. Maybe if I'd held together better…"

"But you didn't." Which was too harsh and not exactly what Thack meant. But in his frustration, he couldn't seem to find the right words.

Maybe you should try.

"I don't blame you, Dad. I don't. And more, I think… Look, it got me ready, you know? I knew how to power through it when Michaela died, because I'd already had to do it. So, in a weird way, I needed that." Dad had drowned his grief in booze and cigarettes, and Thack had had to step up and take care of things. In the moment, it had felt like too much. But he'd learned a lot from stepping up, from taking over, and mostly from watching his father fall apart.

He'd learned how to be strong when he had lost his own wife, when he had to raise his child without her mother. That need to be strong had perhaps been what had kept them all going.

Good things could come from tragedy. Mom had tried to assure him of that as she'd withered away.

"Michaela's been gone for six years, Thack. It's time to stop powering through."

Thack leaned his elbows on the porch rail and blew out a breath. "Hell if I know how."

Dad rested his hand on Thack's shoulder. "Give yourself a break. Let yourself look at that girl. We won't fall apart just because you're not here holding on to the pieces too tight 24-7. One of these days, if you're not careful, you'll squeeze so tight that all the pieces fly right out of your hands."

Thack looked out at the dark. Summer's colors had long since disappeared. He knew his dad wasn't wrong. But he wasn't sure Dad was right either. Thack had kept everything going for so long. How did he just step back from that?

"Your mother would be proud of you. More than you'll ever know. You got her strength—but you know that. What I don't think you know is she would have wanted you to let yourself be weak now and again too." Dad gave him one last pat on the back before slipping inside.

Thack knew he should go inside too. It was too cold to be out here without a coat, and he had a daughter to eat dinner with and watch a movie with and love.

He'd have to figure out how to be *weak* some other day.

Chapter 10

"HOW MANY OF YOUR SISTERS ARE GOING TO BE HERE, Delia?" Summer asked, pen poised over her notebook for Thanksgiving preparations.

"Just Rose this year. The rest of the girls have to work either Thursday itself or Friday morning," Delia replied, sitting very stiffly on the couch with baby Lissa in her arms.

"She isn't going to bite you, Delia," Mel said, doing a terrible job of hiding her amusement at Delia's discomfort.

Delia shot her a killing look. "But I might break her."

"You're doing just fine."

"First, you're sick for, what, months? Then you're gigantic and waddle around, and then you have to shove the thing out of your—"

"You'll be fine," Mel interrupted firmly. "I'd focus on surviving morning sickness before I'd get worked up about shoving things out of places."

"Just think," Summer quipped cheerfully. "Next Thanksgiving, you'll have one."

Delia's eyes widened as she looked down at the bundle in her arms. "Guess what, Summer? Not a comfort right now."

"Oh, don't be difficult. The hard parts will be over, and you'll have a sweet little baby in your arms."

"Well, I wouldn't go so far as to say the hard part is over," Mel replied. "I have bags under my eyes and still wince when I walk."

"Okay, we have to talk about anything else. Anything. Else."

"We could talk about Thanksgiving dinner," Summer gently suggested. That's why the three of them had met this morning, but every time Summer tried to focus on the subject at hand, Mel or Delia went in a completely different direction.

"Ugh," Delia said, shifting uncomfortably with Lissa still dozing in her arms. "How's work with the Lanes going?"

"Oh, well. Good."

"Rose mentioned that Thack came in and asked her about you a few weeks ago."

"He asked me too. I don't remember him being so…" Mel's eyebrows drew together. "I don't know how to explain it."

"Rose said he walks around like he's got a stick shoved up his ass."

Mel pressed her lips together before giving into a laugh. "Well, I suppose if anyone's got a right, it's Thack."

"What do you think of him, Summer?"

"U-um…" Summer tried to smile, but she felt oddly put on the spot. "He's a very dedicated father." Her face was warming, and she couldn't stop herself from fidgeting. Why on earth was she blushing?

She tried to ignore her body's odd response, but Delia gave her a speculative look and Summer blushed even more furiously. Seriously, what was wrong with her?

For the first time this morning, Delia looked at ease holding Lissa. "He's attractive, wouldn't you say, Mel?"

Mel was also studying Summer a bit too closely for Summer's comfort. "Yes, very…classically handsome. Gary Cooper type."

"Who's Gary Cooper?" Summer asked, hoping to change the subject to anything but Thack's attractiveness.

Delia shrugged. "Got me there, but the fact of the matter is, he fills out a pair of Wranglers very nicely, wouldn't you say?"

"I-I don't know." Summer stammered. "I work for him. I don't…look at his Wranglers." Which was a lie. She'd noticed far too many things working for Thack the past few weeks. The exact shade of green of his eyes and the way the tendons in his neck stood out when he was well and truly at his wit's end with his father. She'd memorized the way his arms moved when he reached out to touch Kate's hair or give her a casual squeeze. And, more than she'd like to admit even to herself, she had found herself staring at his butt.

His butt! She didn't even know why. It was just kind of mesmerizing. And it always led to uncomfortable fantasies that made her feel very conflicted and confused. A far different conflicted and confused than she'd felt when Mom had insisted she let some man inappropriately talk to her.

"What does working for him matter when it comes to looking at his ass?" Delia jerked her chin toward Mel. "Pretty sure Mel here was shacking up with Dan when he was technically her boss."

"Shh. Not in front of the baby," Mel hissed.

Delia grinned. "Some day the girl is going to find out her mommy and daddy were getting it on in the llama… What do you call it? A stable? A barn? Crazyville?" Delia closed her eyes suddenly. "Oh crap, I need to throw up again."

"Karma," Mel replied, scooping Lissa out of Delia's arms so Delia could lurch to the bathroom.

Mel crooned softly to her baby, and Summer didn't know what to do with all the pangs assaulting her. That she had sisters who were teasing her like she'd seen Delia's sisters do, that Mel had this beautiful little baby, and Summer knew that… Well, she wanted that. She knew she had so much love to give and…

She kept thinking back to the other day, when she'd been making fairies with Kate while Mr. Lane watched one of his TV shows.

Kate had been frowning at the door ever since she'd come home from school. When Summer had asked what was wrong, Kate had sighed, adding more glitter to her drawing of fairy wings.

"Daddy seems sad," she'd said, playing with a glob of glue. Then she'd looked up at Summer innocently. "Don't you think *you* could make him happy?"

A few days later, the memory still gave Summer an odd, shuddery feeling somewhere in her chest.

Oh, where was her head? She needed to focus on one thing at a time. Thanksgiving, then Christmas. Making it perfect for the Shaws. Last Thanksgiving and Christmas had been a little awkward, but she felt like she belonged now. Almost one hundred percent, so she would make all these holidays perfect. "Well, I'm thinking one turkey should suffice. I'll make the stuffing, maybe a salad. Do you think you can handle the rolls? Well, no, I can make those ahead of time, and—"

"Summer." Mel placed a hand on the arm that was furiously scribbling notes. "You don't have to do it all. This is a family affair."

"I know, but you're busy with Lissa, and Delia's not

feeling well, and I don't think Caleb can cook to save his life."

"No, he couldn't, but that doesn't mean you have to take this all so seriously. It's a meal for us, not for a queen."

"It's a celebration. A holiday." How many had she spent alone or with only Mom for company? Lonely and sad, or trying to make Mom less lonely and sad, because Mom almost never had a steady relationship over the holidays. Mom tended to attach herself to men who had families and didn't want Mom or Summer to be anything more than a hostess, an...object. "It's... It should be perfect."

"It won't be though."

Summer shook her head. "I know you're too busy to make it perfect. That's fine. You can trust me."

"Summer, I'm not... No holidays are perfect. No meals are going to be perfect. Especially with our group. Between a month-old baby, Delia sick as a dog, and Dad in whatever headspace he's currently occupying, no amount of food or preparation is going to make the dinner perfect, but that's okay."

"But..."

"The thing is, life is sometimes poopy diapers and meals that don't turn out and a pain in the ass, really."

Summer might have felt a little depressed at that estimation, but Mel was gently rocking the baby in her arm, while her free hand rested on Summer's hand. It was a comforting, caring gesture. Summer looked up at Mel from her seat, tears pricking the back of her eyes. "Are you big-sistering me?"

"Do you want me to?" Mel started to back away. "Oh

no, not the waterworks. You know I never know what to do when you start blubbering."

"Just think of it as one of those pain-in-the-ass things that you have to deal with," Summer said with a little sniff. "It's just… All I ever wanted was family, you know?"

Mel's expression became concerned, mixed with a certain hesitancy. It didn't take a mind reader to know Mel's thoughts were drifting to the unspoken thing between them.

"So…Mom didn't feel like family?"

Summer shook her head. "Not… I mean, yes, but… all I ever was to her was a trophy or a pawn. Not a person. You guys—even, well, him… I know you see me as a person. You treat me as a person." And she never felt *threatened*. Ignored on occasion, but never like she was in danger. "Even if he pretends I don't exist, at least it's honest."

Mel looked through the doorway to the TV room where their father was likely parked. Quiet and in his own world of misery.

"I know you're still hoping he'll change," Mel said quietly.

"But you don't think it's possible?"

Mel's gaze turned back to Summer and her lips curved, though it wasn't a joyful smile. Something more like an attempt at a reassuring one. "I hope it is. I really do. But I can't get him to hold my daughter, his granddaughter. You know? And I can wrap myself in that misery, or I can enjoy my daughter and my husband and…"

"Your llamas?"

Mel laughed. "Yes, oddly enough. And you, and

my idiot brother and his wife, and my future niece or nephew and… The thing is, even just in a year and a half, I've gained so much. My life isn't perfect in the least, and even if you make the most amazing Thanksgiving dinner, things won't magically *become* perfect."

Summer blew out a breath. "I know." Maybe she'd hoped differently, but Mel was right. Trying to make everything perfect was never going to work. She only had control over herself—her decisions and how she treated the people around her. She couldn't make her father interact with her any more than she'd been able to make Mom care for her.

"But wouldn't it be nice if a carefully cooked turkey could make everything perfect?" Summer asked, resting her chin on her palm.

Mel chuckled. "It would indeed." Lissa fussed and began to wiggle. "And that's my cue to hole myself up and feed her. I will handle the rolls and make Caleb pick up a dessert or something. Don't kill yourself over one meal. The fact that we'll be together is the important thing."

Summer smiled genuinely at that. It was true. She was here. The Shaws had accepted her. She'd give them the best meal she could manage because she loved them, because she wanted to, but she wouldn't obsess. Or, she'd try not to anyway.

Mel grabbed the diaper bag, but Summer had one last question she couldn't swallow down, even though she knew it would mean more teasing.

"When you said Thack had a reason to have a stick up his… Well, what did you mean by that?"

"Oh, are you asking me because you're curious

or because you're interested in the contents of his Wranglers?"

Summer blushed again. "I…"

"Because if it's the latter, I think that's a question you should be asking him. You know?"

Summer didn't really, or maybe she did and she didn't want to admit it. Either way, Delia returned looking gray. "You're going to have to finish any food talk without me, I think."

"We've got it handled," Summer offered, moving to help a very unstable-looking Delia get to the couch. "You just relax and grow that baby."

Delia smiled weakly, and Mel disappeared to feed Lissa.

"Can you believe all this?" Delia murmured, her eyes closed, her hand resting protectively over her stomach.

"All what?"

"All we've got."

Summer swallowed. No, sometimes she couldn't quite believe it, but it made her very, very happy.

———

Thack swung off Midnight and examined the weak spot in the fence. The wire sagged, and it would only take one intrepid cow coming out this far to cause a problem. They were unlikely to in this weather, but it was possible.

He checked his pack, getting more and more irritated when he didn't find the tools he needed. Someone had been messing with his stuff and hadn't put it back properly. He only had one glove, and the fence stretchers were nowhere to be found.

"Crud," he muttered. The November wind was brutal today, and they were predicting significant snow accumulation for later in the week. Getting this fence mended was a priority, but he was already losing the light. The chance of him getting back to the barn, finding the tools he needed, and then getting back out here...

"Crud. Crud. Crud," he muttered, pulling on the one glove. Without the fence stretchers, he couldn't fix the problem, but he could try to pull the lag and see if he could find a temporary solution.

He pulled and tugged and twisted, swearing mildly when he scratched his hand. When he stepped back to survey his work, he rolled his eyes. It would last through approximately one heavy gust of wind, but it'd have to do until tomorrow.

He swung back onto Midnight's back, murmuring encouragingly to the horse and moving her forward into a steady pace.

The sun was quickly disappearing, surrounding him with a kind of eerie gray twilight. Usually the snow sparkled in the fading winter sun, but today was too cloudy and dreary for that.

He glanced at his watch. Kate should be home by now, and by the time he got into the house, Summer would have dinner in the oven.

Alone in the midst of winter, he had trouble not thinking about Summer. The cheerful way she seemed to embody her name.

There'd been a change in his house over the past few weeks, and even if he didn't want to credit Summer, how could he deny it? She was the difference. He didn't have to worry so much now that Kate might escape. He didn't have to struggle every meal to find something she would eat or bargain endlessly with her about how many bites. He didn't have to clean up glitter or paint, and Kate still got to do all those activities.

And yet Summer still left him with a restless sense of trepidation. He couldn't analyze it, couldn't push it away. He watched her with Kate, he talked to her, and something in his chest tightened and shifted in a way that made no sense to him.

Part of it was attraction. He wouldn't deny that, nor would he deny that a man who'd been widowed for six years, no matter how he'd loved his wife, was allowed some attraction. But everything with Kate made all that tricky. It wasn't just noticing the way Summer moved or spending far too much time caught up in the easy curve of her smile. It was that she treated his daughter with an easy warmth and kindness that was far more than was required of any employee.

Even as Midnight followed the trail back to the stables and the house came into view, the world was gray, but the windows glowed. Not just the front window, but the kitchen and dining room windows. Lights Dad always forgot to flip on.

Thack was more than glad when his cell went off, because he didn't like dwelling on all that warmth, all that change.

Of course, when he dismounted and pulled the phone out of his pocket, any relief was gone. Michaela's father was calling, which could only mean one thing.

"Hi, Stan," Thack greeted him, trying to keep his voice light and even, hoping against hope that this time would be different.

"Thackery. How are you?"

"I'm…fine." Thack led Midnight into the stable with one hand, while he held the phone to his ear with the other. "We're looking forward to your visit."

The silence that stretched out was heavy with so many things. Stan and Marjorie had moved out of Blue Valley only a few months after Michaela died. They'd claimed it was to be close to Michaela's older brother and his family, who lived in the far more temperate suburbs of Denver.

But Thack had always felt it was because they hadn't agreed with Michaela's decision to wait to take any treatment until Kate was born. Because they'd been angry that he hadn't pushed Michaela on that score. Angry she'd been pregnant, angry she'd married him, angry that Michaela had sacrificed herself for Kate.

No matter how often Michaela had told them she didn't have a choice, that she wouldn't have even known something was wrong if she hadn't found out she was pregnant. That her survival would have been even less possible, and she owed it to the life inside her to give her daughter the best chance.

Thack led Midnight into her stall. The heaviness on his shoulders had been lighter the past few days, but now it settled right back where it belonged.

"Stan?"

"I'm sorry, Thackery. Marjorie's therapist just doesn't think it's a good idea. Maybe you two could come—"

"I can't leave the ranch." Which maybe was selfish, but traveling this time of year and leaving Dad alone? It wasn't an option. "Maybe…"

"You could send her by herself."

"No."

"I could fly to Billings and collect her. She wouldn't have to travel alone."

"We've made plans for Thanksgiving, Stan. Plans here. Plans we were hoping you would join, and quite honestly, if Marjorie's therapist doesn't think she should come here, I'm not sure how comfortable I feel sending Kate your way."

Again a long silence, and Thack tried to get Midnight ready to bed one-handed while he waited for Stan's response.

"I'm sorry, Thackery. It's not easy for us."

Thack bit back the harsh words that wanted to spill out. He used all his strength and every reminder that Stan was Kate's grandfather and he didn't want any more complications between them. "It's not easy for any of us, Stan."

"We'll discuss Christmas later," Stan replied, ignoring that, ignoring everything. His words were clipped. "I'm sorry it didn't work out this time. I'll be in touch. Good-bye."

"Good-bye," Thack replied, though he was almost certain Stan had hung up immediately.

Thack sighed and pressed his forehead into Midnight's flank. Well, so much for lighter and happier feelings as they barreled toward another Christmas with just the three of them.

Someone cleared their throat, a female someone, and Thack jerked his head off the horse, surprised to find Summer standing at the door of the stables, wringing her hands together.

"Your father wanted me to come get you for dinner," she offered into the gray silence.

"I'm almost done," Thack managed, hoping his voice didn't sound as strained as it felt.

"Is…everything okay?"

"I'll survive." *You need to do more than survive.* He wanted to, damn but he wanted to. But he didn't know how to fix the world for Kate, let alone the people she should have in her life.

"Sometimes it helps to talk," Summer offered, so quietly he almost thought he might have imagined it. But why would it be a surprise that Summer would say that, offer that? She was always offering things, and he never knew what to do about it.

Maybe take her up on it?

"Kate's grandparents… They were…" Why was he dumping this on Summer? But she stood there with her empathetic hazel eyes and, hell, he might as well tell someone he didn't have to pretend for. "They were going to come for Thanksgiving, but they canceled."

"Oh, that's a shame. Do you think Kate will be disappointed?"

"Honestly? I hadn't told her yet, because this is their pattern. A lot of grand plans to visit then…"

"Then?"

"They're still grieving, I guess you'd call it. Michaela, my, um, late wife, she was their only daughter. They moved to be closer to their son and his kids. That's easier, I guess you'd say."

"Poor Kate."

Hearing that eased something inside him that had been clutched tight—a knot he'd been telling himself to loosen for months, maybe years. And yet all it took were those two words from Summer. Poor Kate.

"Poor you."

"Me?" He blinked. On the other hand, he didn't know what to do with that sentiment. "I wasn't particularly... close with Stan and Marjorie."

"But they're your child's grandparents, and I'd think that's tricky ground to cover when, well, I don't know all that happened..."

It was something like an invitation. To tell. To lay it all at her feet, and there was a certain temptation in that. Because Summer was easy to talk to, easy to confide in.

But he didn't want that pity, and he didn't want excuses made for him. No matter how empathetic Summer seemed, no matter how easy it would be, he wanted someone to look at him and not see all the tragedies that made up his past.

"Give me about five minutes, and then I'll be in to dinner." He forced himself to smile, though he knew Summer didn't buy it.

But she had listened, and that was some bright spot in this hell of an afternoon.

Chapter 11

SUMMER TRUDGED BACK TO THE HOUSE ALONG THE path she'd made. It was almost six, and she should have left a half hour ago, but...

She glanced back at the stables. Thack was stepping out of the opening and closing up the door. The wind whipped at his hat and his heavy jacket, but they both stayed firmly in place.

Classically handsome. He was, and more. Something like a tragic hero, all broody and intense, but heavy with burdens that weren't particularly fair.

She knew it was silly to want to lift them from him. Who was she to take on such a task? But it gnawed at her, that want.

She climbed the stairs, knocking the extra snow off her boots. Though a path to the stables had been cleared earlier, dainty flakes were beginning to swirl down from the sky again.

She paused at the door, trying to talk herself out of waiting for Thack and failing. After all, Mr. Lane had asked her to come get his son, so it only made sense to return with him.

Thack walked along the pathway, all certain and sure strides, but he had that air of heavy things holding him down, *pushing* him down. Summer had thought maybe the load had been lightened in the past few days, but this afternoon Thack seemed firmly in his own burdened world. *Sad*. Just like Kate had said the other day. *Don't you think you could make him happy?*

It was foolish to want to.

He walked up the stairs, snow circling around him, oddly reminding Summer of Kate's glitter snow day-dream. Something about the last rays of sun glinting in those fragile flakes.

Their gazes met for a moment, and Summer wasn't sure what she was doing or hoping to accomplish. She had no words for him, no advice. All she had was so much empathy it hurt to look at him.

So, she looked at the door and turned the handle.

"Summer, I wanted to ask you…"

She turned back to face him and he looked…perplexed. Uncertain. He took off his hat, hitting it gently against his thigh, not finishing his sentence.

"Wanted to ask me what?" she prompted when he stood there, eyebrows drawn together, gaze on the western horizon where the sun was nothing but a sliver of gold.

He blew out a frustrated breath. "Well, first I owe you an apology, for the way I was the first few times we met."

"I understand."

"You do?"

"I mean, I would have tried to be more polite if I were you, but I understand you had good intentions."

His mouth curved, just the tiniest fraction. "I appreciate that. I think. Regardless, I behaved poorly, no matter how much I worry about Kate's safety. It was never right to take that out on you."

"Well, thank you," she said warmly. Trying not to be too warm and failing. "But that's not a question."

"Right. Um. I didn't want to ask you in front of Kate and add any pressure, but she's been pestering me about you staying for dinner. So, I wanted to let you know, if you wanted to, you're more than welcome to stay and eat dinner with us."

"Yes."

He blinked as he turned his green gaze on her. "That was…quick."

"I love spending time with Kate, and you're not always so terrible to be around." She offered a smile, hoping some teasing might lift something off those tense shoulders.

He smiled ruefully. "I'm sure I deserve that."

"I'm teasing." She reached out and touched his arm, needing to make some physical gesture or she'd burst. The man needed a hug, some reassurance. She thought maybe he really needed something to go right.

For him. For Kate. He had taken on this burden because Kate's grandparents were doing something he couldn't control, and she…she wanted to help.

She wanted to give something to ease that burden and… "You could come to Shaw Thanksgiving."

The idea snowballed immediately, because it would be so easy to fold the Lanes in, to give them a real holiday. If she could give it to the Shaws, she could give it to the Lanes.

He opened his mouth, presumably to argue, but she had to get it all out before he shot her down. "I'm doing almost all the cooking, so I can say definitively it won't be any problem adding the three of you."

"The three of us?" he asked, sounding confused.

"Sure. You, Kate, your father. It… Well, you know,

it would feel something like family and celebration, and you wouldn't have to feel like... I know it's not the same as having Kate's grandparents here, but it'd be something."

"I don't know what to say."

"Say yes so I don't have to badger you until you give in." She flashed her most convincing smile.

He exhaled, something she thought might have been close to a laugh. "You should talk to the Shaws before you—"

"I am a Shaw," she said resolutely, knowing without a doubt that everyone would be fine with this. Fine because she'd ask them to be. That's what family did. "I'm doing most of the preparations, so I get to invite people if I want. Just think: no cooking, no cleaning, a festive meal for Kate, and all you have to do is show up."

"Why?"

"Why what?"

"Why would you... Why are you inviting us?"

"Because I like you...all... I mean, I like all of you. All three of you." She closed her eyes for a second, wishing she could stop the embarrassed flush creeping across her skin. Smooth she was not. "Ask Kate, ask your father, and then you can let me know. But I'm going to plan on you being there." She said it resolutely, trying to ignore the telling flush on her cheeks.

He stepped forward, and for some reason, Summer sucked in a breath and held it. Some reason that had a lot to do with the insane flutters in her chest. It was just that she could see the color of his eyes so clearly, that vibrant green that seemed so out of place in the dusk of the cold winter night.

He placed his gloved hand on her coat-covered arm, and the only reason she didn't squeak was because she was still holding her breath. The touch didn't have any reason to feel warm or meaningful, not with so many layers between them, but something about the look he gave her made the gesture seem very important.

"Thank you," he offered, sounding grave.

She let the breath out, trying not to step closer even though that's what she wanted to do. "For what? It's just an invitation."

"Thank you for caring." He gave her arm a squeeze. A friendly, grateful arm squeeze. That was all. Certainly not something to get all aflutter about.

Unfortunately, she was very much all aflutter.

"I want to make it clear, if you need to be alone with Kate…I trust you." He blinked at that and exhaled loudly, slowly pulling his hand off her arm. There was a frown on his face, but he didn't take back what he'd said. "Let's go eat, huh?" he offered, inclining his head toward the door.

She nodded, not trusting her voice. Dinner with the Lanes. Thanksgiving with the Lanes. *Trust*. It was friendship, that was all. She'd been so focused on the Shaws that she hadn't really made any other friends, except Rose.

It would be nice to have a friend of her own. A relationship that was just hers. Not that it was a relationship per se, just that…

She rolled her eyes at herself and followed Thack inside.

--- ∾ ---

Thack pulled his truck up the winding drive of the Shaw ranch. Everything in his chest was pulled too tight, and his throat felt like it had closed in on him.

But Kate bounced in her booster seat in the back, chattering happily about turkey and pie and fairy opinions on pie.

Which was a lot better than looking at his far-too-smug father. Because no matter how many times Thack explained he was doing this for Kate and to take a little stress off himself from cooking and cleaning up after a meal, Dad just grinned and grinned and grinned.

Thack parked next to a glossy-looking pickup in front of the Shaws' detached garage. He couldn't begin to count the ways this would be awkward, or the ways he felt terrible for not bringing anything, but Summer had been adamant. Summer adamant was a hard thing to fight.

The Shaw house was shrouded in the dark of early evening. It might have loomed like an impressive-looking shadow if not for the way every window on the front side of the house glowed with light, and the porch light offered a clear pathway to the ramp that led to the front door.

Thack forced himself out of the truck and opened the back door to collect Kate. She'd already unbuckled herself and was ready to jump down, but she stopped. "Oh, my pictures!" She scrambled around in the backseat for the stack of pictures that she'd insisted on bringing as a present to Summer. She'd also insisted on wearing a completely weather-inappropriate dress and then refused to put leggings underneath.

He'd argued until they were going to be very nearly late and then finally gave in to Kate's fashion demands.

Though a path in the snow had been cleared to the front, Thack insisted on carrying Kate to the porch, much to her wiggling chagrin.

"Put me down, Daddy," she whined as he took the stairs.

Since the porch had also been cleared, he finally obliged. "Next time, wear boots and I won't have to carry you anywhere, Katie Pie."

She harrumphed, and before he could knock on the door, it swung open to Summer and the smells of food and a blast of warmth.

"Hi," Summer greeted exuberantly, her arms immediately going around Kate as the girl shot forward. "I'm so glad you could make it with all the extra snow we had this morning. Don't you look pretty tonight, Kate."

"Wouldn't miss it," Dad offered jovially, pushing Thack forward, which meant making him standing far closer to Summer than Thack thought was particularly wise.

She was like a sunrise. She had a bright-red shirt on and some kind of shawl or sweater thing over it that was all oranges and yellows and fringe. She wore one of her long, swishy skirts in some goldish-red and jewelry everywhere.

She smiled at him, that all-too-enticing broad curve of red-slicked lips. Then she turned to Kate who was shoving pictures at her.

"They're beautiful. I'll have to see if I have magnets to put them on the fridge," Summer said, looking at each piece of paper dutifully.

"What kind of pie do you have?" Kate asked as Summer ushered them through a mudroom and into a living room where the Shaws were gathered.

Summer leaned down and whispered something in Kate's ear, and his little girl grinned from ear to ear. Thack would gladly encounter all the awkwardness this evening would entail for just that flash of his daughter's grin.

Dad settled in a chair next to Cal in his wheelchair, and Kate pranced behind Summer into the kitchen. Thack was left standing. Odd man out and certainly feeling it.

Summer popped her head out of the way she'd gone. "Oh, do you need something to drink?"

"No. No, I'm fine." Stuttering like an idiot, about as un-fine as a man could be.

Summer just smiled, everything about her exuding a happy, keyed-up energy. "Sit. Watch football. Dinner will be ready in just a few."

Thack forced a paltry smile and took a few halting steps into the living room. He settled himself onto a chair and tried to focus on the TV, on just about anything aside from the awkwardness of being here and knowing these people but most assuredly not being family.

"How are your fences holding up with all this wind? We've been having a hell of a time." Delia sat on the couch, her hand resting on her stomach, her complexion gray, which seemed odd for a woman he associated with rebellious behavior only possibly eclipsed by that of her sister, Rose, who was sitting next to her looking about as comfortable to be here as Thack felt.

"It's been a struggle," Thack replied, trying not to fidget. "Weather doesn't look like it's going to let up any."

Conversation about the weather and fences went on

easily enough since most of the people in the room were ranchers.

"I have a llama proposition for anyone who's willing to listen," Dan offered, standing off to the corner with a baby cradled in his arms.

"No," just about everyone returned in unison. Dan grinned down at the bundle in his arms.

When Summer called them to the dining room, they filed in. Kate was bouncing next to Summer, a crown of paper turkeys on her head and a suspicious smudge of chocolate in the corner of her mouth, but Summer was having her hand out napkins and appear to be useful, and Kate was eating it all up.

His daughter wasn't particularly helpful at home, so he wondered if this had something to do with having an audience. Or if it just had to do with Summer.

Kate instructed him to sit next to Dad, then she clamored up into the old family-heirloom-looking chair on the other side of him. Summer fluttered around the room, adding last touches and spoons and forks to the ridiculous amount of food that took up the center of the table.

She smiled and laughed, checking on everyone's drink before finally settling into a chair next to Kate.

"Well, before we eat, let's have a little toast," Caleb said, standing at the head of the table. He lifted his glass toward Summer. "To Summer, who made all of this happen."

Thack glanced at the woman in question as they all held their glasses up and toward her. Her cheeks were pink, her eyes a little shiny.

"I just made a meal, guys," she said, pressing her hand to her reddening cheek.

"You brought us all together for a meal. This is a real family holiday, one we haven't had in a long time."

Thack didn't think he imagined the sideways glances at Cal, who sat in his wheelchair, expressly not holding a glass up. There was something in the man's blank expression that bothered Thack, that felt a little too familiar.

So, he looked at Summer instead and repeated the *To Summer* the remainder of the table uttered. Summer smiled prettily, clearly moved and pleased beyond belief.

Dinner was like something out of his childhood. It had been a long time since he'd been a part of any large family gathering, even if it wasn't his family. Those first few years after Mom passed away, Dad hadn't made much an effort on holidays. Thack had always been invited to his grandparents' or aunts' and uncles' houses, but he'd needed to stay close to the ranch, to Dad.

Thack was more than a little humbled that Summer had allowed him to give Kate this. Kate ate it all up, the laughter, the noise, the food—truly a feast. She gobbled up two pieces of pie, and then when Mel's baby fussed, she asked if she could hold her.

While Rose and Summer were clearing the dining room table, Mel obliged, teaching Kate how to carefully support the newborn.

Dad and Cal talked, though it didn't seem to escape anyone's notice that Dad mostly talked and Cal just grunted in response.

Caleb intercepted a stack of plates Summer had begun to carry to the kitchen. "Out."

Summer frowned. "But, I have to cle—"

"We are the cleanup crew. You are officially forbidden from this area until further notice." Caleb glanced at Thack. "Keep her out of the kitchen, huh?"

"Oh, I—"

"Can I help clean up?" Kate asked, bouncing.

"Maybe we—" But before Thack could suggest going home, Kate was whisked into the kitchen.

Thack stood in the hall next to Summer, not knowing what to say or quite what to do. He should collect Kate and Dad and go, but…

Summer was frowning at the kitchen, and something about her expression made him want to soothe her. "The food was great."

She smiled, but it wasn't that exuberant Summer smile. "Thank you. I wish they'd let me clean up. I don't know what to do with myself."

He gestured at the TV behind them. "Well, you could always watch football."

She chuckled. "I hate football. It's so violent. But, you can feel free to watch it if you like it."

"I don't really…have an opinion. Never had much time to sit and watch a whole sporting event. Always seems to be something else to do. Or some kids' show to watch."

"You're such a good dad." Her gaze wasn't on him but on the corner of the dining room where her father and his father still sat.

No matter how perfect the evening had been, no family was perfect, and oddly, that was a good reminder. Thack didn't actually have to be perfect for Kate. He just had to be there and take opportunities like this so she could feel like a part of something.

"Thank you for this. I don't know how to possibly express how much it meant that Kate got to have a meal like this."

Summer's gaze left their fathers and met his. Her eyes were a dark, empathetic brown with the faintest hints of green. Everything about her was soft and sweet, bright and warm. It was becoming an increasingly big problem.

"I was happy to do it. For Kate." She chewed on her lip for a few seconds. "For you."

Uncomfortable with that warmth in her gaze he hadn't quite figured out how to enjoy, Thack moved stiffly to the living room.

He scratched a hand through his hair. He wanted more things like this for Kate, big meals and happy families, and the kind of joy he and Dad couldn't give her being so isolated. He knew Kate was happy for the most part, but he also knew she could have more. He'd been a lonely teen with just his father and too much responsibility. Michaela had come along with her friends and her family.

It had been a bright spot in those days. Then he'd touched that brightness, and look what had happened.

He rolled his eyes at himself. Even if he wanted to wallow in that, he was slowly reminding himself he couldn't. Summer's presence had awoken something he'd lost in the past few years of desperately trying to keep Kate safe.

"I thought maybe…" Was he really going to ask for more help? After everything Summer had done today? But she was standing there, looking up at him expectantly. Maybe even hopefully. "The thing is, I need to start Christmas shopping for Kate, and last year Santa kind of royally screwed up."

"Oh, yes, she was telling me all about that."

"She was?"

Summer nodded, her mouth curving. "The other day she gave me the rundown. Purple instead of pink. I mean, how could you?" But she grinned so it didn't feel like scolding.

"How could *Santa*," Thack corrected, smiling over the mix-up for probably the first time in a year. He'd felt like utter dirt that he'd screwed up something so simple, and as a result, Santa had disappointed his child.

"I need help." When was the last time he'd admitted that? Out loud and to someone who actually could help. "Shopping. I thought maybe some morning you could come with me. I know what Kate likes, but sometimes the details of it all make no sense to me."

"I'd lo—"

"It'd just be an extension of your job. You know, if you can fit it in, that is."

She blinked, something in her expression hard to read. Almost like he'd said something wrong, flipped some dimmer switch on the brightness that was Summer.

"I'd love to. As a favor. Not as"—she made a face—"work. As a favor to Kate and Santa."

Thack smiled. "Santa desperately appreciates that."

Whatever had dimmed brightened again, and Summer laughed, that light, airy sound that never failed to make Thack's stomach feel like it was barreling down some twisty country road far too fast.

"I can't get into town next week," he forced himself to say. "But how about the week after?"

"Whatever morning works for you."

She was standing close again, right in front of him. He could smell that perfume she always wore, and he could hear the faint jangle of every piece of jewelry as it moved with her breathing.

He wanted to reach out and touch...something. A strand of hair, the dangle of her earrings, the line of bracelets on her wrist or the fringe on her shawl thing. He wanted to touch Summer and find out if everything was as warm as she looked, as warm as her name suggested she was.

He wanted. *Wanted*. It had been a long time since he'd let his guard down enough for that.

"Daddy! Ms. Mel let me help change a poopy diaper! It was disgusting." Kate clattered into the room, gleefully talking about the contents of a child's diaper.

It should have eradicated that unsteady, confusing swirl of attraction and want and just plain enjoyment of the woman in front of him, but, sadly, it did not. Especially when Summer smiled and Kate leaned against her, talking animatedly.

No, that feeling lodged deeper, and he quite honestly didn't know how to address it. So, he listened to Kate's tale, he gathered up his family and said their good-byes, and he ignored the feeling as best he could.

But as he drove away from the Shaw house, he could see Summer in the rearview mirror, standing in the circle of light on the porch, watching them drive away.

"You're going to have to figure it out, Son."

"Figure what out?" Thack grumbled, returning his gaze to the road in front of him.

"Just what it is you want."

What he wanted? There was no point in *wanting*. Things got taken away, things weren't easy, and he did have a daughter to protect.

So what he maybe, *maybe* wanted...was a lot easier said than done.

Chapter 12

SUMMER DID HER BEST TO ACT TOTALLY NORMAL AND casual as she sat in the passenger seat of Thack's truck.

Kate was in the back talking nonstop about some art project at school, and the plan was to drop her off there and then go shopping.

Shopping together. Just the two of them. Every time Summer contemplated it, she felt like she was going to jitter apart. It was silly, of course. This wasn't friendly or more than friendly—it was simply work. He'd said that. Like an extension of her housekeeper duties. Not a favor or anything.

But no matter how often she told herself that, the jitters didn't dissipate. The wish that this really was a sign of friendship, a favor given was rooted firm and deep.

Thack pulled through the school drop-off line, and Kate popped out of her seat. "Bye, Daddy." She leaned between the two front seats and gave Thack a kiss on the cheek. "Bye, Summer." And then she gave Summer an identically loud kiss before bounding out of the car.

Summer wasn't surprised anymore by Kate's enthusiastic displays of affection, but seeing one this way, next to Thack, made it feel something like...a family moment.

The three of them. She closed her eyes against the assault of emotions. Too many to name or analyze.

"Have a good day," Thack called hoarsely as Kate

pushed the door closed and skipped toward the school doors with the other kids while the teachers manned the drop-off line.

When Summer managed to glance at Thack, that unreadable green gaze was on her. So many complex emotions, ones that rivaled her own.

"I think people are waiting," she offered gently.

"Right. Right." He focused on the road and pulled out of the elementary-school parking lot, his eyebrows drawn together, his jaw clenched so tight.

She wished there was something she could say, but she could only imagine what he was thinking or feeling. She wondered if he'd felt that family vibe too, and whether it reminded him of his wife.

It hurt a little. That Kate didn't have a mother, that Thack might be thinking about another woman. All jumbled and probably wrong feelings to have.

"She really likes you," Thack said, as if it only just occurred to him that Kate had grown attached.

"I really, really like her." Which was true. She'd fallen in love with the exuberant little girl and her wild imagination. Regardless of who her father was, Summer loved Kate like a member of her own family.

"That's…good." He focused hard on the highway that would take them to Bozeman and the appropriate big-box store with a wide variety of toys.

It would be a long ride if they didn't talk, or at least play some music or something, but Summer didn't know what to discuss when she felt like opening her mouth would only produce squeaks.

Squeak. *Alone*. Squeak. *With Thack*. Squeak. *Think you're really hot*.

"Oh, um, so, I wanted to let you know that if you need help putting up decorations, I'd be happy to."

"I hauled up the boxes yesterday, but I have been stressing a bit about when I'll get it done."

"Well, then let me help."

"I don't want you to feel like you have to."

"You have a real hang-up about that."

He blew out a breath. "Hang-ups? I have a legion," he muttered.

"Don't we all?"

"You seem very happy and well-adjusted."

She laughed. She couldn't help it. "I mean, I try. I am happy." She was. She'd found a whole new world in Montana, and it had given her that feeling of belonging she'd always hoped for. And yet, there were still deep-seated fears inside her and a bitterness she didn't know what to do with.

"But not well-adjusted?"

"Is anyone?"

It was Thack's turn to laugh. "That is an oddly comforting thought."

They talked about Kate for the rest of the drive. She seemed like the safest subject, far safer than whether Summer was well-adjusted or not.

When they reached the store, Thack pulled a piece of paper out of his pocket. "Here's her letter to Santa. Now I just have to remember to send it off to the Man Up North when I get home."

"I'll help you remember," Summer offered happily, grabbing a cart.

They went through aisle after aisle of toys and dolls, Thack studying Kate's list with an adorable amount of concentration. "How am I supposed to understand the difference between Princess Sonia and Princess Perfect Sonia?" he grumbled, looking from the paper to two almost identical boxes of dolls on the shelf.

"Well, the green box has perfect on the side."

"They're both green boxes."

Summer tried to swallow down the laugh, but she couldn't manage.

"I know, I'm hopeless. But none of these things stay the same. Clothes I can get. Books? Easy. I've mastered putting her hair back. I do not get dolls."

Summer plucked the Princess Perfect Sonia box off the shelf. "Here we go." She put it in the cart and couldn't quite help reaching out to touch his arm. "It doesn't have to be perfect."

"She told you about Santa sucking last year," he replied, pushing the cart toward the next aisle.

"She did, but in the grand scheme of things? When she's our age and looking back at every year that Santa came, she…" Summer swallowed, feeling unexpectedly emotional. Christmas had never been about her. Mom had either hosted some man while Summer had to sit in her room out of the way, or she'd been given "pretty" dresses to "show what a pretty girl she was."

"I think, maybe not now, but when she's older, she'll understand how hard you worked, how much you cared, and that will beat any disappointment."

"But you don't want your kid to be disappointed on Christmas or by Santa."

"*You* don't."

He stopped pushing the cart and gave her a curious look.

"There are parents who don't…" She didn't want to discuss the way her parents hadn't cared. It was hardly unique to her. Plenty of parents weren't meant for the job. "Anyway, what's next on the list? The art supplies?" She powered forward, not waiting to see if Thack followed. "Oh, this is perfect." Summer plucked a light-up fairy wand from its perch on a hook. "This is what I'll get her."

"You don't have to get her anything."

"Of course I do. She's…" Summer didn't know how to finish that. How on earth could he think she wouldn't get Kate something, or that she shouldn't? She didn't get it. Didn't want to. "I'm going to get her a Christmas present. Honestly. How could I not?"

"I just—"

"Don't want me to feel obligated. I get it, Thack. What you don't seem to get is that it's not obligation to me." She wanted to yell or stomp her feet or give him a little push or something, which was so unlike her and so…disconcerting.

She didn't want to be frustrated or angry with him, but he was making her feel both.

Sometimes the worst thing is someone you can't trust with your anger. She tried to ignore those words and the thoughtful way the father who only acknowledged her when pressed had said them. She didn't want that in her head.

"You know, you don't say my name very often," Thack said softly.

She blinked at him. "I…" She hadn't thought of that and was a little surprised he had. "I guess I didn't notice."

"I do." He cleared his throat. "So. Art supplies?"

She nodded, trying to absorb all that. All of the conflicting emotions battling it out in her stomach. Up to this point, she'd gone from irritated by him those first few times she'd met him to being blown away by the man he was, the father he was. Now, she thought, maybe for the first time she was realizing he was both those people. A complex man, a combination of all sorts of feelings and experiences and reactions.

Which led to the uncomfortable realization that she too was complicated and not one thing.

They picked out the art supplies, focusing on the task rather than all those pesky thoughts and feelings, and as they moved toward the front of the store with Christmas music piping through the speakers, Summer felt edgy and uncomfortable. Far different from the feeling she'd initially had this morning of being jumpy and excited.

She didn't want complex, hard thoughts. She'd run away from all that. Left it behind. Montana was supposed to be a fresh start and happiness, not confusion and questioning how well-adjusted she was.

They got everything they needed, and Summer talked Thack into some extra Christmas lights and a gingerbread house kit she could do with Kate one afternoon. The more she faked the cheer and the more she hoped she would feel it instead of the constricting tightness in her chest, the less she actually did.

They stood in the checkout line, and Summer hummed along with the speakers. "Joy to the World." She wanted to feel that joy or peace or truth or something. Joy was being here, helping Thack create a great Christmas for the little girl she enjoyed so much. Peace was her caravan, being in charge of her own life. And truth...

What on earth was her truth? The question haunted her as Thack paid for the items, and she paid for the little wand for Kate. Her thoughts took up so much mental space that she wasn't even paying attention to Thack as they walked into the freezing air of the parking lot.

"Um, so I was thinking that…" He pulled open the covered truck bed and began to place the items inside. "We could…" He closed the trunk and adjusted his hat on his head, most expressly not looking at her. "We could go out to lunch."

Summer froze. "Lunch," she repeated dumbly. Lunch? The two of them?

"Unless you're busy, of course. I can drop you off at Shaw and—"

"No!" She tried to rein in her voice before she continued. "I'd love to go to lunch." Because as confused as she was, she couldn't help but wonder if this invitation wasn't, well, what she'd been fantasizing about.

Because it had nothing to do with Kate or Christmas or working for the Lanes. He was asking her to lunch. Just her. There was no way she could turn that down.

⸻

Thack had no idea what he was doing. Not in inviting Summer to lunch and certainly not in sitting across from her at a table in a fairly nice restaurant. Sure, it wasn't fancy, but as it wasn't McDonald's, it was about the nicest place he'd ever been in.

Seriously. What the hell was he doing?

He'd made a specific effort to ask her out to lunch. Her. Nothing dressed up in a favor or doing it for Kate. This was about him. And her. Having lunch. Together.

He felt like one of the men turned to stone in Kate's stories—stiff and frozen and completely helpless.

So, they sat in awkward silence. Him too still while Summer fidgeted endlessly. It seemed an important contrast, though he couldn't work out what was important about it.

They ordered and sat. Silent. Silent. Awkward.

"This is ridiculous," Thack muttered, leaning forward and resting his forehead on his palm, his elbow on the tablecloth pulling the water glass with enough force to spill some over the edges.

Summer laughed and some of the tension eased, because her laughter always felt like sunshine. Never snarky or mean, always joy.

"It's just lunch," she reassured him. Or maybe she was reassuring both of them, because she didn't appear to be any better at this than he was. "Just conversation. Because we're, well, friends. Right? We're friends now?"

He stared into the warmth of her gaze—more hazel than either green or brown. "Right," he managed to say.

Because being friends was important, and more, he thought maybe he needed that "friend" step before...

Aw, sweet pickles, the fact of the matter was that he liked her and was attracted to her, and he didn't know what to do with that anymore. Heck, he never had. Michaela had been the first girl he'd ever asked out, ever dated. She'd been it for him, simply because time had gotten away from them.

Then there hadn't been time. He didn't know how to dive into this whole hog. He didn't know how to flirt or date, so maybe friendship was a good first step.

"So, did you always want to be a rancher?"

He glanced at his hat sitting on the seat next to him. "I think so. It was always a foregone conclusion I'd help Dad run the ranch. There were a few years when I thought maybe I'd go be a rodeo star first, always with the plan to come back, but Mom got sick and passed away, and it… Well, it was never as important to me after losing her."

"I'm sorry."

"Everyone always is."

"It's hard though, growing up with just one parent. But, for as much as you and your father can sometimes argue, it's obvious he's really supported you."

Thack smiled wryly. "He has. It wasn't easy at first, after Mom. She'd always been his anchor or his balance or something, and he kind of fell apart there for a while. It was hard on him to lose her."

"Hard on you both."

"Sure." He shrugged, never comfortable when people offered platitudes. He'd heard them since he was a teenager. One would think he'd get used to them, but all they did was remind him of what he'd lost. If he got mired too much in that, well, he'd turn into Dad. "When we found out Michaela was pregnant, Dad pulled it together. I needed him to."

Summer chewed on her lip, and he knew he should tell her. He should tell her what had happened to Michaela, open up in that way he tried never to do, no matter how many times the therapist in those first few years had told him he needed to open up.

He didn't want to be open. He'd seen Dad opened up and strewn about after Mom, and he refused to be that. Especially six years after.

"That's all depressing stuff. What about you? Did you always want to be a…" Crap.

"Jill of all trades?" she offered with one of her sunny smiles that he was beginning to realize hid something. What, he wasn't sure, but they didn't have that warmth she so often gave him and Kate. "I… My mother was very strict, I guess you'd say. There really weren't many dreams she allowed me to have."

His chest tightened, because the woman before him seemed so effortlessly a dreamer, but maybe that's why she responded so well to Kate. She understood that, understood how it could be tamped down.

"Okay, so we're sad sacks. Tell me something happy. About you."

She grinned, holding up both her arms and moving them so her bracelets jangled. "I get to make all my own decisions now. I painted my caravan blue and purple. I decorate my own place. I come and go as I please. I get to be part of the Shaws, and…"

"Part of the Lanes," Thack finished for her, because as much as she hesitated saying that, it was becoming true. "I hope you know you're far more than an assistant to us at this point. All of us."

Her lips curved, something shy in how she glanced away, her cheeks turning pink. "Who knew you could be so nice when I first met you," she murmured.

"I'm not even sure I knew it myself. I'd been…isolating all of us, I guess. Trying to maintain control to keep everyone safe. You've been a breath of fresh air. One that allowed me to pause enough to realize how… tightfisted I'd gotten."

"Well, I'm happy to loosen—"

Before she could finish whatever she'd been about to say, his phone rang. He frowned at the unfamiliar number. "I'm going to have to answer this just to be on the safe side."

Summer nodded, and he hit Accept before offering a greeting.

"Hi, Thack. I'm sorry to bother you. It's Gabriella."

"Oh hi, Gabby." Thack didn't know what to make of his second cousin calling him out of the blue. Even though she was a doctor in town, they'd never spent much time together.

"Your dad called me, and I came out to the ranch because he was having a rough go of it."

"He called you?" Thack's stomach sank. If Dad had actually called Gabriella in a medical capacity, things had to be really bad.

"I think he needs an overnight stay."

"In the hospital?"

He didn't glance at Summer until she rested a hand on his arm. She always seemed to be doing that, those easy touches of, well, he wasn't sure what it was. Sympathy partially, comfort mostly.

"He needs a better breathing treatment than I can give him at the clinic, and I think he needs to have a checkup with his specialist about adjusting his medications. Of course, he's fighting me on this, but—"

"I'll be right there." Thack was already to his feet before he noticed Summer was gone. When he looked around the restaurant, he saw her smiling and nodding with the waitress who'd taken their order.

After a few seconds, she walked back to him. "I canceled our order, and she'll comp our drinks since it's an emergency."

"But—"

"It is, isn't it? You said hospital?"

"Yeah, Dad. He needs… He has emphysema, I don't know if you knew that."

She shook her head, linking her arm with his and leading him out of the restaurant. "I knew something was wrong, but not that specific."

"He's refusing to go to the hospital, but he needs to go."

"Then we'll head back to the ranch, and you'll convince him to go. Simple as that."

Simple as that, except it wasn't simple at all. Thack was gripped by fear, by the reminder of what happened when he loosened that iron fist of control even a little.

He'd gotten off the ranch, tried to do something friendly with Summer without thinking about Kate or Dad or the ranch, and here he was, rushing to another sick family member, hoping time wasn't running out.

If that wasn't a sign, he didn't know what was.

Chapter 13

MR. LANE ENDED UP SPENDING ONLY ONE NIGHT IN THE hospital. Summer forwent all her duties with the Shaws to help. She stayed with Mr. Lane while Thack took and picked up Kate from school, and she helped with all the meals and housekeeping Thack would allow.

Things had changed since their awkward lunch. In the first few moments, she'd thought maybe friendship had the potential to lead somewhere. As confusing as that was, she wanted it.

But in the last few days since Mr. Lane had come back home, Thack's awkward but sweet earnestness had been replaced with a kind of terse sternness that reminded her of those first few days with him.

She knew he was worried about his father, stressed about Christmas and keeping up with Kate and ranch duties, but no matter how she tried to excuse him, she couldn't get over the fact that something in him had gone cool.

Not quite cold, but something had dimmed. She knew it had nothing to do with her and everything to do with him, but that didn't make it hurt any less.

Summer stirred the chili she'd put together in the slow cooker before turning back to Kate, who was at the kitchen table putting together the gingerbread house. Translation: sneaking as much candy as she could into her mouth instead of onto the house.

"You're not going to have anything left for the shingles," Summer admonished, sliding back into the chair next to Kate.

"Eating it is more fun," Kate said with a grin.

It was hard to argue with that. Kate swirled her finger in the frosting, staring through the open doorway from the kitchen to the dining room. The Christmas tree stood in the corner, bright-white lights twinkling.

Summer had put it on a timer yesterday after Kate complained it was never on, and she'd set out the two boxes of colored lights she and Thack had bought those few days ago, but he hadn't taken the hint or had been too tired to put them up.

"Can't we just decorate the tree without Daddy? He's so grumpy when Grandpa's sick."

Summer didn't know how to explain to Kate that her father's grumpiness was a side effect of his worry. A worry he took on too much and held too tight and let burrow too deep.

Summer wished she had an answer to that. Because as much as his coolness had hurt her feelings, she still felt for the guy. She still wanted to soothe and help him. Bring back the man who'd asked her to lunch.

"Your dad is really busy, and I think he'd be really sad if we decorated the whole tree without him."

At Kate's despondent shoulder slump, Summer couldn't just leave it at that. "But how about this? I'll help you put up the colorful lights, and then you can pick one ornament, and one ornament only, to put on the tree." And if Thack got mad about that, well, she'd give him a piece of her mind.

Even if the thought of giving him a piece of her mind

made her gut clench uncomfortably. Honestly, what about this whole thing didn't?

Kate was already scurrying over to the tree. Mr. Lane had disappeared into his room about ten minutes ago, claiming he had to make a private phone call.

He'd been doing progressively better. His new medication really seemed to help, combined with more consistent oxygen-tank wearing. He was still a little weak, a little gray, but he was on the road to recovery.

Summer didn't know why Thack either didn't see it or didn't think it made a difference in how he should act.

Maybe what Thack thinks or does just isn't any of your business, a little voice in her head whispered.

A voice that sounded a bit too much like her mother for comfort.

Kate went over to the ancient CD player that sat on the table and had been pumping a steady stream of Christmas carols. She pushed Play, grinning happily when the Chipmunks started singing about Christmas.

It was hard not to get caught up in the holiday spirit. Summer was pretty sure both she and Kate had gingerbread frosting in their hair, and Summer had snuck a few pieces of candy too, fully feeling the hit of sugar before dinner.

Summer patiently helped Kate get the strings of multicolored lights around the fake tree. She wondered why Thack didn't have a real one. Caleb had already planned to take her out onto Shaw property and let her pick a tree to cut down since Delia wasn't up to tramping about in the snow just yet.

Maybe she could find a little real tree for the Lane house when they did that. Something Kate could make ornaments for.

"I love the pink ones," Kate said on a dreamy sigh. She slanted a glance at Summer. "What about two ornaments? One for me and one for you?"

"This is your tree, Kate. You and your grandpa and your dad's."

Kate pouted at that and Summer felt bad for saying it, for pointing out she was separate. But she had to point it out to someone, or she might start thinking she actually belonged. Then how would she feel when Thack gave her the cold shoulder?

"One ornament, sweetie." Summer carefully opened the box marked *ornaments* and helped Katie up on a chair so she could see into the box.

"Oh, this one." She picked out an angel ornament made of what appeared to be pearl with gold trim.

"Daddy always calls this one Mommy's angel," Kate said reverently, taking all the care of an old woman as she walked over to the tree and slid the hook onto a branch. "It's my favorite."

Summer shouldn't have been shocked that Thack had the timing to come inside at that point.

"It's my favorite too, Kate," he said, his voice gruff but warm. For his daughter, for their memories, which Summer most assuredly wasn't a part of.

She didn't even know what had happened to his wife. Michaela. But he'd obviously loved her. Losing her had left a mark.

Thinking of how much he'd lost made her heart ache and made her soften that much more toward him because she knew he was only trying to hold on to what still remained.

Summer straightened. "I told her she could put on one. Just…one."

Thack nodded and walked over to Kate, brushing a gloved hand over her hair. "I know you're anxious, Katie Pie. How about tomorrow night we make a special plan for hot chocolate and Rudolph and decorating the tree?"

Kate skipped away from the tree. "Can Summer come?"

She wasn't sure what in his expression changed at that request, but Summer knew she didn't like it. "I c—"

"Summer is always welcome," Thack said before she could get out an excuse.

Summer is also right here, she wanted to say. *Right here wondering what the hell is wrong with you.*

"Where's Dad?"

"He just went to his room to make a phone call."

Thack nodded. "I have a few more chores to do. I know it's getting late, but I hoped you could stay for another hour or so."

"But aren't you going to eat?" she asked, more of her frustration melting into worry.

"In a bit. Just a few things to tie up. You all go ahead. If I get caught up tonight, I'll knock off early tomorrow just for our Christmas party, okay?"

Kate happily agreed, but Summer couldn't get over the feeling that something was wrong, even as Thack disappeared back the way he came.

"Why don't you go talk to him?"

Summer swung around, hand flying to her heart. She hadn't heard Mr. Lane come back in the room.

"Talk to him?"

"He needs a sounding board. I think you'd be a good one."

Summer blinked at where Thack disappeared. Sounding board? That she could do, but she had her doubts about how much he'd let her.

"Let's eat dinner first," she said, forcing a smile. Maybe if she ate, she'd figure out what to say.

———

Thack knew his father was rapidly recovering, but even a few days later, he couldn't get over taking him to the hospital.

How many times had he visited his dying mother, and then his dying wife, in that very hospital? How many more times would that be in his future?

He was struggling to cope with it. All the freezing, controlling techniques he'd used for the past few years were failing him.

He was starting to wonder if he should go back to therapy. If he should introduce Kate to it, but he kept wanting to put that off.

He wanted to put everything off, ignore it all.

For the first time in all this time, that's exactly what he did. Summer had it under control, and where that had once filled him with dread, in the midst of all this damn fear, all he could be was relieved.

He didn't actually have more chores to do. He just hadn't been able to handle Christmas right now. Not Michaela's angel ornament that she'd bought knowing she wouldn't see another Christmas, not pretty lights and happy songs and Summer's beautiful smile at his amazing little girl and Dad in the other room, alive.

It was all too good, and he was so afraid that if he enjoyed it, somehow it would be ripped from him.

So, he did the only thing he could think to do to get rid of the big, pulsing knot of anxiety inside his gut.

He walked over to his father's woodworking shed. He went straight for the little fridge in the corner, filled with bottles of water...which hid the bottles of beer lining the back.

Dad didn't touch the hard stuff anymore, but he always had beer on hand. Thack hated that, but he looked the other way because there were only so many fights he could manage, only so many expectations he could deal with.

Would a stronger man know what to do here? A stronger man would have already set the world to rights. Instead, he was looking the other way when he simply couldn't deal with another *thing*.

Thack popped the top of the beer and gulped half of it without even taking a breath. Then he moved to the back where Dad hid the recyclables. Thack went to work setting up his very old way of dealing with this overwhelming fear.

He pulled out the targets, the glass bottles, and walked twenty paces away.

Dr. Seaver had given him a litany of coping mechanisms for grief and stress during his years of counseling after Michaela's death. This one had always been his favorite. He supposed that breaking things on purpose felt like relief because his entire life was spent carefully balancing things so they didn't break.

He grabbed a bottle, flipped it from base to top, then hurled it at the target hung on the back of Dad's woodshed. It shattered with a satisfying crash.

He downed the rest of his beer before throwing the

bottle, crashing it in exactly the same place. Most of the pressure in his chest stayed tight and hard, but some of it began to ease. He went back into the shed, retrieved four beers, and then set out to drink and destroy.

The people inside that house could take care of things for a while. They'd have to. He was tired of being the only one, tired of all this pressure. He didn't have any fight left. He was giving up.

Yeah, he would give up. What was the point of all this backbreaking work? What was the point of weathering all these disappointments? A ranch he could barely stand to face most mornings? A father who fought him every step of the way until he landed himself in the hospital? No one else who wanted to *really* help. Sure, they wanted to offer advice or food, but they never wanted to step in and step up.

Except Summer.

"Thack?"

"Sweet pickles," he muttered, disgusted with himself that even a crap day didn't keep him from the stupid euphemism. He turned to face the woman in question. Most of her was hidden in the shadow, only the crown of her hair illuminated by the faint glow from the house.

"Sorry, I didn't mean to startle you."

"What are you doing out here?"

"Your father sent me to… Well, he thought you might need someone to talk to."

"No."

"What if I promised to just listen and not say anything at all?"

He knew he should agree to that or go inside. Those

were his two choices. The two Thackery Lane choices of adulthood and responsibility. Instead, he polished off his beer.

"So, I think I'll head home. Unless…you want me to stay."

He finally found his voice. "Stay?"

"I…" She cleared her throat, not meeting his gaze. "I just meant if there's anything else you need help with. Kate and your dad are eating."

If he needed it. What a joke. He needed so much help, and yet he'd finally gotten himself to ask for it, ask *her* for it, and something else had blown up in his face.

What would have happened if Dad hadn't called Gabriella? Would his situation have been so much worse? Thack didn't want to believe in karma or cosmic signs, but weren't they all here? Every time he stepped outside this ranch and his responsibilities, something terrible happened. How did he keep ignoring that?

He drained the last of his beer and then, with no warning to Summer, hurled the glass at the target, the flame of impotent frustration fading a little when the bottle exploded into a hundred little shards.

She jumped and took a few unsteady steps away from him.

"Sorry, I didn't mean to startle you," he said, copying her words. "Here, give it a shot."

She stared at the empty bottle he'd retrieved from the bin. "A shot?"

"I have it on good authority it's cathartic."

"I don't have anything I need…cathartic-ing."

"Don't you?"

She blinked as though he'd caught her in a lie. Had

he? She seemed so serene and happy, but she'd said she wasn't particularly well-adjusted, hadn't she?

So, he prodded where he never prodded. "Don't you have anything you're angry about? Anything that makes you *furious* with the world? Isn't there anyone who's wronged you?"

They were supposed to be generic questions, but suddenly he wanted to know. He wanted to know what had shaped this woman he didn't understand. This woman who wanted to help. Who *had* helped—not with meaningless advice or vague offers of help, but by stepping in and *doing*.

For a second, he thought she might take the bottle and smash it. For a second, he thought she might spill her guts. Eagerness and regret twined themselves inside him. He wanted to know. Wanted to figure her out and unlock the mystery that was Summer.

"There are other ways to relieve stress that aren't so…messy," she said, eyeing the shards of glass that littered the concrete pad below the target. She was uncomfortable, linking her fingers together tightly, keeping her distance.

"Name one."

Her gaze slowly rose from the shattered glass to him. He'd been keeping his distance for these few days, had been overly disengaged from all his interactions with her, and her gaze still hit him like a horse kick.

"Yoga?" she offered, sounding oddly hopeful.

He snorted. Right. He was going to turn himself into a pretzel and magically feel better.

"All right. What about…" She stepped to him, in front of him. Close enough that he could feel her breath and smell the scent that had come to mean only *Summer* to him. Something herby and floral mixed together. The faintest hint of…sugar?

He shouldn't look down. He should keep his eyes on the target, but with Summer so close, so pretty, and so very much here when no one else ever was, how did he focus on anything but her?

Her top teeth were pillowed in her bottom lip in that uncertain nibble that all too often caused an unfortunate stirring in his body. Then, in a move he knew he should sidestep—somewhere in the recess of his brain he knew he should step away—her fingertips trailed across the line of his jaw, and it felt as though she was brushing away half his stress. He all but slumped without the weight of everything resting on his shoulders.

All this from a simple touch, just the graze of her fingertips. But she didn't stop there. No, she took an infinitesimal step closer, then slowly wrapped her arms around his waist, resting the side of her head against his chest.

She was hugging him.

It wasn't a particularly romantic hug. Though her breasts were pressed against his chest, she kept distance between her bottom half and his. Her arms remained still around him.

Comfort. She was offering physical comfort that held no promises, no questions, no added pressure. She was just…giving.

He had no means of fighting selfless giving, no way to push back against someone wrapping their arms around him. He couldn't remember the last time someone who wasn't Kate had offered him a hug. The first few weeks after Michaela's death, people had simply scattered. Her parents had moved, and townspeople had their own tragedies to deal with. Then Kate had gotten old enough to hug him, and she held on so tight. But while those hugs offered him purpose and hope and love, they were weighted down with all the responsibility that Kate represented.

Summer's hug was simply an offer of safety, a respite from all he'd dealt with this week. As much as he knew he shouldn't take advantage, he couldn't resist resting his cheek on top of her head or loosely wrapping his arms around her in return.

Her hair was soft, her body warm and comforting against his. Her arms were loose around him, and yet he had no doubt that if he leaned, she would find whatever strength she needed to hold him up.

He didn't have a clue how long the hug lasted, and he didn't want to think about time. This single moment could last all night, and he was positive it would never be enough. Her comfort was a salve, but the minute she stepped away, reality would crash back.

After who knew how long, she did. Summer stepped away and into the shadows. She hugged her own arms around herself, her expression half hidden in the dark.

"Why did you do that?" he asked, his voice not nearly as strong or demanding as he might have wanted.

"You constantly look like someone in desperate need of a hug."

He wanted to do more than hug her. As platonic as that had been, the absence of her—her arms, her warmth, her smell—all clamored inside him, leaving him desperate for more.

He didn't know what prompted him to say it, to

think it, but the words tumbled out. "There are plenty of things I avoid doing, not because I don't want to do them, but because I can't." *Why can't you? What would be the harm?*

She took an incremental step into the dim light. Her tongue darted out, moistening her lips and making him even more uncomfortably hard. In that restaurant the other day, he'd wanted a friend, and he'd been punished for that want.

But after handling the aftermath of Dad's hospital visit, his defenses were demolished. He had feelings and reactions, but he didn't have the sense to be careful or even awkward.

It had been his sign, that call about Dad, a reminder he didn't *get* things or people. Not like Summer. He couldn't find the energy to accept that sign anymore, not here with her looking so intently at him.

"What…what kind of things?" she asked, her voice soft and breathless. As if she knew. As if she knew exactly what he'd been avoiding.

He swallowed, closing the distance she'd created between them. "Maybe you should go home," he forced himself to say. Before he did something he couldn't take back. Before he did something he'd regret when he had to remember everything he had to do, all his responsibilities, all his stress.

"Maybe," she returned, not making a move to leave or distance herself again. She dropped her arms and took a step toward him, until the toes of their boots were touching. "But then again, maybe I should stay."

Chapter 14

SUMMER'S HEART WAS POUNDING SO HARD IN HER CHEST, IN her ears, she had no idea how Thack didn't hear it. How could either of them hear anything beyond the furious thumping?

This wasn't right. Obviously he was breaking down, and she had no right to push herself into all the cracks that were snaking through his distance and control.

But, oh, how she wanted to fill those cracks. When her fingers moved over his jaw, his shoulders had simply *slumped*, a distinct and visible relaxation. She'd hugged him and felt that hard wall of muscle, strength, and determination losing an ounce of tension.

Surely a hug was better than bashing glass bottles against a wall. Surely understanding was a better salve than violence, no matter how harmless that violence might be.

She wanted to do it again. Her hand on his jaw, a simple hug. She wanted to feel the way it affected him. She couldn't stop herself from wanting something far more complicated.

She wanted to feel his mouth on hers, for one thing. Would it have the same effect on him? Could she help him *and* find out what he tasted like, all at once?

She was trying to find an altruistic reason to force herself to close the distance between their mouths, and that was ridiculous. If he wasn't going to do it, she should. They couldn't stand this close forever, or her heart might actually burst.

Something had happened to him, inside him, after that phone call about his father in the restaurant, and if he couldn't get past it, well, she could.

She could say something. She could grab him by the shoulders and pull him down to meet her mouth. She could get up on her tiptoes and kiss his neck. There were nearly a million things she *could* do. She'd been not-so-subtly fantasizing about exactly this, about the moment when the spark between them would catch and lick to life.

If only one of them would move.

As if he heard the inner workings of her mind, his arm moved. Slowly, hesitantly, his hand rose to her face and hovered just next to her temple.

She didn't breathe. She was afraid if she inhaled or exhaled, it would break the spell. This had to be a spell, after all, a remnant of that fairy magic Kate was so enamored with. But if Summer really had fairy magic, his mouth would already be on hers, and she would know what it was like to get something she wanted.

The very tips of his fingers touched her forehead, gently brushing some stray strand of hair away. She tried to keep her eyes open, to soak up the moment. It probably wouldn't be much more than a moment, after all, and she wanted to relish it forever.

But his fingers trailed down her cheek, and she couldn't keep her eyes open or her breath held. It came out in a whoosh as the pads of his rough fingers trailed across the soft skin of her jaw, just as she'd done to him.

He didn't stop. The backs of his fingers trailed down

her neck, and she had the terrible realization that she'd actually groaned. All he'd done was barely touch her in the most innocent of places, and her chest was tight and jittery, her stomach was doing rolling flips, and a kind of aching need she'd never experienced before was building low in her stomach.

No one had ever made her feel quite this…valued. It was an odd word, an odd feeling, and yet the fact he was being so careful and controlled was the opposite of everything she'd known before.

His hand went around the back of her neck under her hair, so she could feel each finger pressed firmly against her skin. He was *holding* her there, as if he needed her not to move.

She would gladly never move if he'd keep looking at her like she might have all the answers. As if she might *mean* something. So few people looked at her like that. Okay, no one looked at her like that. Even though her family had come to accept her, they still regarded her with an ounce of…*what do we do about Summer*?

Thack seemed to know exactly what to do about her. She needed him to…to… She didn't know. His face was still so close, and she didn't know *what* she needed, only that she wanted his hands. His mouth. Things she'd never allowed anyone to do to her. She wanted to grant him access to all the parts of her she kept hidden. His mouth still hadn't touched hers. He hadn't moved past putting his hand on her neck, holding her there, holding her. It felt as if her heart beat in every place his fingers pressed, as though her entire existence was centered in those five points.

Her breath was uneven at best, everything inside her

waiting and wanting and *wishing*. She couldn't take it anymore. "What are you thinking?" she asked, her voice shaky, her breathing too shallow and quick.

"That I should go. I should be in my home taking care of my daughter, my father, and every other damn responsibility that's on my shoulders." His grip seemed to tighten on her neck, and her head fell back farther, meeting his stark gaze more head-on. Because for all his *shoulds*, he wasn't letting her go.

"So why aren't you going?" She had to know. What was keeping him here? She needed to hear that he felt some inkling of that same energy that had thrummed between them from the beginning. Not just *friendship*, but *this*.

All the potential of this.

"Because…" His voice was rough, and his eyebrows drew together, only visible in the dark because they were so close. "Because I don't fucking want to go."

And then his mouth was finally on hers, soft and hot, demanding. She had to hold on to his jacket to keep her balance, to keep her mouth fused to his, because now that the flame had finally licked to life, she never wanted it to go out.

She never wanted this to end.

There had been so few kisses in her life, and they all paled in comparison to this. To Thack and the way his fingers tangled in her hair, and his palm cradled the back of her head, and the way he held her with a certainty, a sturdiness, that left no room for fear.

He was solid, every part of his body so hard, except his mouth. That was soft, as was his tongue, softer as it trailed across the seam of her lips, asking for entrance. She gave it. Willingly, perhaps emphatically.

Yes, emphatic, as she loosened her grip on his shirt and wrapped her arms around his neck instead, bringing him closer. They were pressed together, her chest crushed to his, her thighs pressed to his, every part of her touching him hot, so hot, and every part of her *not* touching him dying for the pleasure.

His free arm came around her waist, but more, his fingers trailed under the hem of her coat and shirt, so that his bare palm rested against her bare back, pulling her more firmly to him.

There wasn't space between them, nor air, just the hardness of his muscles, like a wall. A wonderful, delicious wall, whose mouth was everything she'd hoped for.

"Summer," he murmured against her lips, his tongue stopping its lovely exploration.

"Don't stop." Because she could tell that terrible idea was floating somewhere in him, muttering her name, and she wanted nothing to do with stopping.

Nothing.

This was out of control. Completely and utterly out of his control, and Thack couldn't care. Where were the pieces that had made up his life for the past seven years? All that control and caution and choices made for everyone but himself.

He wanted something for himself. He wanted Summer for himself. A kiss wasn't enough. Touching, being all tangled together, none of this could possibly be enough. She'd said, "Don't stop," and she was right. Why should he stop? The air had changed when his lips had touched hers. All that heat and pent-up frustration, all that need he'd been trying so desperately to ignore. This *thing* she unlocked in him that he didn't understand. Surely, it was just a symptom of the isolation of the past few years, not…her.

He slid his hand down her back until it met the one under her shirt, and then—because every sensible, respectful, responsible thought in his head had combusted—he inched both hands under the waistband of her skirt and underwear and cupped her gorgeous ass, holding that soft expanse of skin with his rough hands.

She didn't unwind her arms from his neck, didn't stop exploring his mouth with her tongue. Instead she pushed even more flush against him.

He was hard. So damn hard. She was all soft fabric and jangling jewelry and complex scents, and he wanted to bury himself in everything she was, everything she exuded.

Don't stop. No, he didn't want to stop. He wanted her naked. He wanted to be inside her. He wanted what he had denied himself so long, not just because it had been *so damn long*, but because she was the first person, *real* person, to unlock anything like this surge of feeling inside him.

Her fingers trailed off his neck, and he held tighter onto her ass, like his palms belonged on her always. *Belonged.*

But she didn't let go as he'd feared she would, and her mouth never left his. Instead she trailed her hands down his chest until they rested on his belt.

Touch me. Touch me. Touch me. He'd say it if he could stand to be separated from the sweetness of her mouth for one second. But she tasted like heaven, far better than any liquor he could drink. She smelled better than any spring field of flowers, and she felt softer and more perfect than any blanket straight from the dryer.

Summer was this magic thing—better than any other experience he could think to name. Because she enveloped him like he belonged exactly here, as if there was no question.

She traced the outline of him through the rough denim of his jeans, and he'd forgotten. Forgotten that it could be like this, like his blood had turned into molten lava, like he'd never be okay, never be able to breathe again if he didn't get to sink into her, come inside her.

And, *oh shit*, that thought right there. He stepped away from her, pulling his hands so quickly out of her skirt that he might have ripped something. He took a stumbling step back, away, gulping air. He gulped at sanity.

Fuck. Actual full-fledged *fucking damn it*. Because he...

He shoved fingers through his hair, trying to find some center, some ability to breathe. The last time he'd had the thought *Oh, who needs a condom*, it had ended in a daughter.

He'd made a lot of mistakes in his life, but he tried very hard not to *repeat* mistakes. This would be a repeat mistake. Something born of his desperation that would only end with someone hurt or dead.

"Sorry! Did I do something wrong?"

"No, of course not. I just..." Something about the worry on her face, the uncertainty in her voice made him remember how young she was. Not *that* young, but...

Because the only way to make this worse—the thoughts in his head, the desire in his gut—the only way to make this worse would be if she... "You've done this before, right?"

"This?" Her voice was high. Too high. "Oh. Sure."

"Okay, let me rephrase." He took a deep breath. He was reading this wrong. His fears wouldn't be confirmed because this couldn't be any more complicated than it already was. He didn't deserve any more complications. "The where this was leading to part. You've done *that* before, right?"

"Where was it leading?"

Only, she didn't ask as though she didn't know. She asked as though he was being ridiculous. He *was* being ridiculous. In every possible way. But that didn't mean he appreciated her giving him a hard time. Even if he deserved it.

"Maybe that proves my point," he grumbled.

"Are you asking if I'm a virgin?"

It was a little unmanning to realize he was being a complete wuss about actually saying the words, when he'd had his tongue jammed down her throat little more than a few seconds ago. When his bare hand had cupped her bare skin like he had *any* right to lead from a first kiss to an ass grab in five seconds flat.

He'd wanted her so bad, wanted something just for himself. But there was a problem with that. A problem in all of this. As much as he might want Summer, as much as he might be perfectly happy to relieve the tension in his life for a few minutes by screwing her against his father's woodshed, Summer was...well, a person too. With her own wants and problems and tensions to unwind.

She might be just as eager to find some kind of sexual

release together, but she was a woman with her own stresses and baggage, and the two of them didn't get to just walk away and never see each other again. Their lives were intertwined.

He didn't have any space left for more entanglements. He didn't have any extra time in his day for another person who would come to expect certain things. Hadn't the last few days been a glaring reminder of that?

Especially if she had honestly never done this before. "Yes, I am asking if you're a virgin."

"I don't see why it matters."

"See, if you answer with *It doesn't matter*, rather than an actual answer, I think it might matter."

He could sense her frown more than he could see it.

"I have to go."

He almost asked her not to. He *almost* grabbed her arm and kissed her again. There were a million almosts running through his mind, all the things *he* wanted, but...

Hadn't he learned? He didn't get what he wanted. He had Kate, and that meant he didn't have leave to take things for himself. His daughter was everything. If he ever let that slip, he would lose her too.

His chest contracted so painfully at the thought that he almost stumbled. The thought of losing Kate, coupled with all it would mean, nearly brought him to his knees. He had to get inside and check on her, make sure everything was okay, but Summer was walking away into the deeper dark.

"Let me drive you home," he offered, unable to let her face the vast emptiness of the space between their homes alone. It was freezing, and though she had a coat and boots and he'd made a path, in the dark, she could easily fall or get lost. "It's stupid to be walking through the dark and—"

"The moon and stars are bright enough." She stopped walking away, turning to face him. He could only make out her faint outline, and the cowardly part of him was glad he couldn't see her face, didn't know what her reaction was.

She should be relieved, even happy he'd stopped things before they'd gotten even more complicated. Because even if they'd done irrevocable things, he had nothing to offer someone like Summer, so young and vibrant and full of cheer and hope.

"Please let me see you home."

She whirled away from him, the swish of her skirts and jangle of her jewelry a testament to how violent the motion was. "Let me assure you, I'm fine."

"Summer."

"Good night, Thack." She took a stomping step away, and he made a move to touch her, but she grabbed his discarded bottle from earlier and heaved it at the target instead.

The gesture and subsequent crash startled him enough that he didn't even move after her quickly retreating form.

She muttered something that sounded suspiciously like, "Enjoy your erection, jerkface" on her way past the woodshed and toward the line between their properties.

He should go after her. He should go check on Kate and Dad. He was torn in two different directions, and this was the absolute last thing he needed. Another no-win situation.

And he couldn't blame anyone but his own damn self for this one.

Chapter 15

SUMMER STORMED THROUGH THE DARK TREES AND CLIMBED over the fence, wishing she could bust through it like some kind of wild, feral animal. If she had any room in her brain for something that wasn't anger, she might have been afraid. Yes, the moon and stars lit the way, but that didn't make her any less alone in the dark of night in a cold, wild land.

She didn't even know why she was so angry. She should have stayed. They should have talked it out. She should never have thrown that bottle.

But, *damn*, she understood it now—how amazing it felt to fling something and hear it destruct.

Crash.

She wanted to do it a hundred more times, and that scared her as much as it pissed her off. As much as him asking if she was a virgin—without even actually asking it, the wimp.

How dare he? How dare he? And…and…

Damn it. Why was she so mad? She didn't get mad. She was calm and levelheaded. She was a problem solver. And if she couldn't solve a problem, she ran away… Which was how she'd ended up here. Of course she'd run away this time too, but not before her temper had boiled over.

No one appreciates nasty words, Summer. Always smile when you want to frown. Always offer a nice word when you're uncomfortable. For once in your life, try *to be accommodating. For me.*

Summer stopped stomping in the clearing around her caravan. She wanted to cry. She wanted to get in the caravan and drive away from the memories, but more than that, she needed to drive away from the possibility that Mom had warped her irrevocably.

Neither Mel nor Delia bent over backward to make other people happy. They had a way of holding themselves, an inner strength, a belief of purpose and self. They didn't need to make everyone around them happy. They didn't defer to their husbands or their fathers.

They didn't do whatever a man wanted because he might grace them with a few dollars or a pretty necklace.

They wouldn't turn their daughters into servants or try to sell their virginity to the highest bidder. They'd never threaten their children.

"Summer."

She whirled around, only managing not to squeak because she was so lost and upset and angry that it seemed perfectly natural for someone to pop out of the woodwork. She couldn't see him, but of course it was Thack's voice and Thack's ridiculous need to make sure she got back okay. As if she hadn't already saved herself from worse than him.

Once she caught her breath, she planted her clenched fists on her hips. He was still too shadowed to make out, but she glared anyway. "Oh my God, you *followed* me?" She was horrified. Angry. Irritated.

Pleased beyond belief.

Even though she couldn't see him, even though she was so angry she wanted to throw things *at* him, to know that he would come after her... No one ever came after her.

"Yes, I followed you. It's hotheaded and stupid to go off into the woods on your own."

Well, that undercut any pleasure she might have taken in the moment. "The line of trees hardly constitutes woods. And you know what? I got myself here from California alone and without a cent to my name. Without help. Without some pseudo-cowboy who thinks he has to look out for everyone. I have done more alone and in the dark in my life than you have in yours, I can almost guarantee you."

That seemed to shut him up. Why was he here, lecturing her as if he cared? He probably just wanted to make sure he hadn't defiled the poor, innocent virgin. She wanted to laugh at the thought. Sure, technically. But only because her mom had been using it as a bargaining chip.

She felt sick and angry, and he was the perfect target for her anger. Hey, he'd followed her, and this was her domain. She deserved her anger, had a right to it, and he deserved to get the blunt edge. "And furthermore, *you* are going to have to walk through those 'woods' alone and back to your ranch. So, if you want to talk about hotheaded and stupid, go look in a mirror."

Silence followed, and she had to squeeze her eyes shut. Oh God, that was so not the way to talk to someone who had a hand in her employment. Someone she liked, someone she genuinely respected.

Sometimes the worst thing is someone you can't trust with your anger. Why did that foolishness keep coming back to her? Like she was going to believe something her father had uttered. The man was the most nonfunctional person she'd ever met. *Oh, but you'll listen to your mother telling you that you need to be accommodating and sweet?*

"I know this land better than you."

"Whoop-de-doo."

"Whoop-de-doo," he repeated. "You really say the weirdest things."

"And I think I'm over being insulted on my own property, *Thackery*. You can leave now. Or would you like me to call someone to escort you back to your home, so you can be safe? Oh, I know—you want to kiss me again and then grill me on my sexual history?"

It had ruined the entire moment. Because there was no real answer. That was why she was angry. There was no easy answer when it came to her experience, and she never wanted to have to explain that to anyone.

She needed to be alone. She needed to meditate or find some other way to get away from all these thoughts and memories and gross feelings. What she'd really love was a shower, but she could hardly go up to the big house now and explain that one away.

Tears stung her eyes so she whirled away from him and made for her caravan. It was her sanctuary, the place that had meant safety and peace the past two years. She reached the end of her battery-powered string of Christmas lights and turned them on. It was just a little pop of color in an otherwise bleak, dark night, but it made a difference.

Thack's footsteps followed her across the yard. "Summer. Stop. Listen." After a moment when she did not *stop*, he uttered the word that made her finally acquiesce. "Please."

She turned, folding her arms over her chest. Mortification flooded through her for losing her temper over something so silly, but she wanted—she was *determined* to be like her sisters. She wanted to be like *them*, not like what her mother had wanted her to be.

"I apologize."

Her first instinct was to slump and say he was forgiven, smile and comfort him and move on, but that was not the right answer. She didn't even know what he was apologizing for. "For?"

"I don't have…room. In my life. That's not personal. I'm not pretending I'm not attracted to you. I'm not pretending I don't care. I simply don't have room for anything else, not now."

Wait. He…cared?

"So, you shouldn't be angry. Or upset. Because…"

"Because you get to decide whether I'm allowed to be angry or upset?"

"No!"

It was weird to have an argument in the dark. Though it had been shadowy back at the Lanes' bunkhouse, there had been a semblance of light not just from above, but silhouettes made by the lights from the house, from the barn.

Here, there was only darkness. All that filtered through the blackness were the faintest hints of silver moonlight, which didn't offer a true glimpse of either of them, and the little dots of color hanging from the eaves of her caravan.

She and Thack were only voices. It gave her the illusion of freedom and strength—the illusion that she could be whoever she wanted to be. She didn't have to make him happy, or make him like her, or put any effort into helping him.

She could just be her. But who was she? A woman trying to copy her sisters? Or was she her own person?

Or are you just a mess?

"Summer, I need you to understand that what happened back there can't happen again. It doesn't have anything to do with you or your…history. It simply can't happen."

"What part?"

"All of it. The losing my temper. The kiss. Touching. And that is all on me. The way my life is. I don't have room for women in my life. I thought maybe I could try, but lunch reminded me why this is always impossible. There's too much. There have been no women in my life since my wife died because there's just not room for another thing."

"No…women." She tried to make sense of that. *None?*

"None."

"Oh." Now she felt like an idiot. If his wife had died when Kate was a baby, that was…years. *Years.* And he had to have married fairly young.

"There's a reason I haven't been with anyone aside from Michaela, and it isn't that she was my soul mate or one true love or whatever other bullshit people want to believe in. I loved her, I did. I grieved, and there is a part of me that always will, but that's not what keeps me…"

"Alone?"

"I'm not alone. I have Kate and my father. And the ranch."

"But…" Summer chewed on her lip, wondering why she felt so compelled to have this conversation, why she was so bound and determined to push when he obviously didn't want to be pushed. When had her anger vanished? When she learned that he hadn't been with anyone since his wife? No, it was more than that. It wasn't just that he was alone—which he was, whether he wanted to admit it or not. It was that he seemed to think he *had* to be.

She'd been there. She'd tried to make herself believe it had taken two years to get to Montana because of money, because of life, but it had been more than that. She hadn't thought she'd deserved to find this place, hadn't thought she'd be wanted.

She hadn't been, not at first, but Shaw was the one place she would be safe. She'd found that she did belong, that she did deserve the family who actually hadn't known she existed.

So Thack needed a similar push, and she couldn't ignore that. He *needed* someone, and she was good at that sort of thing. She was good at picking up the threads of people's lives and weaving them into something workable. It was what she could give people, what she offered in return for them allowing her to belong.

"You are alone. Kate, your father, the ranch. They're responsibilities. I know you love them and they love you, but that doesn't change the fact they take much more than they can give. That will change with Kate as she gets older, but she'll always be your *responsibility* as much as your daughter."

"Everyone is a responsibility. Having someone in your life is a responsibility. It requires time and care and things I simply cannot give." He was so matter-of-fact about it and so certain. He'd had years to grow certain of it, years spent carrying around the weight of other people.

"Don't you think you deserve someone who can give that *to* you?" Summer asked, taking a few quiet steps toward his shadow. *Let me give you something.* The Shaws let her *do* things. They accepted her presence and her help, but they didn't allow her to give parts of herself. And more than that, in a lot of ways, she was afraid. Afraid to ask them for more than they could give.

"It doesn't matter. What matters is that I can't look beyond those three things. I don't have the time or space for anyone or anything else. I am at the limit of what I can do, and I can't imagine that getting any easier as Kate gets older. So, when I say that…me not saying the right things is inexperience, I mean it. And when I say I can't let it happen again, I mean it."

He sounded so bleak. Not even resolute anymore, just hopeless, and it hurt her heart. That he'd been through so much and still thought he had room for so little.

"Of course, Kate is your world. You have no idea how much I admire that about you."

She could hear a released whoosh of breath. "Good, then you're not angry and we can go back to…"

"Go back to what exactly?"

"I…" He stepped into the clearing, so the moonlight touched his face. It seemed to find all the lines and grooves life had carved into his skin.

He was standing here telling her he had no room for her, no space in his life for a person, for a relationship. Not even for a kiss after his daughter had gone to bed.

But she couldn't resist crossing to him. She couldn't resist thinking through the arguments that were piling up in her head. He might not have room, but he needed someone, he deserved someone to take some of that load he was so determined to carry on his shoulders.

"I've been helping, haven't I?" she asked softly.

"You've been a lifesaver."

"I'm good at that. At helping. At swooping in where I'm needed and setting things to right. You don't need to make any more space for me. I'm already right here." She placed her palm on his chest. So warm and sturdy. So troubled. She wanted to soothe his pain away.

He deserved to have someone to step in and help. He deserved comfort where he wanted it, and if that was in her, why would he resist?

She'd never known a man who would so nobly place his own needs completely behind everyone else's. She'd never known a man so determined to do the right thing for his daughter, no matter the cost.

No, she'd *never* seen that, and she would forever hold him in high regard for that alone.

"I won't kiss you again. I won't be upset that you walked away. But I do want you to know, I am here. For whatever it is you need. You don't need to make *space* for me. I'm very tiny."

"On the occasions when my brain is particularly cruel, I think about the likelihood that someday my daughter will fall in love with some asshole." He cleared his throat, and that glimmer of emotion kept her from asking about this odd subject change.

"I'm forced to think about what I would want for her from that relationship. It would be more than this." He paused and then took a step back, away from her hand, away from her and into shadow. "You deserve more too."

Then she could hear him walking away with his long,

steady strides. He didn't falter because he was so sure he was right. So sure that he was saving her from him.

She stood in the clearing, in the icy cold evening, listening to his footsteps fade and then disappear.

"Maybe I don't want to be saved from you," she muttered into the lonely dark.

Thack walked back to the house through the eerie dark of the old trees lining the property. He needed to check on Dad and Kate.

But more, he needed a few more moments alone to come to grips with what Summer was all but offering and force himself to drop the idea completely. He couldn't consider it. He was cursed.

Don't be an idiot.

He repeated that little mantra over and over as he swept up the shattered glass behind the woodworking shed. He'd seen a new side to Summer tonight, not just the *I want my hands all over you* side, but the angry side. The defiant temper side that she'd kept so well hidden since their first encounters. He'd begun to believe it didn't exist.

Why was that determination so attractive? That fight in her? He had no interest in fighting with people. He had enough of that, and too many people in his way already, disagreeing with everything he tried to do.

Except, she'd... He'd explained himself and she hadn't argued. Maybe she hadn't agreed with him, but she'd put her hand over his chest.

You don't need more space for me. I'm already right here.

He could still feel her palm there on the center of his chest. Right over his heart. His heart didn't have anything left to give. Couldn't she see that? Wasn't that obvious?

But his heart beat painfully as if it were arguing with him too.

He finished sweeping up the glass, wrapping it up in a paper bag and throwing it into the trash bin inside the shed.

He walked toward the house, the warm lights a beacon in the dark. He did love this place. He wouldn't have stepped up after Mom died if he didn't love it.

He loved Kate. He loved his father. But Summer had the right of it, unfortunately. No amount of love ever took away the worry, the weight of responsibility. They were both his everything, along with all the land and animals that surrounded him. They made up his entire life. There was plenty they did give him—love and support—but whether it was his fault or just life, they couldn't lighten the burdens he carried.

He forced himself up the stairs and into the house, trying to ignore the fact Summer had clobbered him with that realization. That Summer was the reason he'd even been able to vent his frustrations tonight, because he'd known she was there. She was in the house and taking care of things. She *had* given him something, something he hadn't had time to contemplate in a long time.

Until she'd come along and ruined that outlet. Because now, forever, when he needed a moment to smash something, to find his calm, his sense of duty and determination, he would think of that kiss, the way she'd pressed against him. The way her ass had felt in his hands.

For those precious moments, he'd forgotten every responsibility, every chore, every burden. She had stepped in and smoothed over what would have been a hundred mistakes and a thousand rough edges.

But if he kissed her again, if he went so far as to sleep with her, if he tried to have some kind of relationship with her, she would be a responsibility too. A worry. She would be another tick in the *have to keep safe and happy* column, adding another need that came before his own.

What would he lose if he gave some piece of himself to Summer? He'd lost too much to believe more wasn't waiting.

He trudged up the stairs, stopped at Kate's room, and nudged the door open. Her princess night-light glowed pink in the corner, and she had a string of pink lights hung up around her window frame, which must have been Summer's doing. Kate herself was a blob of limbs under her blanket, her riotous blond hair sprawled all over her pillowcase.

All of his life was sleeping in that bed. Everything in him had to go to her, because his life would mean nothing without her in it. He could lose everything, but as long as Kate was healthy and happy, that was all that could matter. He'd made that promise to Michaela.

Every time he'd tried to get something for himself, something bad happened. He'd been trying to talk Mom and Dad into letting him do rodeos when Mom had been diagnosed with cancer. He'd been escaping debt collectors when he'd gotten Michaela pregnant, and even that, when it had turned out to be such a joy—a scary joy, but a joy—had ended with his wife gone.

He wanted it all to be coincidence, and maybe it even was. Maybe coincidence was his bad luck, and maybe he couldn't control it. But he'd worked his ass off and put everyone first for years, and look at all he had.

Kate was beautiful and vibrant and smart and happy. Summer had helped keep her safe and from escaping for weeks now, and that was a blessing.

But that was the only blessing he could allow Summer Shaw to be.

Chapter 16

Summer stood in tree pose, her eyes on the trees that separated her caravan and the Lane property. She breathed through the yoga move, trying to keep her thoughts active and proactive.

Yesterday had been…not great. The day after *the kiss*, and Thack had been scarce. Mr. Lane had been well enough to pick up Kate from school and had taken her out to dinner in town, so Summer hadn't seen either of them before it was time to head home.

She had been alone in the Lane house and had felt as lonely as she'd felt in a long time. She'd cleaned and cooked, left a note reminding Thack he'd promised to put up decorations with Kate that night, and felt as though everyone was avoiding her. Only sheer force of will and practice had kept her tears at bay until she'd lain down for the night.

Caleb and Delia were busy with chores and arguing over how much Delia was capable of doing while pregnant. Lissa was sleeping better, so Mel had been working on getting Christmas together at her own place.

No one needed Summer. She should be relieved, even happy to have a day for herself. But she missed Kate's chattering. She missed sharing the details of Kate's afternoon with Thack.

She missed all of the ways they'd begun to feel like family, even knowing she should never have let that happen. The Shaws *had* to put up with her. One way or another, she was a piece of them. She was nothing to the Lanes. Not really. She was only an employee, and it was probably a stretch to even call her a friend.

No, that wasn't fair. Kate considered her a friend. Kate looked up to her, and in turn, Summer was amazed by the little girl who'd made this all happen.

She would *not* be melancholy and self-pitying today. She had come this far. She had gotten the things she'd wanted when she'd gone after them. She would not stop now.

Determined, she leaned back, arms behind her head, palms up, and almost toppled off her platform when she heard footsteps and Kate's panicked voice calling her name.

She righted herself just in time, then hopped off the platform. She made it maybe two hurried steps before Kate was launching herself at Summer, wrapping her arms around her waist with surprising force.

Summer wrapped her arms around Kate in return and squeezed tight, giving Kate the warm place to land she seemed to need even as panic clawed through her. "What's wrong? Is it an emergency? What's happened?"

"I don't want to go to school. Please don't make me go to school."

School? Well, not quite an emergency, but certainly odd. Thack was the one who handled Kate's morning routine, and it was only seven, so school was an hour or so away. But Summer had thought Kate enjoyed school. She was always eagerly chatting about her day in the afternoons.

But she was sobbing into Summer's stomach now, holding tight and shaking.

Summer took a deep breath and tried to think through the way her heart was breaking for the girl. Not wanting to go to school might be a normal kid thing, but Kate being this upset was not.

"Take a breath, sweetheart. Deep one in. Deep one out."

Kate seemed to try, but it ended on a sob so Summer picked her up. "Let's try this." She plopped Kate onto the yoga platform, then climbed up herself. Thack would kill her if he found out she hadn't immediately returned Kate, but…it was easier to determine what was wrong when people were calm.

"Reach your hands up to the sky."

Kate was shaking and crying, but she nodded and mirrored Summer's movement, finally taking a deep breath as Summer did. They went through a few easy poses until Kate seemed to get a handle on her tears.

She needed to get Kate warm and inside, but this outburst was so unusual. Summer knelt next to her, still on the platform, hoping to provide Kate with an anchor. "Now, why don't you want to go to school?"

Kate's face crumpled, and Summer felt like an idiot for thinking yoga would help. Kate was never like this. Summer wrapped her in a hug and rubbed her back. She had to get Kate home, but it seemed more important to find a way to make her okay.

"Whatever it is, honey, you can tell me. I'm here for you no matter what. I think you'll feel so much better if you could tell me what's wrong, and I will do whatever I can to help. I promise. I promise." She ran a hand over Kate's flyaway hair and took a seat on the platform. She brought Kate onto her lap, hoping to keep her warm.

After a few moments of sniffling silence, Kate took a deep breath. "Can you tell Daddy not to make me go to school?"

"You're going to have to tell me why first, Kate. I have to know why."

Again, Kate was quiet. She brought the edge of her coat into her mouth and chewed on the fabric for a few seconds in some kind of self-soothing or nervous habit.

She snuggled closer, the coat dropping from her mouth. When her voice came out, it was soft and raspy. "I-I told on a boy who was being mean to my friend. He said he was going to kill her dog because she cut in front of him." She began to sit straighter. "He's a fifth grader and Greta was afraid, but I said that wasn't right, so I told Mrs. Kinny and he got sent to the principal's office." Kate was so proud of herself, but then she slumped again.

"He got in a lot of trouble. He spent the afternoon in in-school suspension, and then he was walking out when the car riders were walking out, and he said…he said my mom…"

"Whatever he said about your mom, I'm sure it isn't true. Sometimes mean people say mean things because they think it makes them feel better."

Kate snuggled in deeper, her voice coming out muffled and soft. "He said I killed my mom."

The words hit Summer with the force of a physical blow. That anyone would say such a horrible thing to this little girl. That a boy she had to go to school with could even think up such a hurtful thing to say.

"I know it's true," Kate whispered.

"No." Summer took her by the shoulders and pulled Kate back so she could look her in the eye. "It is not true. He is a bully. A terrible, terrible, awful person, and you did not deserve those hateful words."

"But it's *true*," Kate insisted, her voice wavering. Summer brought the girl back to her shoulder simply because she couldn't hold her own tears in any longer. "It's why Grandma won't visit."

"This is all wrong. We need to get you home—" She was missing pieces of this puzzle, and she had to get Kate back to Thack and warmth.

Kate wrenched away, hopping off the platform. "No! Daddy will make me go to school, and I can't tell him. He'll be so sad. You can't tell him. I came to you because you have to help."

Summer followed, reaching out for her, but Kate backed away.

"Promise me you won't make me go back. Please."

"Your father will be worried about you."

"I don't—"

"Katherine."

It was like traveling back in time, all those times Thack had burst through the tree line in search of his escapee daughter, but Summer could find no comfort in that, nothing to smile about. She felt as though she'd been stabbed, and nothing would ever make it all right. "What the heck is going on?" Thack demanded. He must have started running the second he'd found Kate missing, because his chest was heaving.

Summer wished she could find humor in learning that even in a situation like this, he would say *heck* instead of *hell*, but she wanted to scream out every curse she knew approximately thirty-five times. And enact all sorts of violence on anyone who would make Kate think and feel such awful things.

Thack didn't even know what had happened, and he was visibly angry. Summer knew she'd take the brunt of that anger, simply because he couldn't lay it on his daughter. She couldn't even blame him for that. She welcomed taking that anger, if it would help.

"I don't want to go to school. I don't want to go to school!" Kate was crying again, stomping her feet and trying to run off, but Thack scooped her into his arms in one fluid, easy movement.

"Kate. What's wrong? You love going to school."

She wiggled in Thack's grasp, but he didn't release her. Summer had to turn away to try to find her composure, her breath. Find a way to hide the tears that were rolling down her cheeks.

"Please, Daddy. Please. Please."

"What happened, Summer?" Thack demanded, his voice gravelly and brooking no argument.

Summer didn't turn to face him, instead trying to surreptitiously wipe the tears from her face. "Someone said something awful to her at school yesterday, and she's very upset."

"Who said what to you?"

Summer looked over to see Kate shake her head, refusing to look at either of them.

"Put me down. I want to go home."

"Tell me what's wrong."

"No!" Kate wiggled some more, kicking at Thack, and Summer didn't know whether Thack let her down because she was too hard to hold or because he was so shocked by her sudden violence. "I'm not going to school, and you can't make me."

She took off, and Thack took off after her. Summer knew it wasn't her place to get involved. She should stay at the caravan and let Thack handle his own family. But she couldn't let this one be. For the sake of both of them, she had to go. So she started running as well.

———

Thack felt like he was having a heart attack. Not because for the second time in not that many minutes he was running at full speed, dodging trees and a fence. But because his daughter was acting in a way he'd never seen her act. Not since the nonsensical tantrums of tod- dlerhood, but this wasn't nonsensical. She was seven, and she didn't want to go to school, so much so that she was lashing out, and it scared the living hell out of him.

She stormed up the stairs, but before he could follow her, Summer's voice called out. "Thack, wait."

"I will not wait when she's…"

"Give her a few minutes."

He whirled on Summer, a very safe place for his anger and fear and panic to land. "Do not tell me what to do."

She came up short, breathing hard but still glar- ing at him. "Don't yell at me when you're angry with yourself."

He wanted to yell, but what was there to yell? That she was right? That he was so mad at himself for not knowing what was wrong with Kate that he would gladly yell and fight anyone who *did* know?

So mad that he'd come back from his early-morning

chores, Dad still asleep, and Kate had been gone. Just like the months leading up to Summer's interference in their lives. Blind panic had surged through him. Had Kate wanted to explore? Had someone taken her? Was she hurt? Was she gone forever?

He'd kissed Summer, and this was his punishment—losing his daughter forever. But she'd been there with Summer. She'd been there. She was okay. Except for the crying and yelling and running.

"Thack, please. Listen to me."

It was lowering to have to ask. It made him feel like the worst father in the world to ask, but what choice did he have? "What happened? What's wrong?"

"She asked me not to tell."

"Are you fu—"

"Please, just listen. I don't want to kill her trust in me. It's so important at that age to have someone you can trust, but you should know. You should know. I know. I'm…"

He shoved fingers through his hair. He'd lost his hat somewhere along the way, he realized, but he didn't care. All he cared about was that Summer had the answers, and she was hesitating instead of telling him. "I won't tell her you told me, but I have to know." He stepped toward Summer, trying to be honest without being angry. "I have to know what I can do to help my daughter."

Summer nodded jerkily. Her eyes were filled with unshed tears. Her breathing was slowly becoming normal, but she looked as if she were in pain. "Some little asshole told her friend he was going to kill her dog."

Relief swamped through him. If this was about bullies, he could deal with that, even if he had to threaten the little asshole himself. "Please tell me my daughter didn't say *asshole*."

Summer laughed, sort of. There were still tears in her eyes and pain in her expression, and his relief went away, because he realized that wasn't all. Of course it wasn't all. His daughter was a lot of things, but overly dramatic about going to school wasn't one of them.

"No, she did not. She did tell on him, and he got in trouble, but as they were leaving school that day he…"

"He what?"

Her composure broke, and she pressed a hand to her heart, clearing her throat as though she couldn't quite get the words out. "He told Kate she…that her mother had died *because* of Kate. Killed her."

Everything faded. Like he'd been thrown into a cave. He was in blackness, and he couldn't breathe. Even when Summer's hand closed over his, all he could see was black.

"I told her it wasn't true. But she's so certain. Certain that's why her grandparents won't visit. I know it isn't true. I know—"

He pulled his hand away from her, turned away. His vision had returned, but every movement walking up the porch stairs felt like fire. Someone had dared say that to his child. The truth wrapped in a lie. Now he had to talk to her without finding the little fucker and showing him the meaning of a father's wrath.

"Thack. It's…not true. It's not. It can't be." Her voice was so desperate, so plaintive. He wished he could lie to her, but if he wouldn't lie to Kate about it, he wouldn't lie to Summer.

"Killed, no, but it's not as untrue as I'd like it to

be," he ground out, opening the door. He paused at the threshold. "I'm not going to make her go to school, but I'll need some help watching her this morning if you're available."

"Of course. I'll…I'll make some breakfast."

"Thank you," he said stiffly, and then he walked up to his daughter's room. He was facing the inevitable here. It was a small town, of course, and everyone knew. He'd just never expected someone to maliciously throw it into her face like that. Not when she was seven.

Seven.

He leaned his head against the wall next to her door. He could hear her crying. For a second he thought to ask his father's advice, but he didn't think he had the time. And more? His father hadn't been the best at handling hard, emotional things head-on.

Not without being drunk first.

Now there's an idea.

Thack pushed the thought away by stepping into the room, only to find the door locked. He almost laughed. She so rarely got mad enough to lock her door, and it was futile. He kept a little key at the top of the door frame.

But, maybe he should give her the chance to open it herself. A say in her own life. Maybe…Summer was right and she needed a few minutes alone.

"Kate. Please. Let me in. We don't have to talk if you don't want to."

After a few moments when he was sure his heart was being repeatedly ripped out of his chest, the doorknob shook and he heard the click of her turning the lock.

She didn't open the door, but after a few seconds, he

turned the knob and stepped inside. She was curled into a ball on her bed, still in her coat and boots.

There were a million things he wanted to say, but none of them would help. This was what some unthinking ten-year-old had wrought—a pain Thack would never be able to erase for his daughter.

Slowly, carefully, he sank onto her bed. He toed off his boots, gently pried her sodden ones off, then lay next to her, wrapping his arms around her. After only a moment, she turned to him and burrowed into the circle of his arms.

He could feel the dampness of her cheeks through his shirt. He held her tight, giving her all the comfort he possibly could. Hoping she knew that here she would always be welcome and safe.

"Daddy."

He stroked her hair and held her close.

"Did I really... Did my mom... Summer said it isn't true, but..."

Thack swallowed the thick and heavy lump in his throat. He wasn't afraid of showing Kate emotion when it came to this. He never wanted her to think it was easy to lose Michaela, but he also needed to be able to speak, to give her the words she needed.

"When you were growing in your mom's stomach, we found out that she was sick. Her being sick had nothing to do with you."

Kate sniffled loudly. "Are you sure?"

"Positive. In fact, she used to say you were her angel, because if you hadn't been in there, we never would have known she was sick."

"But she died anyway."

He wiped his face on her pillow, then pulled her away so he could look into her eyes, red-rimmed and puffy. He didn't know how to tell a seven-year-old her mother had sacrificed all she could to make sure her daughter would survive. But he looked at her so she would always know. *God, please let her know.* She wasn't at fault. She'd been loved.

"Some people are miserable human beings, Kate. They feel bad, so they want to make everyone else feel bad too. Sometimes people will tell you that your mother dying had something to do with you, but they're wrong. There were some choices she had to make, *we* had to make, to keep you safe and growing, because we wanted you so much. But nothing about that was your fault. Never think that what happened was your fault." *It was mine. I couldn't save her. I couldn't make things right. I couldn't work hard enough to give her what she needed to pull through.*

He paused and dropped his gaze out of surprise. How had he fallen so far backward? After Michaela's funeral, he'd immediately invested in therapy. For him, for Dad, and once she'd been old enough, he'd been on the look-out for any signs Kate would need it as well.

They'd gone through grief counseling, and Thack had tried to come to grips with what had happened. He had thought…he'd thought the feelings of guilt and blame had been worked through. Thought he'd moved on from that. But there they were.

Dr. Seaver had asked him if he'd ever blame his daughter for the choices they'd made in putting off Michaela's treatment. He'd listened as Thack had ranted and raved about anyone ever thinking such a thing.

Then you can't blame yourself either.

But here he was, in one breath telling Kate she was nowhere near to blame, and in the next he was heaping it all on himself.

He pressed a kiss to Kate's forehead. "She got to meet you, and it was the best day of her life. She told me so."

"I wish I could remember," Kate said, her voice small and squeaky.

"I wish that too, Kate. I wish it so hard. But we have to find a way to…live and be happy. Because she loved you. We loved each other. And when you lose someone you love, you can't let that take away all the other love in your life. We'll always miss her, but we owe it to her to have the life she didn't get to have."

He had no idea if he was making any sense, or if he was talking over her head. But she'd stopped crying. She was still snuggled into him, but she didn't seem so rigid.

"Are you going to make me go to school?"

"Not today. I'll go call you in sick right now. You will have to go back tomorrow."

She tensed.

"But, maybe we can go in early and talk to Mrs. Kinny about whatever got you so upset."

She didn't relax, but she nodded. "I think I'm going to go back to sleep."

His cue to leave, but he was loath to let her go. Still, there were chores to do and phone calls to make.

"Summer is going to be here all day, but if you need me for anything, no matter how busy I am, I will come."

Her smile was small, but it was a smile. He'd count that as some kind of victory. "If I want you to come… can Summer still stay all day?"

"Of course." He wouldn't deny Kate anything now, but more, as wrong as it was, as much as he knew he shouldn't, he wanted Summer here too.

"And she can help decorate tonight since we didn't last night?"

"Yes." He eased off the bed, back into his boots, and then pressed a kiss to her cheek. "I love you, Kate. You don't ever have to run away from me like that. You only have to be honest."

"I didn't want to make you sad," she whispered, her eyes filling with tears again.

There weren't many moments of parenting that were like bolts of lightning. He'd had very few times when Kate had said something and he could immediately see all the ways he'd gone wrong. Life with a child was usually too muddled, too gray, too complex.

But this… He saw it all so clearly. He'd shouldered all his feelings and shut them away, kept them under lock and key, to the point where Kate was afraid to share her own, and that…that would never be okay.

"It would make me even sadder to not know what's wrong. It's okay to be sad. It's okay to hurt. As long as you're honest with me, we'll find a way to be happy."

"Are you happy, Daddy?"

What a far more complex question than it should be. Two hours ago, he would have lied and told her of course he was, but this whole thing…

He'd made a hash of his life these past few years, so much so that he didn't even *have* a life, and he wasn't sure how to work through that yet. Wasn't sure how to balance the guilt and the fear that he was cursed, even knowing how stupid that was. He had no idea how to navigate it all, but he'd been ignoring that, pushing it away, and that wasn't the answer either.

"I'm happy that we talked, and I'm happy that you're mine, my wonderful girl." He pressed another kiss to her temple. "I love you, Kate. Always. Forever."

"I love you too, Daddy." She made a big fake yawn, and he took it as his cue to leave, though walking out her bedroom door might be among the top ten hardest things he'd ever have to do.

When Thack reached the bottom of the stairs, Summer was sitting on the couch in the living room. She was crying, and her face was as red and blotchy as Kate's had been. Something in his chest shifted. How could she be so worked up over something that didn't even touch her?

She hopped off the couch and crossed the space between them, wasting no time in flinging her arms around his neck and holding on tight. "Tell me she's okay."

He swallowed, both at how deeply she cared, and how good it felt to have someone come up and hug him after what he'd just been through.

He rested his hand on Summer's back. She was cold, wearing some spandex-y excuse for clothes. "She'll be all right."

Her body slumped, and he held her upright. The funny thing was though, she seemed to be holding him upright too.

Chapter 17

SUMMER PULLED AWAY, FEELING SILLY SHE'D SO COMPLETELY lost it. Kate wasn't hers. Thack wasn't hers. She was a friend at best, an employee at worst, but the bottom line was—she cared. She cared so much, and it hurt to see them hurt.

"Sorry," she mumbled, trying to pull herself together.

"You don't have to be sorry. I owe you… Thanks doesn't even begin to cover it."

She worked at cleaning up her face, though she knew she had to be failing. She felt wrung out and empty. She couldn't even begin to imagine what *they* were feeling. "I didn't do anything."

"Kate came to you. You listened. You've given her someone she can trust. Someone safe to run to when she's afraid of…" His throat moved. "She didn't want to make me sad. But, if you weren't there, where would she have gone? Would I have ever even heard about this?"

Summer blinked, feeling emotional all over again. "I'm just so sorry it happened."

"Me too." His face looked pained, but there was something else in his expression, in his manner. She wasn't sure how or why, but he didn't seem so tense, so on edge. He wasn't happy or relaxed by any means, but whatever had passed between him and Kate seemed to have eased something.

"I'm behind with the cattle checkup, so I'm going to go work. But, if she needs me, if she wants me, even for something quick or small or silly, she can come get me, or you can."

Summer nodded because she didn't have a voice, and even if she had one, she didn't know what to say. She didn't know what to do for him or Kate.

"Summer…"

Whatever he was going to say was interrupted by laughter. Male and female laughter, coming from the back of the house. Both of their heads turned toward it, and she assumed Thack was just as surprised as she was to see Mr. Lane walking from his main floor bedroom… with a woman.

"Oops," the woman said, trying to suppress a smile. "I think we've been caught, Merle."

"You're supposed to be taking Kate to school. And you're not supposed to be here," Mr. Lane said gruffly. "Mrs.…Bart?"

"Hi, Thackery. I better scoot. I'll call you later, Merle." She patted Mr. Lane on the face and then, face averted, *scooted* toward the door.

"What's going on here?" Mr. Lane demanded, staring at Summer intently. She supposed he noticed her puffy, red face and eyes, but she was still trying to process him leaving his bedroom with a woman. In the morning.

The front door clicked closed, and Summer glanced at Thack. He was wide-eyed, his mouth dropped open. On the positive side, she supposed he'd moved on from dwelling over his own terrible tragedy, at least for the moment.

"You…in your… Morning… But…Mrs.…Mrs. Bart?"

"Hell, Son, I'm only fifty-five. We can't all live like monks." He glanced at Summer, and she knew her face was going thirty-five shades of red, even as Mr. Lane disappeared back into his bedroom.

Ticking moments of silence followed, and Summer wasn't sure that Thack moved. She wasn't even sure he breathed.

"Are you all right?" she finally asked.

"My father is sleeping with my kindergarten teacher."

Oh. "Well, I suppose that doesn't happen every day."

"God. What if it happens every day? In my house. With me in it." He shuddered and shook his head. "I can't… Nope. I need to get to work." He glanced up the stairs toward Kate's room.

Poor guy was really running the gauntlet this morning. "Don't worry about a thing. I'll take good care of her."

He nodded, eventually turning and leaving. Summer made breakfast and then had to have an uncomfortable conversation with Mr. Lane about why Kate was home.

"She wasn't feeling well."

"Is there more to that?"

"Yes, but I think Thack should be the one to tell you."

Mr. Lane nodded and went to work in his shed.

Then Summer spent the rest of the day trying to make Kate smile and eat. It was slow progress, but by the time Thack came in for dinner, Kate was almost her old self. A little more clingy to Thack, so quick to crawl up into his lap at dinner, still not quite one hundred percent seven-year-old exuberance, but she wasn't crying, and she wasn't silent. Most importantly, she wasn't broken.

Helping the Lanes put up the remainder of their

Christmas decorations while Rudolph played on the TV—Kate happily squealing every time the Abominable Snowman came on—was like something out of a dream.

In the grand scheme of things, it wasn't perfect. Summer could see that even more clearly after all the upheaval this morning, but that this morning could be followed by Christmas decorations and hot chocolate and happiness was a miracle.

"All right, Katie Pie, bedtime."

"But, Daddy, what about Frosty and—"

"School bright and early tomorrow, kiddo." He scooped her up in a way that made Kate squeal and giggle, and Summer could only sit on the couch and smile at them, at the love there. Even when things were hard, even when Thack didn't think he had any more room in his life, there was so much love between these two that it could only make Summer happy.

Thack caught her gaze. "Would you mind sticking around? I'd like to talk to you."

She nodded, even though it sent a jitter of nerves down her spine. What was there to talk about? Kate escaping? More help with Christmas maybe? That kiss from two nights ago that she couldn't get out of her head?

Probably not that.

She made one last check that everything in the kitchen had been put to rights. Mr. Lane retired to his room to make a "private phone call" to someone she had a sneaking suspicion was Mrs. Bart.

So, Summer settled herself on the couch, enjoying the twinkle and color of the Christmas lights and the way they sparkled off the different ornaments. She leaned her head against the back of the couch, "Rudolph the Red-Nosed Reindeer" stuck in her head on repeat, and apparently promptly fell asleep. Because the next minute, Thack's hand was on her shoulder, gently shaking her.

She blinked her eyes open, realizing most of the lights had been turned off. Only the tree was lit, casting a magical glow over the room.

"Sorry," he offered sheepishly. "Would have liked to have let you sleep, but I'm not sure this is the place for it. You'd get quite a crick in your neck sleeping like that."

She pulled her head up, trying to think past the fuzzy sleep brain. The only solid thing she could focus on was how handsome he was in the glow of the Christmas lights. So tall and sturdy and infinitely amazing.

She let out a dreamy sigh before she remembered this was real life, not her imagination. "Oh, right, well you wanted me to stay."

"We can talk about it tomorrow."

"But if we wait until tomorrow, I'll never sleep." She flashed him a grin and patted the spot next to her. "Sit. I'll rub your shoulders, and you can tell me what's up."

"You'll rub my shoulders?"

She tried to pretend that was a totally normal offer, not a ridiculous mistake on the part of her still-dreaming brain. "Sure. You're always so tense. You could use someone to rub your shoulders. No funny business. I'm just going to give you a little massage. It's been a long, trying day—let someone do something for you."

He looked at her skeptically, but she offered her hands, palms up. After a moment of hesitation he slid onto the cushion next to her, back toward her.

What she really wanted to do was lean her cheek there between his shoulder blades and tell him how strong and wonderful he was. But that would cross a line. They might have kissed, he might have even thanked her for the role she played with Kate this morning, but that didn't mean his *no room for romance* edict had changed.

But him allowing this gesture was a step toward *something*. So, breathing deeply, she rested her palms on his shoulders. Much like when she'd touched his face the other night, his posture immediately relaxed. Not fully, but enough that she could notice.

She dug her fingers into his shoulders, trying to loosen some of the muscles he held so tight. He groaned, and the sound hit her where it absolutely shouldn't.

"Sweet pickles," he muttered.

She couldn't stifle the laughter that bubbled out of her mouth. It was just so ridiculous when he said that.

But he laughed too. "You have no idea how badly I wish I could go back in time and stop myself from ever starting to use those words, never mind using them enough that they became part of my regular vocabulary."

"I think it's adorable."

"Adorable. I say *sweet pickles*, and beautiful women are calling me adorable. I'll have you know, once upon a time, I was considered smooth and cool."

She giggled, couldn't help it. Smooth and cool. He was ridiculous, and adorable, and she wanted to slide into his lap and do not-adorable things.

She kept rubbing his shoulders instead, working out the kinks of those tight muscles, so gratified when he relaxed and all but slumped forward. It felt like she'd done something for him, which warmed her heart, and the massage allowed her fingers to explore all those firm, contracting muscles. Hot and sturdy under her hands, carrying such a great burden.

That jittery feeling that centered itself in her chest so often when he was around intensified—an awareness. An intense need to know what those shoulders might feel like without the shirt.

Smooth over steel, still warm, capable, and endlessly strong. What might it feel like to explore him completely, everywhere?

Summer's cheeks were on fire by this point, a coiling, needy want centering itself deep inside her. Something no number of platonic shoulder massages or chaste, friendly hugs would ever assuage.

"Thank you," Thack murmured, shifting so he was no longer sitting sideways on the couch. Her hands had to slide off his back, and she sighed over not being able to touch him anymore.

You could hold his hand. You could touch his face. You could *kiss him.*

No. No, she'd promised not to do that. Of course, if *he* wanted to…

He let out a gusty sigh, eyes closing as he leaned his head and rested it on the couch back.

She almost opened her mouth to ask what he had wanted to talk to her about, but he seemed so peaceful. She stayed where she was instead, wondering how this moment could feel so perfect. Exciting and nerve-racking and still a little raw from this morning, but still…somehow that all together made it perfect.

His breathing evened out, and his body relaxed even

further. Her fingers nearly twitched with the desire to explore.

"Thack?"

Nothing. Not a change in breathing or a flicker of response. Now she was the one wishing she could let him sleep. He deserved some rest, but that probably shouldn't be found on a sofa when he was so close to a bed.

She really needed to not think about his bed.

Still, instead of talking louder or poking him or doing anything that might actually wake him up, she rubbed her palm against the scruff of his chin, soaked in that rough scrape against her palm.

Still nothing.

She sat back, watching his even breathing, noticed the way his face looked at least five years younger in sleep, with the low, warm light from the Christmas tree softening all his hard edges. Unable to resist, she leaned over and brushed her lips across his cheek.

"Liar."

She screeched and jumped, high enough that coming back down made an audible thump against the couch cushion. When she'd caught her strangled breath, her eyes met his green ones, and she couldn't even be mad because there was a tiny glimmer of humor in his eyes.

Had she *ever* seen that in him before? She'd seen some moments of ease and hope and happiness, but never *humor*.

"You promised not to kiss me."

She tried to glower and probably failed. "I never said anything about *where* I promised not to kiss you."

His mouth curved into a smile, and it was possibly one of the top five most wonderful things she'd ever seen. It hovered somewhere around the blazing sunset behind a mountain that she'd seen her first night in Blue Valley, and just behind the smile of her niece. *Especially* after this morning.

As if he'd read where her thoughts went, he sobered up. "I couldn't have managed this morning without you. I really couldn't have." He reached out and cupped her face, and she wasn't sure she'd ever be able to breathe when he willingly, purposefully touched her.

"I didn't do anything special."

"You did." Only two words, but they were emphatic. His gaze never broke from hers, his hand didn't leave her cheek, and she never wanted to change this moment where she mattered. Where she'd done something that truly mattered.

~~~

It was hard to know what to do in this situation, when all Thack wanted to do was keep touching her, keep telling her how much she meant to him right now. He wanted to forget about this morning, about two nights ago, and bury himself in *Summer*. He wanted to kiss her, and not in that angry, desperate way he had the other night. He wanted to sink and explore, to lose himself in something that wasn't dark or hard.

Summer's smile had never been either of those things.

What held him back wasn't what he'd said the other night. If there was any positive to take out of this morning, it was that he realized he'd lost sight of things. He'd lost at least half the answers he thought he'd found in therapy those first few years after Michaela's death.

He'd forgotten, somehow, that his happiness mattered.

His happiness affected Kate. And he couldn't get over the idea that his happiness might be tied up with Summer. He still wasn't sure it was the best idea, but he was…less opposed.

He deserved something too, right? To be the example, to show Kate she deserved things for herself, that it wouldn't do for her to be the martyr. Worse yet, for her to think she was to blame, to think *she* held the responsibility to keep him from being sad.

It might be that every time he reached out for something for himself, his hand got slapped, but if he put Kate in his shoes, he would want her to keep reaching. He also knew, without a shadow of a doubt, that the wonderful, loving women he'd loved and lost would want that for him too.

But even if he needed to be better about finding his happiness and not taking everything so seriously, that certainly didn't mean Summer wanted to fling herself into all of this.

But she was here, and she wasn't moving away from his hands on her face.

"Um, well." Summer cleared her throat. "I'm so sorry. For blubbering all over you this morning. My heart just breaks thinking about it, but that's unfair. She was your wife. Kate was so little."

"Yes, I recall." The anguish on her face made him sorry. "What I'm trying to say, badly, is…it means something. That you care. It does."

"I…love her," Summer said, looking at her lap. But he couldn't take his hand away. He couldn't stop touching the soft skin of her cheek. Couldn't stop himself from leaning in or feeling the full impact of her words, even if he didn't know what to do about them.

His world, Kate's world, it had all become so small. He'd been so intent on keeping her safe, keeping her away from all the bad things life could bring. What good things might he have been keeping her away from as well?

"I know that may seem strange since she's not mine," Summer said softly, still avoiding his gaze. "But she reminds me of myself. And she's so sweet, so open, and to have that little piece of absolute shit say something so horrible to her at *school* when she's *seven*… Oh, I wish I could strangle him. And burn every possession that means anything to him."

It was such a strange thing to watch his own feelings be expressed by someone else. His own hurt. His own anger. Quite honestly, he hadn't given as much thought to the boy who had done this to his daughter, because he'd been caught up in the damage control.

He didn't want to tap into that anger though, because he was afraid if he thought too much about it, nothing would stop him from punishing the kid himself. "I'm going to do my best to talk to his parents without throwing any punches."

She laughed, though it was harsh, not joyous. "I've seen a lot of people do terrible things, but to be so young and be unnecessarily vicious to someone younger still. I am not a violent person, but I can imagine doing a *lot* of violent things. If you *did* punch someone, I'd probably applaud."

He didn't know why that moment in particular prompted him to move. Why were *those* words the ones that made touching her face not nearly enough? Whatever it was, he lowered his mouth to hers and took what he should have been so much more careful about taking.

But she made it hard to remember caution when she wrapped her arms around his neck and pressed closer, touching her tongue to his bottom lip. Caution flew out the window under the lulling warmth of her mouth, the way her eyes fluttered to closed, and the bright colors from the Christmas tree lights reflecting there and against the glossy strands of hair that teased her jawline.

He let his hands travel over her face, into that hair that smelled of flowers and felt like silk between his fingers. He slowly tangled his tongue with hers, pulling her closer, his own eyes closing as he sank into that sweet, dizzying taste of Summer.

He lost himself in the lazy, sensual kiss. It had the same effect as the angry, frustrated one of the other night. It held the same danger, just a softer danger, and he was more inclined to try to navigate it, to dive deep into the sizzling heat that somehow mixed with the comfort and softness that seemed so essential to who this woman was.

She made a little sighing noise into his mouth, and he shifted so they could be closer, so he could hold her soft chest against his hard one. He held her closer so he could delve deeper into the beautiful mystery and comfort of her mouth. Her slender arms tightened around his neck, and he could feel the press of her bangles into his skin as she held him just as close as he was holding her, meeting exploration for exploration.

All the muscles she'd relaxed with her back rub tensed tight with a new kind of burden. Hard, unrelenting *want*.

But there were things that had to be said before he could allow want to take over, and more importantly, there were things Summer needed to understand. Things that had to be untwisted before he could even think about trying to be the kind of person she would need. So, he pulled away a hair. Just a hair, their mouths still so damn close.

The lights from the tree twinkled in the moisture on her lips, and he wanted to sink there again. Again and again.

Was talking really necessary before more kissing? More Summer?

She didn't unwind her arms, just blinked up at him. "Was that a particularly seductive statement?"

The laugh that escaped his mouth was rusty. "No."

"Right. Um. So. As much as I hate to point it out, because I'd prefer to keep doing this, the last time I kissed you…"

"I know." He forced himself to sit back, to remove his hands, to remove *hers*. To be a rational, reasonable adult. He'd made a promise not to pile blame on himself, but that didn't mean he should jump into things he wanted without thinking, without weighing the consequences. His life would always be complicated by the challenges that had come before, and they could never totally go away.

He blew out a breath. "After Michaela died…I did a lot of counseling. Made Dad do it too. I knew we had to be one hundred percent healthy with everything to give Kate what she needed."

Summer's hand slid over his and squeezed. "You have no idea… Not all parents would put their children first. Not like you do."

He blinked at the emotion in her voice, the admiration. He felt unworthy, but so damn pleased by it.

"Thack…what did you mean? When you said that it wasn't as untrue as you'd like?"

He looked at her hand on his and wondered how he would get through this explanation without feeling like… Well, just feeling, he supposed.

But, at this point, there was no choice or going back to a time when she didn't have a right to ask him that. "During one of Michaela's exams after she found out she was pregnant with Kate, they found a tumor. It turned out to be colon cancer. Because most of the interventions posed a risk to the baby, Michaela refused treatments until Kate's chance of survival was greater than her own."

Summer made a sound, not as dramatic as a gasp but something close to it. Her hand gripped his tighter.

He never thought he'd have to explain this to someone. Not for himself. Maybe for Kate, but never for him. He could stop or gloss over the rest, but as hard and painful as it was to say, he was finding that doing so also lightened the load.

"It was an impossible situation, but Michaela didn't think she would have found out about the cancer in time if she hadn't been pregnant, so she refused to risk Kate. Her parents weren't particularly supportive. They wanted me to change her mind or do what I could to override her decision." He wanted to kiss Summer and forget this. He wanted to walk away, but the months, maybe years, of tenuous, strong-armed over-control seemed to have been a way of doing just that.

He didn't want to set that example for Kate. He

wanted her to be able to move forward, blameless, happy, even if she would always wish she could remember the mother who had sacrificed so much for her.

Which meant that was what he had to give himself. He had to move forward, blameless and happy, even when things were hard. "The thing is, sometimes I wanted to. I wanted to fight her and beg her to give herself more of a fighting chance, but I couldn't… She was dying—how could I argue with her? I'd been down the cancer road. I knew where it ended up. And I blamed myself, because it seemed like every time I stepped out of line, someone I loved suffered the consequences."

Summer touched his cheek, that way she had that was soft and strong at the same time. He didn't want to look at her, because it was hard enough keeping his emotions in check as it was, but she rubbed her thumb along his jaw and he forced himself to be strong.

Her eyes were full of tears, and she swallowed before she spoke. "But, you know that it was normal to be confused and right to take her side. You know that…cancer isn't karma used against you."

She said it so certainly, so forcefully. Where had she come from, this miracle in front of him? "I try to know that. I fail sometimes, and I don't think some of that guilt will ever ease, but it doesn't eat me up like it used to."

"Good."

"Summer, I don't know what I could have to offer you." Which was true beyond measure. He wanted to be able to offer her everything, but all he had were broken pieces.

She didn't move away and didn't falter. "We could find out."

Even knowing it would probably bring him pain, that it would be another impossible facet of his life to navigate, he found he wanted to. He wanted to find out how he could fit her into their world. Because as much as he was attracted to her, as much as she made him feel more alive than he'd been allowing himself to feel, as much as all that mattered and made him want to try, the core of it was so much more.

He'd grown to trust her. Completely against his will, while he was looking the other way, she'd shown that he could trust her not just with himself, but with his daughter. His daughter, whom Summer loved.

It wasn't the same as if she were their blood, but that didn't mean her feelings weren't important. Without even asking, he knew he could trust Summer to put Kate first. Together, they would put Kate first, trying to navigate all the rest.

It was scary as hell, but it felt like a new chapter in his life was starting. For once, he was looking forward to it.

Chapter 18

SUMMER HAD NEVER FELT SO ODD. ON THE ONE HAND, her heart ached for all Kate and Thack had been through. Even when she woke up the next morning, there was a kind of heavy hurt in her chest. It didn't go away, and she didn't know how she felt about that. Was it strange that she should hurt for them the way they hurt for each other? Or did it speak more to what she'd admitted to Thack?

She loved Kate. She did. And sometimes her feelings for Thack were…strong. Really strong. But then again, last night she'd realized how little she really knew him. So, it was more like a seed. She didn't love him, because the seed hadn't sprouted yet.

But it could. It wouldn't take much.

Which led her to the other hand, the hand that was giddy and happy and ridiculously excited over the prospect of *finding out* where this could lead.

It was how things were supposed to be in a normal life. And, yes, Thack and Kate's tragedy wasn't exactly *normal*, but a relationship could be. It could be easy and sweet and good, just what she'd always wished for.

That hope, that giddiness, didn't erase the chest ache, but it buoyed it. It was a lot like those first few weeks after she'd first come to Blue Valley. She had ached at her father and Mel's response, but Caleb, in his gruff way, had accepted her on sight. She'd found her family.

For the first time in her life, she'd felt safe and happy, even if the situation wasn't perfect. No one would harm her here. She was safe from the whims of a volatile woman she'd never understand.

Summer sipped her tea, thinking about the Shaws. She was a part of their lives. She felt valued and like she belonged. Her father's coolness toward her was the little hangnail that bothered her, but she never pushed. She was so afraid to push—in case one day she'd push too far and he'd admit that she wasn't his.

But why would he have admitted he knew her mother was pregnant and not admit he wasn't the father? Unless Mom had...

She shook her head and finished off the tea. She didn't want to think about that. She had work and people who needed her. She mattered to the Lanes. Thack had *thanked* her for being someone Kate could trust.

That was what she would focus on—the places where things made sense. Where she could be of some help.

Of course, that didn't mean she could head over there first thing. Mr. Lane was obviously feeling better if he was...entertaining, so he would be getting ready to take Kate to school. Thack would be working.

She had a normal routine to see to, and it was Friday. She'd be singing at Pioneer Spirit tonight. She needed to get back to her usual to-do list: yoga, shower, tidy up the main house, and check in on Delia. Make lunch for the Shaws, make lunch for the Lanes. Tidy up there.

She smiled as she pulled on her yoga clothes. Her life was full. Full of giving to people. Full of using skills she not only enjoyed, but was good at.

She didn't have to entertain strangers or make creepy

men feel comfortable. She didn't have to let anyone do anything to her that she didn't want them to do. Her life was her own, and she'd never, ever been happier.

When she stepped outside, she frowned. Her yoga platform had been flipped over. Odd. It was too heavy to have been tipped by the wind. Surely an animal wouldn't have been able to do that either. But what could?

All the contented excitement that had built in her chest dropped to her toes. *You don't deserve it. Remember that, Summer. Whatever happy you get, you'll never deserve it.*

Her mother had whispered those words to her, time and time again, once while she'd calmly, deliberately loaded a gun.

Summer squeezed her eyes shut. No. She wasn't going to think like that. She was happy, and nothing could ruin it. She *did* deserve to be happy, and she was going to have joy in her life.

She opened her eyes, forcing herself to look at the overturned platform. It had to have been a wild animal. Maybe a scrap of food or a tinier animal had gotten underneath, and the bigger animal had turned it over... somehow. *Oh*, maybe Caleb had wanted to move it so it didn't sink farther into the ground. It had been dark last night when she'd returned home. Maybe he'd done it yesterday, and since she hadn't been around, he hadn't been able to tell her.

Yes, that was it. Had to be. She put the platform back to rights, working through her normal routine and doing everything in her power not to think of all the sinister things that this could signify.

That was just silly. As silly as the creeping sensation

that she was being watched. No one was in those woods. No one was messing with her. What would be the point?

There was no point, but even though she pretended she was fine, her limbs didn't feel sturdy. She hurried through her routine and packed her bag with only half a brain dedicated to the task.

Even as she walked to the Shaw house, she kept her eyes on the tree line. She was a believer in following her gut, but her gut was being ridiculous right now. There was just a lot of good happening in her life and she wasn't used to trusting that.

She stepped into the Shaw house, headed for the stairs and the upstairs bathroom, but before she could take a step, she heard Caleb call her name from farther inside the house.

Odd. Usually everyone was out working at this time of the day. Still, she made her way to the voice, stopping short in the entry to the living room when she realized everyone was there. Well, not their father, but Caleb and Delia, Mel and Dan, and Lissa snoozing in her little playpen in the corner.

"There you are."

"Here I am," Summer replied, feeling as nervous as she'd felt since those first few weeks. "Was I supposed to be here earlier?"

"No, but you were supposed to be here yesterday, when we would have talked to you about Christmas."

She couldn't fight the flush of embarrassment that swept over her cheeks. It would be easy enough to tell them there'd been an emergency with the Lanes. After all, it wasn't like she had a set schedule for helping out here.

It was just… It felt like they knew. Knew that she was throwing herself at Thack and didn't approve.

"Sit down," Mel said, though she added a smile and an odd gesture as if she was trying to make it sound like less of an order.

Stiffly, Summer moved to the couch. All eyes were on her. It made her feel weird, but she plastered a smile on her face. "What's this all about?"

"Well, yesterday we were going to start planning out Christmas Eve and day, but you didn't show up. Which isn't like you."

"We're worried about you. You've been scarce," Caleb added.

"I have two jobs. The Lanes had a minor emergency yesterday, and I pitched in to help."

They all exchanged a look. Summer frowned. As much as she appreciated their concern, she did not appreciate…whatever this was. It felt a heck of a lot like judgment.

"I don't think you understand the gravity of the situation you're dealing with over there. The Lanes have been through a lot," Mel finally said, her tone and expression deadly serious.

"Yes, I know."

Mel and Caleb exchanged another look, then Caleb zeroed in on her. "You know?"

"Yes, I know. I know what happened. I don't know why that's cause for all this." She waved a hand to encompass the room. "What exactly are you all afraid I'm going to do?"

"We're just worried. You're too kind for your own good. You give too much and take too little, and it'd be awfully easy for the Lanes to take advantage of that."

"Before my husband continues," Delia said, lounging in a recliner, feet tucked under herself, "I'd like to point out I objected to this and suggested they let you handle your own affairs. My opinion—that you are an adult and capable of making your own decisions, just as Mel and Caleb are capable of making theirs—was vetoed."

"You're not helping," Caleb grumbled.

"Dan agrees with me," Delia returned.

"I agree with no one. I'm Switzerland," Dan replied.

Summer wanted to feel cheered that they cared, that they were worried. She wanted that to be love, and she supposed in Mel and Caleb's roundabout way, they were showing their love. But...it wasn't what she wanted. Especially after getting the creeps with everything this morning, she'd wanted to come here and feel normal.

Not like a chastised child.

"Thank you for standing up for me, Delia," Summer said as evenly as she could manage. "As for the rest of you, I appreciate the concern..." No, she didn't. She almost said it. Almost let her temper slip through, but she didn't want to make anyone *mad*. "But, I'm quite capable of handling hard things."

"You're too softhearted."

Summer ignored the sting of tears and got to her feet. "Excuse me. I need to take a shower," she said overbrightly.

"Running away isn't the answer," Caleb said softly as she walked past him.

She whirled on him, surprised by the force of anger inside her. But she fought it. Because she didn't want to cause a scene or make them mad. Didn't want to be unwelcome here, not now.

Of course, the last time she'd yelled at Caleb hadn't exactly resulted in that. In fact, it had helped. She and Mel being firm with Caleb had helped him repair his relationship with Delia.

When she was firm, when she lashed out, Summer tended to get…maybe not what she wanted, but at least forward movement. It was a shocking revelation. Her father's stupid words about trusting people with your anger rung in her head again.

She loved Mel and Caleb. They were her siblings, and even though they hadn't all grown up together, she'd been around for the start of their new lives with their spouses. That had built a bond.

Did she trust that bond?

She swallowed and glanced at Mel, then Caleb. "Screw you both for thinking so little of me," she said, surprising even herself. "I came here, and I had to fight to be accepted. It was very kind of you to let me into your lives, and I love you because you are my sister and my brother, but…that doesn't mean you can treat me like the stupid baby of the family. Do you know what I've gone through to even be here?"

"You've never told us."

It hurt to have Delia point that out when for a shining second she'd been the one on Summer's side.

"Because I don't want to. Because I want to forget that part of my life ever existed." She fixed Caleb and Mel with twin glares. "But make no mistake: I can handle the Lanes, I can handle you lot of crazies, and I can handle myself."

She stalked out of the room to the sound of applause—which she assumed came from Delia. A few whistles that had to be from Dan. She wanted to laugh. She wanted to cry.

Instead, she got ready to face the day, because she could handle it. She could handle *all* of it.

———

It had been a long day. Of course, that could be said almost every day. It had been a long two weeks of scurrying to get ready for Christmas while still running a ranch, making sure Kate was getting along at school, and trying to find a few extra moments to spend with Summer alone.

Thack had been failing at that last part, but Summer had been there helping with the rest, and that would do for now. Maybe once the holiday fervor died down they could go on a real date and share more than a quick kiss on the porch before Summer headed back to her caravan at night.

Thack was a little edgy with the waiting, but he'd deal. Besides, tonight his mind was occupied with the phone call he'd made asking Stan and Marjorie to please, for Kate's sake, come to Blue Valley at least for a small portion of her Christmas break next week.

To his surprise, Stan hadn't just agreed, he'd *promised*. Marjorie had supposedly started seeing a new therapist who suggested facing her grief rather than avoiding the triggers for it.

Thack still wasn't sure if he'd tell Kate beforehand. Though it seemed promising, he didn't want her hurt if her grandparents' plans fell through.

Maybe he'd talk to Summer about it. Ask her opinion. He couldn't help smiling at the thought. It was something of a miracle to have found someone he trusted.

As he approached the house, however, his smile dimmed. Dad had Mrs. Bart over for dinner. In Thack's house. At his kitchen table. Where his mother had once served them meals.

He wasn't angry with his father for that, could hardly blame him when Thack seemed to be starting something with Summer, but it didn't make the situation any less weird.

He really didn't want to have to face the thought of his father with his kindergarten teacher. He was running out of other options though, and staying outside any longer would only make things weirder. So, he trudged across the yard, up the porch stairs, and into the warm entry of his house.

Laughter greeted him. He smiled. It was nice there could be laughter even without Summer, who would have already have left for her gig at Pioneer Spirit.

In the living room, his father was sprawled in his recliner watching one of his shows with the volume too loud. Mrs. Bart and Kate had their heads together over the coffee table, both drawing something on red and green pieces of paper.

"Hi, Daddy," Kate greeted without even looking up. "You missed dinner. Mrs. Bart made mac and cheese with *hot dogs* in it."

"Oh…"

"There's some without too," Mrs. Bart said, giving him a wink. "Though I sent most of it home with Summer. She was flitting around here so much she barely ate."

"Um, well. I'm sure either will be fine."

Mrs. Bart cleared her throat, giving a meaningful look at his father. Dad straightened in his chair.

"Oh right. You know, it's a Friday night. Lillian and I can get Kate to bed if you'd like to go paint the town."

Thack could only stare at his father. "Paint the town?" He looked around the room, but he was the only person standing here. "Me, paint the town?"

Dad shrugged, eyes never leaving the TV. "Hear they've got some good entertainment down at Pioneer Spirit."

"At Pioneer...oh." Oh. His dad was trying to get him to go out. To Summer. On a Friday night. While Dad and Thack's kindergarten teacher watched his daughter.

"If something comes up with the cows, I can see to it."

"But—"

"And I can see to Kate." Mrs. Bart smiled reassuringly as Kate furiously scribbled whatever image was part of their little game.

Thack could only stare. A few short months ago, his life had felt too heavy, falling apart at the seams, and now suddenly people were stepping up to help. What's more, he was actually thinking about letting them—something he never would have been able to do before Summer came into his life. Lights twinkled on the Christmas tree, and paper chains Kate had made with Summer were hanging from just about every available surface.

He still had wrapping to do and stockings to find and meals to figure out, but this was the most on top of it the house had probably ever looked before Christmas. Enough so that it wasn't crazy to entertain the possibility of a night away.

Part of him was afraid to trust the idea, but part of him was starting to think he owed it to Kate *to* trust it. She wasn't begging him to stay. She was so caught up in whatever she was doing with Mrs. Bart that he might as well not even be here.

"I…suppose I could find something to do for an hour or so," he said slowly, not at all sure.

"Daddy." Kate finally looked up. "You should go listen to Summer sing. She's so good, and you're never here to hear her. Oh, can I go?" She hopped to her feet, ready to run for her shoes, but Thack stopped her.

"Summer plays at a place that's only for grown-ups. But I can stay home and play games with you if you want."

Her shoulders slumped, but she kind of shrugged, like she didn't care much one way or another. Kids were such ego builders.

"Or, you could go," Mrs. Bart said, getting to her feet and holding a hand out to Kate. "Kate and I can have a little fun in the kitchen. What if I told you I knew how to make the best Christmas cookies in the world, but I'd need a helper?"

"Really?" Kate started hopping. "I can help? Like measure stuff? Daddy always says I do it wrong."

Mrs. Bart clucked her tongue. "Your daddy is too precise. A true baker goes by the feel, and I can tell that with the right guidance, you'll be a true baker."

Kate was already heading into the kitchen without even a good night, and Thack could only stare.

"Go on, boy. Enjoy yourself."

"If anything…"

"Trust me, I'm no hero. If we're in over our heads,

I'll summon you home immediately." Dad grabbed the remote and started clicking through the channels. "But, Son?"

"Yeah?"

His father gestured at him with the remote. "You might want to clean yourself up a bit. Change your clothes. Brush your hair."

"It's Pioneer Spirit."

The corner of Dad's mouth quirked. "It's Summer."

Thack didn't have an argument for that.

Chapter 19

SUMMER SANG HER FIRST SET. USUALLY THE ROWDY Friday crowd made her a little uncomfortable — something she'd learned to breathe through and ignore. Rose helped by keeping the rowdiest customers toward the back. But tonight, Summer was still angry and jumpy enough from this morning with her family to enjoy the heady mix of drunk and soon-to-be-drunk revelers.

She shifted her usual playlist around a little, started with some of the faster-tempo songs, and got into them much more than she usually did.

When Summer took her break, Rose handed her a bottle of water. "You need some whiskey to go with that? You seem a little on edge."

"No, I'm fine."

"Everyone's eating it up. Come to work angry more often." Rose grinned and then sauntered back to the bar. Summer drank the water, re-situated herself, and then played into the second set.

Usually she enjoyed singing, even for people too drunk to notice, but she was feeling antsy and irritated, and the energy she'd been able to push into her first set began to wane. Her songs got slower, and people got rowdier. Exhaustion closed over her, and she just wanted this to be over.

She moved into the second-to-last song of her second set, scanning the bar for Rose. Maybe she could take off instead of doing a third set. Rose had a jukebox, and by this time in the evening, most people weren't listening to *her*. They were drunk. They were falling over each other or getting into fights, making out in a corner, or stumbling out the front looking for more trouble.

She didn't find Rose, but her eyes landed on a familiar set of green eyes, and she thought her heart stopped. Or that she was hallucinating. But even after she blinked, there he still was.

She realized she'd stopped singing and playing, and people were yelling at her. Blushing furiously, she found her place in the song and finished it. Even though what she really wanted to do was jump off the stage and ask him why he was here. Was he here to see her?

Oh God—was he here to see someone else?

She finished out the set. She was distracted and her playing was all off, but no one seemed to notice as long as the background noise kept on. She wasn't sure what to do. He was sitting at the bar. Alone. And he kept his eyes on her.

Rose sauntered over, offering Summer her usual post-set water bottle. "Hey, kid, why don't you take off?"

"But...I have another set." She didn't know why she was arguing when she'd been thinking about leaving early anyway, but there was something about the way Thack was looking at her so steadily. There was an intensity to it. Kind of like that night when he'd been angry, only nothing about his relaxed posture seemed angry or threatening now.

It was intimidating and exhilarating. She wasn't sure what to do with it yet. She knew she *liked* it, but how did she *respond* to it?

"Honey, the way that man is looking at you, take off and don't look back."

Summer blinked, trying to look at Rose instead of Thack and failing. "Is he...looking at me a special way?"

"You're a trip, Summer. He wants you naked. If you don't want him naked back, I'll be happy to go over there and offer my own services."

Summer frowned, but Rose gave her a push. "I'm joking. I could go over there in pasties, and he wouldn't give me a second look. That man's eyes are all for you, and you aren't much better. So, get out of here, huh?"

The word *naked* made Summer feel giddy again. She tried to smooth down her hair, but it was always a mess after she played. She felt sweaty and wished she had a second to put herself together, but...there he was. So she had to cross the room to get to him, and she found once she took the first step, the rest were easy. "Hi."

"Hi."

"I didn't know you were coming." It was amazing that even though she'd kissed him and he'd kissed her, even though she knew the tragedies that made up his life, he could still make her schoolgirl nervous.

"I wasn't. But Dad and Mrs. Bart thought I could use a night on the town, and Kate didn't seem too broken up about it. Except the part where she couldn't come listen to you sing too."

"I'm sorry she couldn't come." Summer looked around the bar. "I don't think there's much hope of this being an appropriate venue for her for a while."

"Uh, no. Possibly never if I have a say in it." He smiled and her heart did that stopping thing again, and her stomach rolled, and she barely noticed the noise or the jostling bodies or the smell of spilled beer. Nothing really mattered except the space between them.

"Do you have to sing more?"

"Um, no. Rose said I could go."

"There's not much to do in Blue Valley after nine, but maybe we could…uh…take a walk down Main Street." He squeezed his eyes shut. "That's so very lame."

"It sounds *wonderful*." She grabbed his hand and led him toward the corner where her gear was stashed. She snapped her guitar case shut, pulled on her coat and gathered her bag, and then beamed up at him. "Just let me put this stuff in my car. I'm parked in the back."

"Lead the way."

She started walking, but he took the guitar case from her. "Here, let me help."

It wasn't necessary, but it was awfully nice. Especially when his free hand took hers, their fingers intertwining. It was like the culmination of so much desperate belief—that not all men were like the men Summer had met through her mother. That something sweet and easy and normal could exist, and that it could be something she might earn. She swallowed at the lump in her throat. How silly she was to be emotional over something so…little.

The frigid, dark air helped her get her bearings. She led him to where her car was parked, and he helped her load the guitar in the back. When she shut the door, she turned to look at him and managed her best flirtatious-if-nervous smile. "So. Walk?" Though she didn't know how long they'd last in the freezing temperatures, she thought she might tempt frostbite if it meant spending time with him.

"Yeah. Just…one thing first."

Before she could even ask what, his mouth was on hers and she sighed into the kiss, leaning into him. She loved the way his hands tangled in her hair, that even though they weren't exactly at ease around each other one hundred percent of the time, this was easy.

No, *easy* wasn't the right word. It just *worked*. Their bodies fit and somehow his mouth always knew exactly how to move against hers, like they had been built to match in all of the right places—two puzzle pieces that on the surface hadn't looked like they would fit together.

But the surface was never the whole story, and while for the past two years she'd desperately tried to make the layers fit, she couldn't erase those first twenty years of her life.

Somehow, kissing Thack in the middle of a dark Montana town, she found she no longer wanted to erase the experience of those years. It was a part of her, a part of how she'd gotten here, to this place where his kiss, his hands, *he* felt like magic.

She wanted more. He wanted more. They wanted each other. She didn't want to freeze her butt off on a walk down Main Street. Not when, for the first time, their time together was truly just the two of them. No matter where this took them, that was something to grab with both hands and not waste.

"We could skip the walk," she said, holding on to his coat, ignoring the press of the car door handle in her back.

His eyes narrowed as if he wasn't quite certain she was suggesting what he thought she was suggesting. "Um. What exactly would we do instead?"

"You could take me home." She sounded breathless and probably ridiculous, but she didn't care. This was something she'd dreamed about. Over the years, she had put a great deal of thought into the details—when and how, and what type of person would be the one she would want to give those last pieces of herself to.

Thack wasn't exactly what she'd pictured, but at the same time, he was more. Strong, steady, dedicated. Everything about him awed her. He had her pressed against a car door, and she was deliriously excited with it. How could she not want to jump in feet first?

"But we have two cars and… I'm taking this too literally, aren't I?"

She couldn't stifle the laugh, both happy and nervous. "You are. I mean, if you have to get back to Kate, I understand. But you could escort me home. If you have the time. If you want."

"Dad said he'd call if he and Mrs. Bart needed me, so I could take you home. You know, I…I'm kind of curious about what the inside of that thing you live in looks like."

"I'll give you a tour."

"Thank you for being ten times better at this whole flirting thing than I am." He brushed a kiss against her mouth.

She smiled up at him. "Luckily, you make up for the bad flirting in the kissing department."

He gave a short laugh. "Not a bad trade."

She took a deep breath and mustered all of her courage and all of her determination. She set goals, and she reached them. Thack didn't have to be any different. "So, follow me home?"

He gave a short nod and held the driver's side door open for her as she slid in. She started the old clunker, only partially sad when it actually started. It would have been kind of nice if he'd been able to drive her home.

Oh well. "Parked around front?"

"Ah, yes. Meet me there?"

"Yup."

He hesitated again, then smiled. "I'll see you soon." Carefully, he closed her door. In the rearview mirror, she watched him walk away, her heart pounding wildly. She'd invited him to her place. She'd offered a *tour*, which she hoped was obviously more euphemism than reality.

Well, it didn't matter. Because tonight…tonight she was going to go after exactly what she wanted.

———

Thack parked his car in the little gravel square next to Summer's caravan. He'd tried to keep his mind blank during the drive, but now that they were actually here—with only a line of trees and a fence separating her odd little home and his sleeping daughter—he blew out a breath and forced himself to get out of the car. It didn't matter. Everyone was fine back home, and in a way, he was doing this for them as well as for himself. To prove to them all that he could live a full life and not be completely burdened by the people he loved.

He never wanted them to feel like burdens again.

Summer was lugging her guitar case out of her car, and he moved to help. The moonlight seemed to search out her beautiful smile, and he forgot any reservations his brain had come up with.

Virgin. Virgin. Virgin.

Okay, except that one. Why did that make him nervous? Why did that make *him* feel like a virgin again? Probably because if virginity *could* grow back, his might as well have.

"Well, come on inside. It isn't much, but it's mine." She led him to the little stairs of her caravan, flipped on what must have been a battery-powered string of colorful Christmas lights, unlocked the door, and climbed inside. She held out her hands for the guitar, and he offered it up before following her inside.

It was tiny. Even tinier than he'd imagined. His head was very close to skimming the ceiling.

"I haven't had very many people in here," she said, flipping on a battery-powered camping lantern and then lighting what appeared to be some old-fashioned kind of kerosene lamp. "I never realized how low my ceiling was. Or how tall you are."

He reached up and touched the ceiling. "It's a bit close, yeah. But I fit."

She beamed at him. "Yes, you do." She averted her gaze. "Um, do you want something to drink? I don't keep much on hand, but I could make you some tea."

"Uh, no, I think I'm all right. But if you want some, go ahead."

"Sorry, I just… It helps after singing so much."

"No need to apologize." Or to be this stilted and awkward, but he didn't know how to fix it.

"Take a seat," she instructed, pointing to a little bench next to what must serve as a table. A tiny Christmas tree sat in a little pot on the center of the table, covered with paper ornaments he recognized as Kate's drawings cut into little shapes.

He reached out and touched one, surprised at how much it could mean that she'd taken to Kate so wholly. It was hard to reconcile that great openheartedness and care with a woman who would isolate herself in this tiny caravan. "Do you like living like this?"

She looked around as if considering it and set to making herself some tea. She suddenly stopped, and a concerned look flitted across her face.

"Everything okay?"

"It's just…" She poked around an open cabinet. "A few things are out of place. Odd, I'm usually more organized. I must have been in a rush this morning."

But there was a line across her forehead, as if she wasn't convinced.

"Does anyone else have a key?"

"I have an extra one up at the Shaw house." She chewed on her bottom lip, which made it hard for him to concentrate on anything else. The slight moisture on her lip gleamed in the odd light from the lamp.

She shook her head, and her hair, already falling mostly out of the intricate little braids that she'd tied back with a beaded ribbon, fell even more. The caravan was so small he could sit where he was at the far corner and still reach out and touch the ends of her hair or run his fingers through the strands.

But he wouldn't be content with just touching her hair. He wouldn't be content with anything that wasn't *everything*—every inch of her bared to him, so that he could explore it with his hands.

She put the mug back on the little shelf she'd retrieved it from, then faced him and smiled. It was one of those forced-cheer smiles though, and he longed to make it real. But damn, he was rusty and off his game.

"Forget the tea. I promised you a tour."

"There's more?"

She grinned at him, most of her concern over her misplaced things morphing into humor. "I don't sleep on the bench."

Sleep. Bed. Right. She grabbed his hand and pulled him with her to the far side of the caravan. Nudging aside a quilt hanging that seemed to serve as a door, she brought him into a tiny room almost completely full of mattress.

"This is my room."

He had to clear his throat, a lump sitting there at the realization that he was looking at a very soft place to land. Somehow they were standing upright and looking at it, instead of all the more intriguing options.

"So it is."

"It isn't much, but it's comfortable."

"Uh-huh." He blinked at the bed. Okay, she'd brought him. She'd made her interest clear, and though she was an enthusiastic people-pleaser, she *did* have the ability to say no. All he had to do was stop overthinking and go for it.

Sweet pickles.

He turned to her and noticed this area of the caravan was rather dark. Though the two lamps in the kitchen area still were going strong, the light was weak by the time it reached this far, shining around the edges of the hanging quilt. He could see her, but the view was shadowed.

She moved to the farthest corner of the room, fiddled

with something, and then multiple strands of red, white, and green Christmas lines popped on.

"You are certainly a bearer of Christmas spirit."

"I try."

"You have a place that's very…"

"Unique?" she offered.

"You. Unique, yes, but it's so…you." He turned to her, and their eyes held. Much like the first night he'd dared touch her like this, he lifted an uncertain hand to her temple and brushed the hair back, reveling in the silky texture, in this woman who'd somehow undone him completely.

"You haven't done this before."

She scowled. "If you can't say it, you don't get to comment on it."

He supposed that was fair, though he really, really didn't want to have an actual conversation on the subject. But then again, he didn't know how to just move into action without saying anything. Not in this situation. "Okay." He cleared his throat. "You've never had sex before."

She crossed her hands over her chest, the scowl not leaving her face. "Not exactly, no. I don't know why you keep bringing that up."

"I just want to make sure…"

She raised an eyebrow and tapped her foot, and he felt like an idiot. But, hell, at least he was being a *considerate* idiot.

"You can stop me any time. All you have to say is no."

She studied him intently, but her expression had softened. She took a step toward him, so that very little space still separated them. She placed a hand to his abdomen. "I won't."

There was a second or two of silence, as if they were absorbing the presence of each other.

He placed his hand over hers on his stomach, the solid weight of her palm centering all cartwheeling feeling there, a sharp pang of need lower. Though he *wanted* to push her hand to that lower, he pulled it upward instead—over his stomach, his chest, then to his jaw, because few things in the world were as perfect as the way she rubbed her palm across his jaw.

"You shaved," she murmured, her hand moving of its own accord now, up and down his jaw, and then down his neck, trailing a drugging warmth across his skin.

"I do clean up on occasion."

He placed his hands on her hips, gently urging her forward, closing what little distance remained between them.

The array of Christmas lights bounced off her hair and her smile as she wrapped her arms around his shoulders. For several quiet, content moments, they simply held each other in the small, glittering space of Summer's bedroom.

His heart thudded steadily against his rib cage, loudly in his ears. Everything felt hypersensitive—the air, the gentle pressure of Summer's fingertips on his scalp, the aching, desperate erection straining against the constraints of his jeans.

He wanted his skin pressed to Summer's, wanted her scent all over him. He wanted to breathe and see, feel, and taste nothing but *her*.

He kissed her forehead, her cheek, her jaw, not

trusting himself to take her mouth quite yet. He wasn't sure he could resist all that open warmth to give her what she needed if he sank into that lush mouth of hers.

He kissed her neck, just under her jawline where the concentration of perfume seemed to be its sweetest, and then for a moment he just breathed her in, his head in the crook of her neck, his hands on her back. She was this soft, warm place to land.

She lightly trailed her fingernails up the length of his spine under his shirt, each bump she traveled lighting a new wave of need and desperation. He wanted, *damn* but he wanted in ways he hadn't let himself want for a very long time. It was alarming, so he pressed his forehead to her shoulder, trying to find some sense of her inner peace.

But Summer didn't seem all that peaceful. Her breathing was coming in short spurts, and she was clutching his shoulders, arching against him until he groaned.

There was no calm, no peace. There was only the delicious need that had been building between them for weeks. Maybe months. They both wanted. For the first time in a long time for the both of them, they were going to get what they wanted.

He was determined—determined—there would be no adverse consequences.

"Kiss me, ple—" Before she even got the please out of her mouth, his lips were on hers. They became a tangle, grabbing each other—arms, fingers, mouths. Every spot their bodies connected was a sparkling burst of pleasure, of perfection.

He had the fleeting thought they should take things slow, but her fingers were easily, quickly working open all the buttons of his shirt. Then she pressed her palm against the hot skin she had bared. He supposed he could try to be nobler about it, but wouldn't the noblest thing to do in this situation be to give her whatever she wanted?

He'd worry about that rationalization later. Much, much, so much later. She slid her hands over his shoulders, pushing his shirt farther and farther open, until she gave it a little tug and it fell to the floor.

He had forgotten what this was like. Not just to feel desire toward someone, but to have someone feel it back, that ridiculous heady pride that came from knowing someone wanted him as much as he wanted them.

Any thoughts of going slow or giving her only what she wanted dissolved into fractured dust, and he gripped her T-shirt and tugged it upward. Without hesitation, Summer raised her arms, but the shirt wouldn't go any further. He gave a little tug and she squeaked.

"I'm tangled in my necklaces," she said, her voice a mix between a laugh and the breathy excitement neither of them seemed able to control.

"Well, crap."

She laughed again, scooting away from him and pulling her shirt back down. But before he could grieve, she quickly pulled off all her jewelry—much quicker than he could have ever done. *Thank God*. Before he could reach for her again, she lifted her shirt up and over her head, and dropped it to the floor.

He'd had no doubt she'd be as beautiful underneath her clothes as she was with them on, but her appearance still hit him with the power of a blow. How soft and fresh she looked, between the swell of her breasts covered by her bra and the dip of her waist emphasized by the waistband of her long, flowing skirt. The way the lights made her skin seem to glow and the threads of different colors in her skirt sparkle.

Summer was Kate's fairy queen, brought to life. She was beautiful. *Magical*.

They crossed to each other, the tiny distance between them suddenly seeming huge. He tumbled her onto the mattress, bracketing her head with his hands, arms locked tight so he could hold himself above her.

He was breathing harder than was probably manly, but he was long past caring as long as she was panting too. As long as she felt as tightly wound and desperate as he did.

Her hair was tangled around her head, everything about her pale against the vibrant color of the sheets. She was beautiful, and she meant something bigger than he'd ever imagined he would allow into his life again.

It was terrifying. It was everything. "This might not…" He cleared his throat, trying to find the words. More because he needed to say them than because he thought she needed to hear them. "It might not be fantastic, but it will be…eventually. I promise."

She only smiled. "It will be perfect. Because it's you." She placed her hand over his heart, like she had in her clearing all those nights ago. Telling him she was small, that she didn't take up any space. But she was wrong. She took up so much space inside him. She filled him with something he couldn't ever remember feeling, and what he hadn't realized until this moment was that someone could come into your life, find what little space you had left, and make it feel like more than enough.

Chapter 20

Summer's chest was so full it felt as though it might burst open, and every messy emotion would spill out between them. Thack's green eyes held hers so intently that she was tempted to look away, but she couldn't.

She could feel the hard length of his erection pressed where he was nestled between her legs, and she had the fleeting thought she should be scared. Nervous. Anything but anxious and desperate and *needy*.

But excitement was all she seemed to have room for. She trailed her fingers down his chest, completely taken by the curve and dips of his muscles, the trail of dark hair that lured her toward the buckle of his belt. He could be smooth and rough, hard and soft, always so strong, so…good.

He was unlike any other man she'd ever known, unlike any man she'd known *existed*, and he wanted her as much as she wanted him. It was some kind of magic. Or a miracle. Or just…one of those little beautiful things life gave you to remind you anything was worth this.

She paused when his mouth lowered to hers, distracted by his soft lips, the velvet of his tongue. Sensation took over her entire body in fascinating ways as his mouth trailed down her neck, her chest, and he traced the outline of her bra with his mouth. It spiraled through her, a tumble of heat and longing.

Even with her breathing uneven, her heart racing in

some unknown contest, her insides felt warm and lan-guid. The way his fingers brushed her skin, rough and smooth, sent licks of pleasure through her entire body.

Her breath caught when his mouth closed over her breast, the sharp surprise of pleasure causing her to instinctively arch against him, and he groaned against the fabric of her bra.

He sat up, straddling her legs, knees pressed against her thighs. "Sit up," he instructed, his voice harsh, almost strangled. It whispered along her skin, turning her insides to liquid honey.

His rough fingers undid the clasp of her bra so quickly it was a wonder he hadn't been practicing.

"I know you said there hasn't been anyone"—probably not best to bring up dead wives in the middle of this—"for a long time, but you're awfully good at that."

He sat back, grinning as he slowly pulled the bra off her arms. "Just good with my hands."

She had to smile back. Seeing levity in him was so rare. That smile, that wink, the ridiculous statement. She never wanted that light in his eyes to go away.

But it melted into something just as potent when his eyes drifted to her breasts. It was like desire, but sharper. Like attraction, but hotter, deeper. He looked at her as though she was magic, the center of everything.

Her nipples tightened, even before he brushed a finger across them. He could do so much with a look, then even more with his hands. She'd never known this before. No one had ever looked at her like this, touched her like this, with the kind of intensity that meant more than excitement over the act to come. This was excite-ment over her. Over them.

She could scarcely breathe. Then he was touching her and she *couldn't* breathe, because every stroke of his hand, his fingers, everywhere he touched her seemed to morph into something else. Something warm, liquid.

Precious.

She'd never felt precious before. And not only that, he was *reverent*. Reverent in his touching, the way his fingers skimmed along her ribs, his palms gliding over her hips as he pulled off her skirt, leaving a trail of goose bumps. He dropped the skirt to the floor, then kissed her knee, her hip, her shoulder—as if each body part was beautiful and equally important. He explored her, and she didn't have the brainpower to do anything but let him and be willingly, enthusiastically taken, savoring each warm press of his mouth.

Except it was taking *forever*. Forever. She wanted more. She wanted him. She was naked, and he still had his pants on. He touched her everywhere, except where she wanted it the most.

"I knew you'd be beautiful," he murmured against her shoulder, his mouth nibbling the sensitive spot underneath her jaw so that she shivered, shuddered in unfulfilled need. "But even without all the sparkles and jewelry, you are pure magic."

It was a beautifully romantic sentiment, one that pleased her immeasurably, but it also made her antsy. She didn't have words—she didn't even have cohesive thoughts. All she had was this coiling, restless thing inside her.

He could fix it. She knew he could.

She arched against him, the rough denim sending a bolt of electric need through her. "Thack. I need..." More. Everything. Him.

He groaned, something between a sound and a curse. He got off the bed, standing awkwardly because his head was at the dip and he was a little too tall, but he pulled a condom out of his pocket.

"I, uh, bought these when I went to town this morning. Just so you're not thinking I've been carrying it around for seven years."

"You went and bought condoms today?"

"Well, I had to go to Billings to pick up Dad's present for Kate, and I figured if I was going to buy condoms, the last place I wanted to do it was at Felicity's, so it was then or never."

Thinking about the word *never* made her shudder. Never experience this? However it ended, it was already too much and too perfect. But never? That would be a tragedy. "I'm glad you chose then."

She loved the way his smile went so wide when they joked. It lightened him, suffusing the air with a giddy kind of joy.

He placed the packet on the edge of her bed and unbuttoned his jeans. She thought for a second to reach out and help, to take off his clothes as reverently as he'd taken off hers.

But she wanted to watch. She wanted to see. She wanted every second of this moment seared into her brain for all the years to come—whether they would be with him or not. She wanted this for eternity.

He unzipped and pushed his jeans over his hips, stepping out of them so that Thack Lane stood before her in nothing but his underwear.

How lucky she was to have this gorgeous, warm-hearted, complicated man all to herself.

She reached out for the waistband of his boxers, ran her fingers along the edge where cotton met skin, cool and hot, smooth and hard, and smiled when he groaned.

Not just him all to herself, but wanting her right back. He wanted her. He cared enough to say she could stop him. He cared enough to be here and give.

Give, give, give. He was constantly giving. She wanted them to give together. So she grabbed the condom from the edge of the bed and motioned with her other hand for him to lose the boxers.

His mouth curved, smooth and potent. So many sides to this man, and she would gladly spend however long necessary to find them all, to indulge in every single one.

He pushed the boxers down and Summer breathed slowly, carefully, indulging in the *sight* of him—powerful thighs, lean hips, and the thick jut of his erection.

She handed him the condom, everything inside her chest a jittery mess of anticipation and whatever nerves existed there simply mixed with the giddy excitement.

He tore the wrapper open and withdrew the condom from the packet, and she watched with her bottom lip between her teeth as he rolled it on. Again, she knew intellectually she should be nervous, but this *need* inside her was so big, so bright, and she was so used to shame and not wanting… She couldn't find it in her to care about nerves.

Then he was above her again, those strong arms on either side of her chest, and it felt like he belonged there, one leg between both hers, the other tucked against her right leg. She felt the press of him where she was *so, so* ready. But he didn't enter. He simply lowered his body until it covered hers without crushing her.

His mouth brushed her ear. "You have no idea what kind of dirty things I want to say to you. I apologize in advance if one of them slips out."

"You can't *shock* me," she returned, running her hands down his back because she could. She could feel how oddly smooth his skin was there, the hard muscle—evidence of how much he worked. She sighed, so excited, so happy that words she didn't really mean to say slipped out. "I may be a virgin, but I'm not innocent." She paused, mostly because he did—a slight recoil, a flick of a glance. As though he was going to ask what that meant. She didn't want him to. It would ruin everything. "Though if you say *sweet pickles*, I might laugh too hard to finish."

His eyes narrowed, even as his lips quirked. "I will not be saying *sweet pickles*." Again he was at her entrance, and this time he slowly pushed, and it wasn't exactly what she expected. No magic. No ecstasy. In fact, it was kind of uncomfortable, but the way he watched her, the way he groaned, everything about him, and the sudden feeling like she was becoming a part of him made the discomfort an afterthought.

She wrapped her arms around him, holding him tight as he paused. She buried her nose in his neck where he smelled like soap and something so different from any of the many scents she had in the caravan. Even if these first few moments were uncomfortable, *he* wasn't—*this* wasn't. She'd *chosen* him, and that was everything. This would always, *always* be important.

"You feel so damn good, Summer. I'm going to be

so deep inside you, and it's going to be good, baby. I promise." His fingers trailed to where they joined, finding sensitive spots that had her arching against him and made the discomfort fade more and more. "I can't wait to feel you come around me," he whispered into her ear.

A shiver of excitement went through her. She hadn't been lying when she said he couldn't shock her, that she'd heard it all, but never had words had this effect. She was filled with desperate wanting, needing exactly what he said. Wanting the rough words, wanting his desperation alongside her own.

Each withdrawal, then slow slide back and deep felt better. And better. The hard press of his fingertips in her hips, the bolt of pleasure when his tongue flicked over her nipple. She arched to meet him, finding the spot that made her feel like she was on the edge of something. Something powerful.

Because it was him, them together, because it was right and what she *wanted*. What she'd *chosen*.

Her fingers slid off his slick shoulders so she grasped his forearms, urging him faster, chasing that elusive moment when everything would go from ache to pleasure. She watched, fascinated by the tightness in his jaw and how it was so much different than his usual tension.

She released one of his arms, brushing her fingertips across his jaw as he thrust and withdrew. His gaze met hers, that fierce green that sent tremors through her, matching the way her body was responding to his easy strokes.

He kept that gaze, his movements against her going slower, teasing. She whispered his name, arching against him, desperate for the coiling need at her core to release, unfurl.

"Meet me," he said, his voice an edgy scrape of need. So she did, arching against him with every thrust, and it sparked some foreign feeling, hot and greedy. Close, so close.

She didn't expect it to be more simply because he was inside her, but it was. The moment wasn't just an explosion of physical pleasure—it was…emotional. She pulsed from the inside out, wave after wave of *satisfaction*, even as her eyes stung with tears, and her heart ached and grew at the same time.

Thack moved against her one last time, a hard, deep thrust that gave her some unknown swell of power as she wrapped her arms around him.

He moved to his side, but his arms were around her as tight as her arms were around him. She held on, because if she didn't have him as an anchor she might cry in earnest. She wasn't even sure why. It wasn't a sad cry, but more of an emotional release.

She'd finally dictated the way something that had to do with her, with her body, would happen. She'd gotten to choose. She'd gotten to participate, and none of it had been tied up in her past.

He'd given her a gift, and he'd never fully understand how meaningful it was. He'd given her an experience no one, not even her mother, could take away.

She didn't want to let him go. She didn't want this to be once or twice. She wanted it to be *it*, which meant she was galloping ahead too fast. She knew that. Her brain rationally understood that, but her heart was used to doing the leading these days.

"I hope that was as amazing for you," he said, nose pressed into her hair. "But if it wasn't—"

"It was. It couldn't have been anything but."

"I could have said *sweet pickles*."

She laughed, scooting closer to him, enjoying the coarseness of his chest against her back. She felt warm and satisfied, and the glitter of her strands of Christmas lights swathed them in the most delicate glow.

This was all she really needed for Christmas. Thack. This man who'd given the worst first impression and had come to take up so many pieces of her heart. She felt like she belonged to him, and she hoped—even if it was too soon for such things—she always would.

She turned to press a nose in his neck, wanting to exist in this warm aftermath for as long as they could. "It still would have been perfect. You're exactly who and what I wanted, and I wanted this to be fully *my* decision. It was." And that would always, always mean the world to her.

He was quiet for a few moments, the relaxing movement of his fingers trailing up and down her arm never stopping. "What decision wasn't?"

And suddenly it was as if everything went to ice.

———

It shocked the hell out of Thack when Summer rolled away from him, scooting off the bed and retrieving her clothes. She didn't necessarily put them on, but she collected them, *all* of them, and held them in front of herself. "Are you thirsty? I'm so thirsty."

"Summer."

"Water? Juice. I have grape juice. I like…grape juice."

He pushed himself into a sitting position, trying to get any kind of handle on the situation. They'd had sex. She'd been fine afterward, all sweet and pliant. And then he'd asked… Something wasn't right, and it made a knot tie in the pit of his stomach because he didn't think it was about him.

If it wasn't him, he couldn't fix it. "Tell me what's going on."

She shook her head back and forth, but the light of the lantern caught her eyes and he could see tears shimmering there. Without even thinking, he was on his knees on the mattress, moving so he could be closer.

"Summer, tell me what's wrong. You can't be walking away and about to cry and not tell me what's wrong."

She shook her head again, and this time a tear spilled over. "I don't want you to think differently of me."

"How could I think differently of you? You're…" He got to his feet. It felt a little foolish to be trying to have a serious conversation completely naked, but this seemed too important to take a second to go searching for his clothes. "Summer, what happened?"

"It's complicated," she said in a raspy voice.

"I'm pretty understanding of complicated. I am intimate with complicated," he managed to say, his voice only a shade too tight. But even if his voice didn't betray his tension, everything else had to. He felt like he'd been dipped in cement.

He couldn't stand to be naked any longer. He located his jeans and tugged them on and tried not to feel claustrophobic in this bizarre little place. How had it gone from cozy and *her* to dark and scary and…

Complicated. Tears. Hell if that's what he needed.

Summer didn't look at him. She stared at the floor, those delicate eyebrows drawn together in a riot of pain, confusion, and fear. But she didn't open her mouth to tell him what any of it meant, and that was almost more than he could bear.

"Do you…" He had to clear his throat or his voice would break completely. "Do you want me to leave?" It would kill him. In fact, even if she said yes, he wasn't sure he'd be able to leave her alone right now. Maybe one of the Shaws…

But her arms came around him, a tiny sob escaping her mouth as she held on to his neck so tightly he almost couldn't get a full breath. She pressed so tightly that the clothes she'd clutched to herself were stuck between them.

"Please don't leave."

He held her against him, trying to find his equilibrium, trying to find his strength. He wielded it so much that he couldn't let it desert him just because he hadn't expected this.

"Then you have to explain it to me, all right?" He held her tight, rubbing circles on her back, tucking his chin onto her shoulder, trying to give her strength even as his was faltering. "You have to tell me what's wrong. I can't guess, and you can't let my terrible imagination fill in the blanks, because I have dealt with a *lot* of terrible." It probably wasn't fair to throw that out there, but it was honest.

Hell, if whatever they were starting here in the mess of his life, and apparently hers, was going to go somewhere, it had to begin with flat-out honesty. That's what had gotten them here in the first place.

"So, you have to tell me what's wrong or what I can do. If you can't…"

Her grip tightened. "Don't finish," she said, her voice little more than a squeak. "Please don't finish."

"Summer."

"I just need a minute. This wasn't about you. Or us. Or even sex."

"It was about my question." He unwound her hands and slowly pulled her body away from his. He grabbed the shirt she'd dropped and pulled it over her head. She finished by pushing her arms through the armholes. It was long enough to skim her thighs, so he didn't bother to pick up her skirt.

She looked impossibly young, and he felt like a complete and utter failure. Yeah, it wasn't about sex maybe, but it wasn't… It was *something*, and he hadn't handled that something correctly.

"There were a lot of decisions that weren't mine," she said faintly, not meeting his gaze. "In my life before I came here. I don't like to talk about it."

"I don't particularly like to talk about all the crap that's happened in my life, but I did."

She squeezed her eyes shut and tried to turn away, but he kept her rooted with his hands on her shoulders. "Tell me about your life before Blue Valley." He waited until her gaze met his again. "Tell me. I want to understand. I need to. You want this to be something, don't you? As much as I do?" He needed her commitment here, and he knew it wasn't fair to need it. She was young and inexperienced, but he had a daughter and he simply couldn't afford to be fair—no matter how much he'd like to.

She finally nodded, even though she looked terribly pained.

"Then you have to let me in. I have too much at stake."

Her eyes studied his, some kind of war going on behind them. He wished he could soothe it, take it all away, but he'd learned the hard way that he didn't have that kind of power. No one did.

"Do you mind if I get a drink first?" she asked.

He let out a whoosh of breath. "As long as that's not code for running away."

Her mouth almost curved, and he realized how desperately he wanted to see her smile again. She had so many different smiles, and he hadn't noticed how dependent he'd become on them until now.

He reached out and touched his thumb to the corner of her mouth, and it lifted farther. "Whatever it is, it won't change how I feel," he said, knowing he shouldn't make promises he couldn't guarantee. But he couldn't help himself or deny that light, jittering feeling lurking around his heart.

"My mother was very…controlling," she began, fingers twisting together, eyes looking longingly at the door, at escape. But then her eyes met his again, and she seemed to square her shoulders, determination shadowing over all that fear and doubt. "Will you say…say the part about wanting this to be something again?"

"You mean, that I want this to be something?" She nodded, and he slid his thumb over the line of her lower lip. "I want this to be something. I want you. I…*care* for you."

She swallowed, and he felt like he *could* guarantee that what she said wouldn't change this feeling. Not as he watched her shore up all that strength, all that determination, and give a piece of herself she was scared to give.

No, nothing could change this feeling ricocheting in his chest. He just hoped that meant nothing could stand in their way either.

Chapter 21

SUMMER WAS SHAKING. THE LAST THING SHE WANTED TO talk about after the first time she had sex was her mother. She wanted to be curled up on that bed in the warm afterglow, or maybe even moving toward a round two.

Instead she was crying and shaking, and she didn't totally understand why or what had happened. She'd enjoyed it. Thoroughly. It had been everything she'd hoped for, physically *and* emotionally. He'd been sweet and sexy, and it had felt *equal*.

She'd felt like a queen when they'd lain there snuggled together.

Then he'd had to ask the question that ruined everything. The one that made all those before things come crashing back, invading her mind like little evil spirits driving the two of them apart.

"Your mother was controlling," he offered, pushing her along.

She didn't want to be pushed. She didn't want to do this. Not *now*. But, she couldn't get over him saying he had too much at stake. He did—she so understood he did—but didn't she have things at stake too?

"Summer."

She squeezed her eyes shut, tried to block out everything except a deep breath in. A deep breath out. He couldn't spend the night here. Not with Kate back at the Lanes'. Even if Mr. Lane and Mrs. Bart were watching

Kate, Thack was not the kind of father who would take spending the night elsewhere easily.

She had to hurry up. She had to…

Why was she doing this? She couldn't *tell* him. She couldn't share all those gross, wrong things that she'd allowed to happen to her.

She couldn't stop shaking. She couldn't do this. "I can't. I can't."

There was a silence, a dead kind of silence that could only preface bad things to come. This wasn't the silence before he said he understood and pretended the last ten minutes hadn't happened. This was the silence before things shattered.

"Then *I* can't. Then I have to go."

There was another silence. She didn't open her eyes, but he wasn't moving. He was standing still. Was he waiting for her to change her mind? She didn't think she could.

But the sound of him rustling around for the rest of his clothes, the sound of his footsteps moving out of her tiny room…it was worse. The thought of losing this was so much worse than the fear of showing him the ugly parts of herself.

"Wait," she choked out, following him.

"I'm sorry, Summer, I can't stand around and—"

She stepped between him and the door, placing her hand on his chest, keeping him away from the exit. "Wait," she said forcefully. "Wait, please. I don't want you to leave."

"I don't *want* to leave," he said through clenched teeth, and it hurt that all the tension was back in him, the weight on him, and she'd put it there.

"Thack." She meant to talk, to tell him everything. She meant to, she really did, but her hands slid up to his neck and she tugged him down until his mouth was on hers and she gave everything to the kiss.

She just needed a moment. A moment of this, his mouth on hers, his arms wrapping around and holding her. A moment to pretend that his words were true, that nothing she could say could change how he felt.

But when she wanted to cling, to be held tighter, he loosened his grip, reached behind his neck, and loosened hers. "Don't…" He shook his head. "This isn't the answer. I wish it could be. I wish it could be easy. But my life is too complicated to fit in something 'easy.'"

"Well, if it's already complicated, why add more?"

"Because that's how life works. You care about someone, and their complications weave into yours. If they don't, then what's the fucking point?" He watched her. Waiting.

She tried to say something, to tell him some glossed-over version of the truth. Something that would explain vaguely without putting a black mark on everything that had happened here.

But she waited too long, because he shook his head. "I'm sorry," he said in that gravelly, world-weary voice, and he reached for the knob and turned it, pulling the door open to the dark night that surrounded the caravan.

"When I was little, we'd move from house to house based on who Mom was seeing," Summer blurted out, not sure where she was going or why she was starting all the way at the beginning. She stared at the little colorful dots reflected from her Christmas lights onto the snowpack. Maybe if she focused on something good…

Thack slowly closed the door, with him still inside. So, she had to keep talking.

"We'd stay a year or two—I managed third to sixth grade in the same school district, actually. But, basically, she'd find a guy to live off, and that's where we'd be."

Summer hadn't realized how odd her upbringing had been until she'd gotten older, managed a few friends of her own, and had that weirdness pointed out to her in glaring detail. Oh, she'd never liked it, but she just thought that was life in the way kids simply accepted their circumstances because what else can you do?

"Mom considered it a service. Like a paid companion. She was a hostess of sorts. Moved in the same circles of wealthy men who had certain…tastes."

"Tastes?"

"Um…" Because this was where it got sticky. Weird. Uncomfortable. This is where she always worried people would realize she was tainted. Because she was. Mom had said she was marked.

Because Mom was always so damn honest?

Summer clutched her hands together, pressing them to her chest, where the pressure was too much, where pain and fear swirled and threatened to ruin this. But that would be letting Mom ruin what she'd only just begun to build.

No, she couldn't let that happen. "They were always involved in these parties. Lots of drinking. Lots of sex stuff. I don't remember it when I was really young. I think Mom kept me away from it for a while, but once I was old enough to be useful—"

His hands were gripping her arms before she had

even registered him crossing the distance between them. "What do you mean *useful*?"

"No. No. Not like that. I mean, like serving drinks and cleaning up and things like that." She swallowed, the intensity in his gaze, the strength in his grip, the barely restrained fury making her feel hollow and weak, but also...she desperately needed to soothe him, to take away his sudden hurt. "She didn't bring me into that other stuff..." The *until* hung on the tip of her tongue in the air between them. She *had* been a virgin. She could keep that part forever secret—the things she *had* done. The things her mother had tried to auction off.

But Thack didn't seem like he'd be satisfied unless she gave him everything. He wouldn't trust her if she didn't give him the dark parts of herself, because she knew the dark parts of him.

"Until I was thirteen. And it was never sex. It was gradual. Things got...more involved as I got older."

His grip never loosened, his tense jaw never relaxed, and that blazing fury in his eyes never receded. She had to force the words out and fast, so he didn't misunderstand. So he didn't think it was worse than it was.

God, how had she gotten here?

"Sometimes she would want me to listen to them say things. Sometimes I had to...watch things. Be touched a few times, but it was all very peripheral."

His hands on her arms loosened and slid up, over her shoulders, up her neck, cupping her face with a gentleness that had fresh tears forming behind her eyes. "They touched you?"

"Just...a little."

He pulled her in to him, until her cheek was pressed

so hard against the wall of his chest that she wouldn't be able to enunciate words. "Oh, baby," he said on a pained whisper, brushing a kiss over the top of her head.

It hurt to tell him, it hurt to cry, it hurt to remember, and it somehow hurt to have him hug her and kiss her. But it wasn't all hurt there. There was an odd cleansing feeling. Where she'd always thought saying it all out loud would make everything dirty, tainted, *marked*, it somehow felt more like a winter blizzard.

Dangerous. Scary. Painful like the cold could be if you stood there for too long, but…clean. Austere. *Powerful*.

She felt…new. And she hadn't even laid it all at his feet yet.

Thack felt sick to his stomach. Everything in him revolted at the idea Summer had had to *see* any of that, let alone be *involved*. That her mother would *do* that to her. He wanted to hold her here, where she would be safe, for as long as he could.

"There's…more," she said softly, a little slurred, he assumed because he was clutching her too tightly to his chest for her to be able to speak properly.

He loosened his grip, steeled himself. It was something of a shock to realize that not only had he isolated himself from other people—and their issues—but that he'd gotten to the point where he'd assumed he had it the worst of anyone. Hard to beat a dead mom and wife, right?

But he was struck by how foolish it was to think the tragedies and travesties that befell people could be measured against each other that easily.

Her eyes met his, still watery with tears, but filled with so much damn determination and bravery that it humbled him. Had he thought *he* carried the entire world on his shoulders? Because he wasn't the only one dragging around baggage. He was just the only one between the two of them who was letting it drag him down.

Not anymore.

"Um." There was distance between them now, but he couldn't let her go. His hands still gripped her arms, and her palms rested on his chest. It was becoming something of a familiar gesture. Her hand on his heart.

She shook her head, and it was odd how it made no sound without her usual tangle of jewelry jangling. "So, the more." She took a deep, shaky breath, but he could sense something easing in her. Something like he'd felt after talking to Kate.

This was terrible. It would never not be terrible, but sharing the terrible with the right person somehow made it easier to carry.

"My mother was…entertaining offers for…me."

"You?"

"Um, there were two men who wanted to…" Her deep breaths became shallower, so he tightened his grip, trying to give her the strength she'd given him.

"They wanted a virgin. She was pitting them against each other for more and more money. She didn't tell me, but one of them did. And…" She tried to turn away, but he wouldn't let her. Couldn't let go.

"Hold on to me," he offered, voice feeling scraped raw.

She looked at her hands on his chest, then slowly curled her fingers into his shirt and held on.

"I confronted her, and she told me to play along. That

this could set us up for a long time, and I was lucky she hadn't sold it off earlier."

"Sold...it...off." He couldn't make sense of the words, even as he spoke them. How could... How... How?

"I told her I wouldn't. She said I would, whether I wanted to or not. And I... So much had happened against my will, but without me ever really fighting back. A few times I resisted or backed away, but mostly I just let her, let *them*."

It killed him that her gaze dropped, that she looked ashamed, that she sounded as though she were confessing to something she'd done. Only none of this was her doing.

He grasped her chin, tilting it so she would look him in the eye. "You didn't *let* anyone do anything. Your mother... She should have protected you with everything she had. You never should have been a commodity. You shouldn't have been put in that position *to* feel as though you were letting anyone do anything."

She blinked at him. "Do you...do you really think that?"

"Of course I do. The thought of my child in that situation... I'd never allow it, Summer. Not on my *life*. What she did to you is on *her*. Her. It's unconscionable. It's *hideous*."

Her eyes were wide, but her hands clutched tighter into his shirt. "It's how I felt. I... She always manipulated me into thinking it was okay, it was my job, but the...selling me off... Basically, I *felt* it was wrong. In my gut. In my soul. I couldn't let her do that. I couldn't let whoever she chose..." She shuddered and he gentled his grip on her chin, cupping her face with both hands, hoping it would keep her anchored. Keep her here, with him, in this little room.

"I couldn't. So, I started planning. I saved any money I could that Mom didn't know I had, which wasn't much. And the night it was supposed to happen, I ran. I guess it was lucky I'd never fought back before. Mom wasn't expecting it, and she couldn't catch me."

"And you made it here."

The first glimmer of a smile moved her mouth. "Yes, I did."

Emotion swamped him. Deep, powerful, scary as hell, and he knew he didn't have the words. Not for her. So, he dropped his mouth to hers in a kiss that sang in his veins, so gentle, so reverent. Because she was such a precious gift that even a few *days* ago, he didn't think he could have.

She pulled away, but her slim fingers circled his wrists. Her eyes met his, that fierce determination emanating from somewhere so deep inside that he could only be in awe of her.

"So, when I said you were a choice, I hope you know how much that means. How important it was to me. Because it was everything I wanted and was afraid I'd never get."

He had no words for that. For the responsibility she was placing on his shoulders—some piece of her heart, her experience—for the privilege to be the one she'd chosen.

He had no words for the realization that she was the same for him. She was everything he thought he wouldn't be afforded again: a chance he'd want to take with a relationship, with another person. The belief he *wasn't* cursed, that bad things didn't have to always end the good.

"Boy, do we make quite a pair," she said, obviously trying to inject some cheer into her voice. He recognized the attempt at humor, at levity, and he tried to hold on to it.

"Baggage attracts more baggage—that's the saying, right?"

Her eyes searched his, looking for something, and if he knew what she was looking for, he would find it and give it to her. Wholeheartedly and without reservation.

"It really doesn't change anything?" she asked on a whisper.

"All it changes is that I think you're braver, stronger, and more resilient than I already *knew* you were."

"But...I didn't f-fight. I didn't argue." She swallowed, though seemed to have trouble with the action. "Not for a lot of years." She swallowed again, her gaze faltering. "I've never even told anyone."

"I can't tell you what to do. I *won't* tell you what to do, because that is your life, your experience, your choice, but I would..." He searched for the right words, for the right path down this tricky road. "You should. Tell people. Talk to someone."

"You mean therapy."

"I mean... Well, yes. Because I know that it kept us from shattering to pieces. I only mean it as a possibility."

"For the girl with no health insurance who barely exists?"

"For Summer Shaw, who deserves some healing."

She bit her lip and averted her gaze, but her hands made their way to his chest again and rested over his heart. He placed his hands on top, holding hers there. He could stand here forever. Well, he wished he could. Unfortunately the ticking clock of single parenthood rattled through his brain.

"You have to go," she said, a statement, all but reading his mind.

"I can't spend the night. I'm not sure I feel comfortable asking you to spend the night with me. It's not that I don't want you to, I—"

"I understand. We'll have to work up to that sort of thing when it comes to Kate." She smiled, and he had no doubt it was real. That it wasn't hiding anything but understanding. Because when it came to Kate, she really did understand. Probably more than for most people, his dedication to Kate would resonate with her. Wasn't that something of its own miracle?

He had to smile. He had to lean in and kiss her. "We'll figure something out."

She nodded, her fingers still clutching his shirt. He didn't want to leave. She didn't want him to leave. He glanced at his watch. He had to do chores in four hours. "I could stay for another hour or so, I guess."

Her smile curved into a grin. "We can probably find something to do in that time."

"If we hurry, maybe we can find two somethings."

She laughed, taking his hand, intertwining her fingers with his. Somehow they'd ended this whole thing with laughter and jokes and hands clasped together.

For the first time in a very, very long time, Thack looked at the future with at least as much hope as worry.

Chapter 22

Summer woke up feeling like a completely different person.

Okay, that was a bit of an exaggeration. She was still Summer Shaw, still living in an odd little caravan because she was just a few shades too scared of showing her entire self to her family, especially her father. But little weights she hadn't even *realized* were holding her down were suddenly gone. Even waking up alone, she felt...not really alone.

Thack had snuck out around three, and she knew he'd probably gotten no sleep before he was hard at work at the ranch, hard at work being a dad. Hard at work being someone she was tumbling into love with.

She rolled onto her stomach, buried her head in her pillow, and let herself *wallow* in that giddy, amazing, scary, wonderful feeling.

He'd given her everything she could ever have wanted last night. He'd been *perfect*. She should be satisfied with that, satisfied to exist inside that right now, but she wanted more. That want was a sharp-edged pang.

She wanted to wake up with him. She wanted her days and his to exist on the same plane. She wanted so much more than she already had, and that was always dangerous business.

She blew out a breath and crawled out of bed. She was already behind her usual routine, and today was a singing day, which meant her time at the Lanes was shortened as it was.

What would walking into that house be like after the events of last night? She held a hand to her heart, pausing in her tea making to think it through.

It would be good, she decided. Like coming home.

Oh, stop getting ahead of yourself.

She abandoned the tea, trying to ignore how everything in the caravan had been just a bit out of place when they'd come back last night. Obviously, she'd been distracted. What would be the point of someone somehow getting into her caravan just to mess with her stuff? It was nonsensical.

She pulled on her yoga clothes and then her winter gear, determined to go through her yoga routine slowly and mindfully despite the low temperatures, but when she stepped outside, her stomach sank.

The platform was turned over again. This wasn't right. Between that and her things being rearranged…

Something was definitely wrong.

She leaned against the caravan, trying to fight the rush of disappointment. *Of course something is wrong. You always ruin it.*

No. No. She wasn't going down that road. She had bared her *soul* to Thack last night, and she was not going to believe in some kind of karmic punishment coming down on her for being honest. For finding someone she could give so much of herself to.

She deserved that just as much as anyone.

This morning, she didn't right the platform. She was running late anyway, and she wanted to check on Delia and her almost all-day morning sickness. Summer grabbed a change of clothes and shoved it into her bag, trying not to linger over thoughts of her disrupted kitchen.

Last night, it had been easy enough to forget about the way her space had felt invaded. This morning, it felt more sinister without the promise of sex luring her away. Without Thack's strong and steady presence as a distraction.

She walked away from her caravan, looking back occasionally and expecting to see some random visage of evil. But there were only mountains and white, glittering snow.

She was being ridiculous. She walked the rest of the way, forcing herself not to look back, not to panic. This was a normal, regular day. But instead of heading straight for the house, she headed for the barn, hoping to find Caleb. Because there'd be a sensible explanation, and surely Caleb would have it.

She found him hanging some tools on the barn wall. He looked tired, and she was suddenly wary of saying much of anything.

"Hey, Summer, what are you doing up here?"

"I…" No escape then. "Just wanted to talk to you real quick."

"Sure. I'm about to head down and check on Delia. Walk with me."

She nodded, trying to push away the nagging feeling in the pit of her stomach. "Um, Caleb…" She tried to match his long strides, though she was all but scurrying after him. "Have you or Delia been around the caravan at all?"

"I haven't. Delia hasn't mentioned it, but I can't imagine she's gotten out of bed the past few days and not told me." He glanced back at her, worry etched in the lines of his face, but he shook it away and gave her a considering look. "Why are you asking that? What happened?"

She shouldn't tell him. He had so much on his plate. She knew he was worried about Delia's almost constant morning sickness, and he was running the ranch down one hand and with less help from Summer herself.

But wasn't she going to apply the feeling she'd gotten last night to the rest of her life? To open up. To not just want to be accepted but to…do some accepting of her own?

"My platform has been overturned twice."

Caleb stopped walking completely, furrowed brows and stern expression focusing on her. "What do you mean *overturned*?"

Summer twisted her fingers together, trying to find some source of nonchalant calm. "Well, flipped over on its side. Which is…odd. I'm not sure what could be doing it."

He immediately started walking again and she had to jog. "Hey, wait!"

"I'll tell Delia and call Mel. We'll have a meeting tonight. Should we call the police?"

"Police? Caleb. Stop. Nothing's been damaged. And I…I'm singing tonight."

He didn't stop and didn't falter. He was already on the porch pushing the front door open when she reached the bottom of the stairs. "Call in sick."

She frowned at his back. She'd gotten less and less content to obey his harsh orders, even when he meant well, and last night was a turning point. "No."

"This is important, Summer."

"So is my job, Caleb."

"As important as someone messing with your stuff while you're by yourself and out of sight of the house? No. Go pack your things and take Mel's old room. I don't want you out there alone."

"What do you think is going to happen?" Summer asked breathlessly, following up the stairs to the second floor.

"I have no clue, but someone is messing with your stuff. It'd be stupid for you to stay out there alone."

She thought about telling him she *hadn't* been alone, but that seemed irrelevant to the conversation at hand. Mostly.

Caleb stopped abruptly at the closed door to his and Delia's room. He rested a palm on the door frame. "Maybe we should keep Delia out of this."

"There's nothing to keep her out of. It was nothing. Just…weird."

A door from the end of the hall slammed. "I'm pregnant, not on my deathbed," Delia offered, though she was using the wall as a kind of crutch as she walked down the hall toward them. She blew out a breath. "Even if I *feel* like I'm fucking dying," she muttered. "Now, what's going on?"

"Your husband is overreacting."

"How very like him."

"She says, incapable of walking down the hall without leaning on something," Caleb grumbled, taking Delia's hand and pulling her till she was leaning against him instead of the wall.

"What's going on, Summer?"

"The yoga platform Caleb made me… It's been overturned…twice."

Delia's eyebrows drew together. "Well, that's weird."

"Yes, a little weird, which is why I mentioned it, but certainly not worth people getting all worked up about it."

Delia frowned, and she and Caleb shared one of their married looks. Summer wanted to be frustrated that they were taking this more seriously than they should, but the connection in their eyes softened her. She couldn't help it. They were so prickly on the outside that it made her a little mushy when they were sweet.

"I'm sorry I worried you two. It's weird, but no one's doing anything threatening."

"Still, you should stay here for a few nights. That's a little too close for comfort when you're out there all by yourself."

Caleb flashed her a self-satisfied smirk.

Summer blew out a breath. "I'll sleep here, but only because it'll be easier to get ready for all the Christmas celebrating. *And* I'm not going to be here every second of every day."

Caleb opened his mouth, no doubt to argue, but Delia started talking before he could begin. "You know, I think I might be able to stomach some toast. Could you make me some, Caleb?"

He frowned a little, but Summer knew as well as Delia he wouldn't be able to say no.

"All right," he muttered, brushing a kiss over Delia's temple before he disappeared down the staircase.

"Spill it," Delia demanded, walking slowly, as though every step was difficult, into her bedroom.

Summer followed. "I did spill it. The platform was overturned twice. That's all." She was still determined to pretend the inside stuff was her. Her being careless. No one could have broken into the caravan and then relocked it.

"Not that. You've got Caleb on high alert, so we'll have *that* figured out in no time. I'm talking about Thack Lane."

Summer tried hard to act nonchalant, but her face was on fire. "What do you mean?" she squeaked.

Delia crawled into bed. "Rose called me this morning. Said a Mr. Thack Lane escorted you out of the bar last night."

Summer frowned. "Why are you two gossiping about me?"

"Small towns," Delia said with a shrug. "And we care about you, little girl," she muttered.

Summer sat on the edge of the bed, taking in Delia's pale face and the obvious signs that she'd been losing weight. "I care about you too. I feel like what you're going through isn't quite normal."

Delia laughed with only a hint of bitterness. "I went to the doctor yesterday at the insistence of my husband. If I've lost more weight at my next appointment, they'll put me on some medication."

"You're worried."

"I'm fine."

"Caleb's worried."

"I know." Delia rested a hand on her still-flat stomach. "But unfortunately, there's nothing I can do to keep him from worrying except, well, take care of myself and the little demon."

Summer placed her hand over Delia's. Delia groaned. "You're going to be a belly rubber, aren't you?"

"I don't know. Mel slapped my hands so many times, and you're a little meaner. I might have learned my lesson. Maybe."

Delia laughed, and Summer was gratified that she'd brought some levity to the conversation.

"Look out for yourself, Summer. And tell Thack so he can look after you too."

"Because I can't look out for myself?"

"Because the more people looking out for you, the better. I learned that one the hard way, so don't be stubborn. Got it?"

"Yes, ma'am."

"Good." They sat in silence for a few minutes. "You really don't have any idea what's going on with the platform? Or who might want to spend time to freak you out a little?"

"No, I don't have a clue." But the idea that it might be someone deliberately trying to put her on edge instead of…whatever…settled like a heavy weight in her stomach. She could think of one person who would want to mess with her. Who'd know how to get in and out of her caravan without a problem.

It couldn't be.

Two months ago, she thought she'd seen her mother, but it had been Kate.

It had been Kate.

Her mother couldn't be here. Wouldn't be here. She'd always said she'd never set foot in Montana again. Even Summer being here wouldn't change that.

Would it?

—∿∿∿—

Thack had a million things to do. He was more than a little exhausted, but his daughter was standing on the porch, all bundled up, begging him to make a snowman.

How could he possibly refuse? Summer would be here soon to make lunch, and it would hardly kill him or the ranch to take a break.

He might break out in anxiety hives, but maybe that was necessary to figuring out this whole *balance his life* thing.

"Maybe if you put your hat on him, he'll start talking. Like Frosty," Kate offered, grinning at him as she rolled a small ball of snow for a head.

Once she was satisfied with it, Thack lifted the ball onto the body he'd created. He winked at his daughter, then plopped his hat onto the snowman's head. "Nothing."

"He needs a mouth first," Kate returned, rolling her eyes at him even as she grinned. "I need some rocks." She darted off toward the landscaping around the porch where, if she dug far enough, she'd be able to unearth some rocks from under the snow.

The sun glinted off the endless landscape of white, and Thack decided to focus on that, how pretty and pristine everything looked, instead of all the things he knew he needed to do before the snow melted.

It was almost Christmas. He could take a week off from worrying and focus on Kate, focus on enjoying what he had. He could make the *choice* to give just as much energy to thankfulness as worry.

"Daddy, look! There's Summer." Kate used the hand not carrying rocks to point to the tree line where Summer had just stepped into sight. Something in his chest caught, a weird little jab. Like looking into the future, exciting and scary at the same time.

Into the future. That concept—the future—hadn't been a very fun prospect the past few years.

Kate growing up and going out on her own. Dad getting older and struggling more with his emphysema. Thack in charge of it all. Worried about it all.

But there was something about the possibility of having someone to share it with that made a difference. "You like Summer, right?" It was a stupid question. He saw the way his daughter's eyes lit up every time Summer entered the same room. Probably the same way his did.

"I *love* Summer," Kate replied, arranging the rocks into eyes and a smile on the snowman.

"So you'd be okay if she spent more time with us? And, um, more time with me, sometimes just Summer and me?"

Kate's head whipped around. "Like you guys would get married? Greta's mom just got married and now she has a stepdad, and if you and Summer got married, she would be my stepmom and—"

"Whoa. Hold on there, tiger." Holy crap, he had not expected her to jump on *that* so fast. "Um, so, when you're old enough to get married you have to, um…" Sweet pickles, how to get himself out of this one? "You have to spend time together first, to make sure…that you can make that kind of promise to each other."

"So, that's what you're going to do?"

"Well, um, we're going to spend some time together and—"

"And Summer can spend the nights and eat meals with us and take me to school and—"

"One step at a time, honey," Thack replied quietly as Summer approached. "Afternoon."

"Afternoon," she replied with one of her warm smiles. "But you two don't mind me. Make your snowman. I'll go get lunch started. You come on in whenever."

"Sure."

"Oh, here." She unwound the colorful fringy scarf from her neck and handed it to Kate. "He's missing a magic scarf."

Kate squealed and took the scarf, happily fussing with getting it around the snowman's neck.

Summer winked at Thack and began walking past, but he couldn't resist taking her arm and pulling her a little closer, then brushing a quick kiss over her lips.

Her smile made him want to forget everything except her and find a way to repeat last night.

But his daughter was right there. Grinning from ear to ear, even as Summer gave a little wave and headed off for the house.

"It's like Eric and Ariel," Kate said on a dreamy sigh.

"Let's hope without the evil octopus," Thack muttered, feeling one hundred percent out of his depth. But since that was true of about ninety-five percent of his parenting experience, he knew to just roll with it.

Chapter 23

"CAN SUMMER STAY AND READ ME A BOOK TOO?"

Summer knew she shouldn't eavesdrop, but Kate's loud voice made it nearly impossible not to. Summer had just finished the dinner dishes, and Thack and Kate had gone upstairs to call Kate's grandparents to confirm their Christmas visit.

Mr. Lane had gone out with Mrs. Bart, and though no one was saying anything to anyone else about it, Summer got the feeling that things were getting *quite* serious in that department.

Still, she had liked washing the dishes while listening to Thack and Kate thump around upstairs, the steady hum of deep and high voices going back and forth.

But now they were downstairs, and Kate was asking for Summer to be added into the evening routine. She all but held her breath waiting for Thack's response.

"I would say yes, but Summer has a job singing on Saturday nights."

Oh right. She'd forgotten all about that. What had once been one of her favorite parts of the week was quickly becoming an annoyance. It meant she couldn't spend as much time here. She didn't want to leave here. Didn't want to spend the night at the Shaws. She wanted to insert herself into the Lanes' lives completely.

Which was probably too much, too fast. Overkill.

"But I want to *gooooooo*," Kate whined.

"Sorry, Katie Pie, only grown-ups can go. But I'll read you an extra book. Okay?"

Kate groaned, but then she appeared in the kitchen, darting over to Summer and wrapping her arms around Summer's waist. Summer held her there, glancing up at Thack who was standing in the opening between the kitchen and the living room. He had a wistful smile on his face that made her heart ache, and she wasn't even sure why.

But then he glanced at the clock behind her. "Running a little late, aren't you?"

She looked at it too. Running a lot late, actually. No time to practice or change. If she wanted to be on time to start her set, she had to leave now.

"I guess I am." She hadn't told him about the platform being overturned like Delia had wanted her to. But what could happen between now and her walking to her car and driving into town? Nothing, surely.

Even if it's Mom? She felt cold at the thought. Quite honestly she'd rather face some crazy person or a burglar than her mother. A stranger was, well, random. Mom was…unpredictable. Overpowering.

Summer forced herself to release Kate and step toward Thack. "I can come by in the morning and make breakfast if it would help with Christmas Eve."

He took her hand and squeezed it. "You can come *help* with breakfast. Because we want you here."

She wanted to cry. She wanted to burrow into him and tell him everything. And she would. Just…not yet. Her smile must have wobbled because concern crossed his features.

"You okay?"

She'd tell him after Christmas. She'd tell him every-thing, even that she was afraid it might be her mother. Day after Christmas. She forced a convincing smile. "Yes. Everything is fine. Wish I didn't have to go."

Thack brushed his fingers down her cheek. "Me too." He pressed a chaste kiss to her lips, probably due to Kate's eager eyes following every movement.

"I'll see you both tomorrow." Summer forced herself to be casual, to grab her things and keep a smile on her face and pep in her step, even as she stepped into the dark and dread filled her again.

Why couldn't Delia and Caleb have blown the whole thing off this morning? Why'd they have to think it was something? And why did she have to have that stupid, horrible, terrifying suspicion filling her soul and weigh-ing her down?

She drove to Pioneer Spirit feeling anxious and out of sorts. The absolute last thing she wanted to do was sing in front of a bunch of drunk people. But this was her job, and sometimes you had to do things you didn't particularly want to do.

Or you could run. Far, far away.

She could do it. She could leave behind the Shaws, the Lanes, the love and belonging and hope she'd found here. She knew she *could* do it. Instead of pulling into the Pioneer Spirit lot, she could keep driving. Out of Blue Valley, out of Montana. She could make it all the way to the East Coast if she wanted to.

But what would be waiting for her there? Maybe a new kind of freedom, but was that worth the loneliness and emptiness? Was it worth leaving all this behind?

She dropped her forehead to the steering wheel once

she was parked. "You are being so damn overdramatic," she muttered into the quiet of her car. But she'd been following her gut all along, and now her gut wouldn't let the idea go. That her mother might have followed her here.

If that was true, then she had put the Shaws in Mom's path, and she didn't want to be the one who'd brought her here. Mel and Caleb had moved on from that betrayal. They had families of their own now, and Summer wanted to protect them from all the damage their mother could inflict.

But she had to know first, didn't she? That it was Mom. She had to be able to prove to herself and then to others that there was no mistake, that this wasn't a random event. That her mother had actually followed her from California and was causing trouble for Summer on purpose.

It was so hard to believe and so hard to ignore. She could be going crazy. She could be paranoid. This could all be a figment of what Mom had always called her overactive imagination.

Or it could all make sense. She was finally feeling at peace. Happy. And Mom sensed it. Like a carrier pigeon had sent her a message—*Summer is happy. You have to ruin it.*

The worst part was, as much as she wanted to fight, when it came to Mom, Summer didn't think she'd win. But if it meant protecting the family who had come to accept her and fold her into their lives, then she'd lose. She'd accept her loss.

Of course, where that left Thack and Kate, where that left her, she wasn't sure.

It had taken ten books to get Kate to fall asleep. Thack was trying hard not to be irritated by that or the emptiness that seemed to cloak the house. It wasn't empty. His daughter was tucked into her bed safe and sound.

But Dad was off with someone, possibly for the night. Summer was at the bar, singing, and he was alone.

There wasn't even work to do. Summer had cleaned up and helped to ensure the house was completely Christmas-ed, Dad had paperwork caught up and had been working with the company to fix the porch, and Thack couldn't leave Kate alone in the house, so any ranch work was out.

He could go to bed. He *should* go to bed, but somehow he knew he wouldn't sleep. He'd think of Summer. He'd go over every possible way Stan and Marjorie coming for Christmas could blow up in his face. But they had agreed. They'd *told* Kate they were coming. He had to have faith in that.

He'd try to, anyway.

He stood in the middle of his living room, illuminated only by the colorful lights of the Christmas trees—the big fake one in the corner and a small real one Summer had arranged by the entryway to the kitchen.

His life was changing, and it felt a little like this. Familiar, a living room he'd known his entire life, and yet different in the glow of Christmas lights, with the clear stamp of Summer's influence.

He knew for certain he was exactly where he was supposed to be. Despite the changes and the murky future in front of him, the past few months had brought him out of a dark period. A probably necessary period, one marked by selfless survival. But Kate was safe and happy and healthy. She was ever his cheerful, strong-willed, loud girl, a bright light always.

And here he was, alone and without too heavy a weight on his shoulders for the first time in... It felt like forever. Long enough, he supposed. Long enough to know he needed to summon the courage to keep moving forward. To not let himself go back to that place where he couldn't find this peace.

As if God was listening in on his thoughts, a knock sounded at the door, interrupting that momentary peace. He frowned at the door. Dad had a key, and even if he'd forgotten it, he wouldn't knock that loud. It could be Summer—his heart kicked a little at the thought—but surely she would have texted first. He doubted she would have left her set early two nights in a row. That wouldn't be like her. She took her responsibilities to people very seriously.

Still, Summer was who his heart hoped for. For a second when he opened the door, he thought for sure it was her. But then the woman stepped into the warm glow of the porch light, not Summer at all.

A stranger's presence here was a complete and utter anomaly, because they were too far from the main road to get passersby. Something about the woman standing on his porch struck him as familiar. He couldn't put a finger on how or why. "Can I help you?" he asked cautiously when she said nothing.

"Oh, I hope so."

Something about her smile—and the weirdness of a random stranger popping up on his porch—made him hold the doorknob harder and keep the open space slim so she couldn't see beyond him.

"My car broke down, and I've been walking I don't know how long trying to find someone." She pulled an old and battered-looking cell phone out of the pocket of her vibrant red coat—something that should have looked Christmassy, but just made this all seem very… threatening. "Thing's useless."

"Where'd you break down?"

She inclined her head, and if it weren't for Kate upstairs, he might have chastised himself for being so damn suspicious of a middle-aged woman.

But his daughter *was* upstairs, and his gut feeling about this woman was not a good one.

"Oh, along the main road. Goodness, I don't know how far back. I'm not from around here."

"So, what are you doing here?"

She blinked and he knew he was being an asshole, but he couldn't get himself to loosen up. She *was* familiar somehow, but it was hard to make out how in the dark around them. Maybe an old relative from years ago? A lot of Mom's family was from Virginia, people he'd met maybe once as a kid and that was about it.

It didn't get him to open the door any farther.

"You're alone?" the woman asked, ignoring his question.

"If you wait here, I'll get you a phone you can borrow."

"It's awful cold, and I've been walking for a while. You don't think I could come in?"

"No." Thack shut the door in her face and locked it. If Dad were here, he'd be getting an ass-chewing, but he couldn't shake the feeling this woman was trouble. He didn't even want to give her his phone, but he supposed that was a reasonable compromise between being a dick and being so helpful he let a strange woman into his house late at night.

He grabbed his cell off the kitchen counter and returned to the door, unlocking and opening it—only to find the porch empty.

He was tempted to step out and look around, make sure she wasn't messing with something on the property, but though he avoided them like the plague, he'd still seen enough horror movies and police procedurals over Dad's shoulder to know that would be a dumb move.

He closed the door, locked it, went through the house checking every window, every door, and dialed the number of the Valley County Sheriff's Department.

He glanced out the front window as he related the incident to the dispatcher. She seemed bored, but she agreed to send one of the deputies to check for any broken-down cars.

He clicked End, wondering if he'd be able to sleep at all now, when a little flash of something near the tree line made his heart feel as though it had stopped.

The tree line. The property line between his sturdy house with a foundation and locks, and Summer's unmoored little caravan.

He couldn't go running out there, not when he was on his own, but he couldn't let Summer head back there tonight. What if this was some crazy woman or a thief looking for an easy mark?

He might love Summer, but she would be one *hell* of an easy mark.

Wait.

Love Summer.

"Come on, brain, give me a break here," he muttered. He had to deal with one thing at a time, and love was going to be there no matter what he did. The rest? He needed to act.

You're an overreacting idiot. But better to overreact than live with the guilt if something went wrong. He had a hard enough time dealing with the guilt he already had. He looked up the number for Pioneer Spirit and asked if he could speak to Summer when Rose answered.

He could hear her yell over the din of a bar on a Saturday night, something about *your man* being on the phone. Funny that it could make him feel a certain amount of pride. Pride without the crushing sense of responsibility that sat at the foundation of so many of his relationships.

Love. Yes. Well. *Sweet pickles.*

"Thack?"

"Hey. Sorry to bother you at work, but something weird happened here. A woman stopped by. She wanted to use my phone, but then she disappeared. Anyway, I called the cops to come check it out, but…I don't like the idea of you being out in your caravan if she's wandering around. If you want, you can come stay with us, or maybe stay up at the Shaw house tonight. Something wasn't right with that lady."

A buzzing silence followed, and if he couldn't hear the din of the bar in the background, he might have thought they'd lost the connection. "Summer?"

"Yeah. Hi. Um, wow, that's weird. A woman."

"I know it's a little creepy," he said, hoping to soothe the freaked-out note in her voice, "but we'll figure it out once it's daylight. I just want you to be careful."

"Right. Careful. Um…" Again a long stretch where he only heard the sounds of the bar.

"You don't have to be worried."

She made a weird sound, one he couldn't quite make out. It almost sounded bitter, but that must have had something to do with all the background noise.

"I'll stay at the Shaw house. I have a key, and I don't want you and Kate waking up to let me in."

"I wouldn't mind."

"I know." Something about her voice was off. Distracted, he supposed. "The Shaws will be easier. I have some stuff there, and…it would just make more sense. I wish it would make more sense to come to you, I do."

"You really don't have to worry. I'm probably being paranoid."

"Yeah. Of course. Um, I'm so sorry… I have to go…"

"Yeah, no, I totally understand. Hey, I…" No. He wasn't going to tell her over the phone while she was at her job. There were better ways to do it. "Be careful, huh?"

"I will. I'll, um, text you. I don't want you to worry."

"I can call Caleb, have him pick you up if you don't want to drive alone."

"No, it's okay. If I'm worried, I…I'll see if Rose can drop me off. If not, I'll get Dan or… It'll be fine. You just stay put and keep Kate safe."

"All right."

"Thack…" She blew out a breath. "I have to go, but… um…I just wanted you to know…" Someone shouted something that sounded like her name. "I love you," she said, almost in a whisper, almost inaudibly.

But he heard it. He'd absolutely heard it. "I love you too," he replied, clutching his phone a little tighter, clutching his handle on this whole thing a little tighter.

He had the sneaking suspicion she'd ended the call before she'd heard his response.

Chapter 24

SUMMER HATED LYING. SHE WAS TERRIBLE AT IT. HER mother had been the one to tell her that, time and time again. Why couldn't she pretend better? Why couldn't she fool people? Just smile and tell them everything was *wonderful*?

Well, she was fooling people now, better than she ever had. She'd keep doing it to the best of her ability, because she was going to save the people she loved from the woman who had given birth to her.

It would be so easy to be willfully obtuse and ignore the signs—ignore the slight messing with her stuff, the platform, the fact Thack had had a *woman* come to his door with a vibe that worried him.

But ignoring it all put everyone she loved in a vague kind of danger. Mom could be unstable, and Summer had no doubt that if Mel and Caleb came across her, or knew she was here, it would hurt them badly.

They each had a complex relationship with their images of Mom, thanks to the way she'd abandoned them, and Summer had never known how to broach that or fix it. The reality was just as grim as their feelings, if not more.

It would hurt them. Mom could hurt them. Just by existing, really.

Summer had no doubt that Caleb and Mel would step between her and hurt. Even when Mel hadn't been sure about Summer, there had been moments when she'd stepped up and acted like an older sister, like a protector.

Now it was Summer's turn. It was her fault Mom was here, so she would make sure to fix this without Mel or Caleb ever being the wiser.

Summer killed the lights of her car as she crested the hill that led to her caravan. She didn't want to chance Thack seeing headlights through the trees and knowing she'd ignored his warning. Besides, the moon was bright and she knew the way.

Because she *knew* the woman wandering around the Lane property *had* to be her mother. There were no other explanations left. Summer was the only one who could face her, who could fix this.

Her heart pounding so hard it felt as though her whole body vibrated, Summer stopped the car and pulled the keys out of the ignition. Everything was silent and dark and eerie, but she would not be brought down by fear.

Her legs might shake, her breath might come in shallow puffs, but as she crossed the yard and walked to her caravan, she was determined to be strong. Determined to do what needed to be done.

She wouldn't let Mom make her a pawn again. She would face Mom, and she would fight, no matter the consequences. But most importantly, she would not let her mother level a threat at the people she loved. Summer might have to leave behind the world she'd built, the world she loved, but at least everyone else would be safe. All that love would be safe if she could be strong and draw Mom away.

Summer smelled the invasion before she saw it. It was Mom's heavy-handed, cloying perfume, and it was amazing how that scent could throw her back years. Summer trembled, but *she* was the reason Mom was this close to the Shaws.

Which meant she had to be brave. She had to take on those lessons in courage and strength she'd learned watching Mel and Delia the past year.

"Hello, Mother," Summer offered into the dark of her caravan.

"Hello, darling daughter." The battery-operated lamp clicked on. "Not surprised to find me here?"

"I think I got your messages loud and clear."

Mom was blond now. She didn't look any older. Aside from the different hair and the trendy clothing, she looked exactly the same. A pettiness that Summer never felt except with her mother bubbled up and out. "Dating a plastic surgeon?"

"Just excellent genes, darling. You'll thank me eventually." Mom looked her up and down. "If you ever get over this ridiculous flower-child hippie nonsense."

"Why are you here? You said you'd never come back to Montana."

"I did?" Mom tilted her head, pretended to ponder it. "Hmm. You must have heard me wrong. I've missed my home like a…like a missing limb. I grew up here. The mountains are a part of me. I've longed for the way the world goes gold on a summer evening."

Summer could almost believe it. If she hadn't been away for so long, if she hadn't discovered what real love was, she might have believed it. Mom was a convincing actress. But her mother had been warped when it came to love a long time ago. Something had twisted inside her so that she could only see herself, her needs, her wants, and everyone else was simply standing in her way.

Summer had people to protect now, people she would keep from being bulldozed by Mom's self-obsession, which meant she couldn't fall into the trap of feeling sorry for her. She couldn't take time to try to get Mom to see the light, to change. Summer could only try to get her away from this place.

Even if Summer herself had to leave everything she'd come to love. It would be a noble sacrifice. She had to believe that.

"Are you here for me?"

"No. Though you'll do for now."

Summer wouldn't show her mother the ice that skittered through her limbs. Mom would eat all of that up—Summer's nerves, her fear—and use it against her, so Summer stayed as ambivalent as her poor acting skills allowed. "What does that mean?"

"Your man has quite the cattle operation. Do you know how much it's worth?"

She could deny having a man. She could deny Thack's existence, but that would only give Mom more ammunition. "No."

"Hmm. Well, we can work on that. I've done research though, since you left, since Richard—the son of a bitch—left." The anger that flashed out was smoothed away almost immediately. "Your older sister has done *quite* well for herself. I think the Sharpes have millions."

"You will stay away from Mel."

Mom pressed a hand to her heart. "You wound me, Daughter. I've found out I have a granddaughter. I need to meet her."

It took everything Summer had ever learned growing up under her mother's thumb to keep from exploding in outrage. It took every ounce of control, every unit of brainpower to keep from yelling, threatening.

Mom would not touch Lissa. Not on Summer's own life.

"What will it take to get you away from here?" She could try to outmanipulate Mom, but she knew better. Her best bet was to be as straightforward as possible. She would do everything she could to get her mother away, and then she could worry about how to find a way back.

"I want my family."

"You want your family's money."

Mom shrugged. "I've become accustomed to a certain kind of lifestyle. The kind of lifestyle my darling son-in-law could offer me." Mom looked her up and down. "Possibly your man too."

Mom was digging around, trying to find a sore spot. She was succeeding, but Summer thought she was doing a reasonable job of not showing it completely.

"I imagine you'll have better luck with a former professional athlete," Summer forced herself to say. "I'll even help you."

"Oh, they didn't welcome you with open arms?"

Summer swallowed the need to defend them, the need to tell her mother just what the Shaws had done for her. She had to fight Mom with Mom's own tactics, and maybe even apply a little bit of the truth against Mom's lies. "Funny, they didn't even know I existed."

"Is that what they said?"

She would not let Mom make her doubt them. She

had seen Caleb's face, and Mel's. They hadn't known. Her father might have, but her brother and sister hadn't. Mom would not force her way in and make a rift there.

"If we do this my way, I can get Dan to give you the money you need. But you have to do what I say."

Mom's mouth slowly curved. "Aren't you Ms. Calls the Shots these days. Maybe I taught you something after all."

Summer's stomach roiled, but she did her best to look disinterested. Dan would do anything to keep Mel and Lissa safe, anything to keep them from this hurt. There were so many ways Mom could hurt people. "They won't give it to you if I don't help you."

"Why would you help me? You ran away from me. You ran from the life you could have given both of us. The life you were supposed to give me." Mom rose from her seat on the bench, and Summer felt like a little girl again, shrinking away from that gleam in her mother's eye.

She hadn't always been afraid of her mother, but there had been times—when things were bad, when they were running out of money or men, when Mom had looked at her like that or loaded that ever-present handgun—that Summer had known true fear.

"You were supposed to be the key," Mom said, her eyes narrowing. Because nothing could ever be Mom's own fault.

Summer raised her chin, trying to meet Mom's gaze without letting the shudders rack her body. "I still can be, if you let me lead this one." Lead Mom far away, hopefully with a little help from Dan.

"Well, you do surprise me, Summer. Pleasantly this

time. I'm interested to see what you can do. I'd come to believe I hadn't instilled anything of importance in you, but this gives me hope."

Mom gracefully sat back down on the bench. "You have twenty-four hours to show me some results." Mom tapped a long, French-manicured nail on the table. "Don't disappoint me, Summer. You know how I get when I'm disappointed."

Summer swallowed. Yes, she knew. Locked in her room, without dinner. Forced to endure more of whatever she'd failed at. Public recitations of her many failings. Having to hear the things Mom had to do with men because Summer had failed.

You failed me, Summer. Why can't you do anything right? You're supposed to help us. You failed.

Only Summer wasn't a child anymore. Mom couldn't send her to her room or force her to do anything. She couldn't use that guilt against her because Summer had finally seen it for what it really was.

Manipulation. And more, the fact Summer wasn't a *daughter* to Mom. Or even a person. Summer had only been a *ticket*. A *thing* to use to get what her mother wanted.

Summer was so much more here—more than an object to be used—so she wouldn't allow Mom to do that to the people she loved. There would be no threats, no manipulations. Summer would save them from that.

"I do wonder about this granddaughter of mine," Mom said conversationally. "From what I could scrounge up online about the wedding, my older daughter looks as much like me as you do." She fussed with her hair. "Or did, when I was a brunette. What's the little girl like? Her father's quite the—"

"She's a baby," Summer snapped, disgusted that she could see where Mom's mind was going. "You won't touch her." She realized her mistake too late.

Mom had found her vulnerable spot.

"Then make sure you get me what I want, what I need, and what I deserve, because if you don't…" She let it trail off, patting the purse strapped across her shoulder.

For years, Summer had thought she could change her mother, thought something horrible had happened to Mom to make her this way, so calculating, so cold, so conscienceless. Summer had tried to unravel the reasoning and find the motivation.

But it remained locked away, held somewhere deep under her mother's pathological need to take from people. Summer's love had never been enough to change that, and she'd given up trying. To save herself, she'd given up being the *ticket*. She'd just wanted to be Summer.

She'd felt guilty about that for a long time, but with her mother threatening Lissa, threatening the Shaws' happiness, Summer didn't give much of a damn about what had brought her mother to this point.

She only knew she had to stop her.

"If you promise to stay put, I can have this whole thing set in motion by tomorrow." Summer hoped. She hoped with all of her might.

"That eager to be rid of me?"

"You don't want to be here." She wouldn't allow her mother to ruin Christmas for everyone.

Mom gave a little shrug as though she didn't care, but Summer knew a few of Mom's quirks that could work in her favor. Her distaste for closed-in spaces like the caravan was one of them. The bitter hatred she had for the state she'd been born in was another.

As far as Mom was concerned, Montana had cursed her, and her life had begun once she'd left. She'd once broken up with a gravy-train kind of man simply because he had property in Montana.

Her being here reeked of desperation, and Summer would use that. "If you want this to work, you have to stay here. No one can know you're in town."

"Or I could tell them I'm here and ready to be one big, happy family," Mom said, studying her nails. "Just in time for Christmas. A miracle, really."

"And stay in Montana until they believe it?"

Mom's hand dropped and her chin came up. "All right. Twenty-four hours, Summer. Then I start going after what I want myself, and you know it'll get messy."

Yes, Summer had no doubt about that, but she could do a lot in twenty-four hours—including saying good-bye.

———

Thack couldn't sleep after Al left, saying they hadn't found any evidence of a broken-down car or a woman creeping around his property. Thack had checked on Kate at least once every ten minutes and then given up. He was going to be up all night.

Now, if only Summer would text him. He glanced at his phone for the umpteenth time. He wasn't really sure what time she got done at the bar, or how long it would take her to be picked up and driven to the Sharpes' or the Shaws'.

Why hadn't she wanted to come here?

He plopped onto the couch, frustrated with himself, with Summer, with the whole damn world for being so infuriatingly hard to predict and control.

When a knock sounded at the door, he didn't even jump. He wasn't sure anything tonight could shock him. Still, he took the rifle he'd gotten out of his gun safe after he'd called the police and placed it out of sight but within easy reach of the actual door frame.

When he looked out the peephole, he thought for a moment that woman was back, but the sparkly scarf and the dark glint of hair identified the woman on the other side of the door as Summer.

Wait. The resemblance.

He felt as though he'd been pushed back in time months to when he hadn't wanted to open his home to Summer. To a time before he loved her. It took him a minute to push past that and open the door.

But when he opened it, she was alone, and he felt foolish for the millionth time tonight.

"Hi," she said breathlessly.

"Hi." He glanced around. "Where did you come from?"

She shook her head, quickly stepping inside as he closed the door behind her, locking up before turning to face her.

She all but launched herself at him, arms around his neck, mouth desperate on his. If it hadn't been for the sight of the gun propped up against the wall, he might have fallen into it. But the woman on his porch before — the reason she looked familiar was *Summer*.

He pulled her away, and there were tears on her

cheeks and a kind of frenzied desperation in her expression that he'd never seen there before.

"Kiss me, please. Just one more time."

"One more time?" Confusion dulled some of the shock, but not enough of it. *One more time*. "Summer. What is going on?"

"You don't have to worry about the woman who came to your door, and you don't have to worry about me. You don't have to worry period, because what's happening doesn't have anything to do with you."

"What are you talking about?"

"I have to…go away for a while. It might be a long while."

Everything inside him stilled for a moment before crashing back into real time. "Go away for a long time?"

She nodded. "I don't want to, but I have to keep Mel and Lissa safe."

"Safe?" He grabbed her arm, the fear of her disappearing competing with his fear of her being in danger. "Do I need to call the police? You aren't making any sense."

"No, no police. She hasn't done anything wrong, nothing that we can call the police for. But I know her, Thack. I know what she's here to do, and I can't let her."

She still wasn't making much sense, but he wasn't a dumb man. The resemblance, Mel, the thing Summer would fear. "Your mother?"

She nodded. "I know. I look…like her."

The woman had been blond, and it had been dim, but he could see why he'd found her familiar. Same fairy face, same build, same coloring.

"You need to sit down and tell me things from the

beginning." Because he needed details, facts, sense. She was panicking. She wasn't just going to run away.

She shook her head, releasing her arm from his grasp. "No time. I have to talk to Dan. I have to... Anyway, I only came to say good-bye. I couldn't not say good-bye."

A word he'd had his fill of, and that had anger sneaking into all the cracks that surprise and confusion had left in their wake. "That sounds a hell of a lot more final than I hope you mean."

Her tears were back, flowing down her cheeks in a steady drip. When she spoke, her voice was little more than a croaky squeak. "I don't know how long I'll be. I don't know if I'll be able to come back. I only know I have to get her away from here. For everyone's good."

"You're going to run away from us?" he demanded. It was so...out of left field and insane that he almost thought he was having some kind of warped nightmare.

That she would say she loved him.

That she would leave.

Or is that just the way your life works?

"No, I'm going to... I have to get her away from here. Away from them. She's...she's poison, Thack. I know that sounds like an overreaction. Or like I've made her into some one-dimensional villain, but she's not. It's so much more complicated than that."

Complicated. But was it really? It didn't feel complicated. It felt stupid. Damn fucking stupid, not one euphemism for the curse words forming in his mind. "So, instead of telling your family, instead of rallying all the people who love you together to fight whatever poison she could inflict, you're going to run away?"

"Stop saying that!" she said on a choked sob, desperate and panicked.

A part of him wanted to comfort her, to get to the bottom of this crazy plan and find a way to soothe her panic away, but his anger had grown beyond that nurturing part of him. He was furious. Furious that he would finally have a *partner* within his grasp. Someone who cared as much about him, as much *for* him, as he did for her.

And she was saying good-bye. Two days before Christmas. Once again, the world was taking from him, but this was all her doing, not the world's. "It's what you're doing. Why should I stop saying it?"

"I am saving Mel and Lissa, and I'm sorry you don't understand. Actually, no, I'm glad you can't understand this. I'm glad this makes no sense to you, because it making sense is awful." Her tears seemed to have stopped, replaced by that inner strength he was so used to.

She was good at projecting that—the way she seemed to have it all together, all worked out. That way she seemed to know just how to navigate the world, just what the right thing was.

There was no doubt in his mind that she was dead wrong right now.

"You need to tell Mel. You need to tell Caleb. You need to tell your father, and you need to not run away. What can your mother do if we're all around you?"

"She can *hurt* them. If Kate was in danger, and you had to leave behind the things you loved to save her, wouldn't you?"

"I don't believe you have to."

She straightened her shoulders. "Fine. In fact, that's good. Don't believe me. It makes everything easier. Good-bye, Thack. Please tell Kate good-bye for me." The tears were back, but she didn't slump. "Tell her that I love her."

"You said you loved me too."

"I do."

He took a step toward her, wishing he had something besides anger and hurt settling into his gut, but he couldn't find anything else. "If you knew what that meant, you wouldn't walk out that door."

Her lips firmed together, her hands clenching into fists. "I have to walk out that door. If Kate were on the line, you'd walk out that door too. Love isn't black or white. It isn't stay or go."

"No, it isn't. But it is fighting. It's trusting. It's giving yourself over to be loved, as much as it is to love. It is more than swooping in and saving someone. More than sacrificing yourself for someone else. Fuck it all, Summer, *you* taught me that. If you walk out that door, determined to do this thing, you might as well spit on the past month."

"You don't understand."

"Then go. But if you were looking for a sweet send-off, you're shit out of luck." He turned away from her then, because if he didn't, the regret would swamp him. The uncertainty. If she was going to leave, if she was going to abandon everything *she'd* built—even in the name of her family—he couldn't relent. He couldn't soften, because in all the times in his life that he'd lost, he hadn't had a choice. Love had been yanked away from him by death, cruelly, irrevocably.

But this…this was all Summer's doing, and he couldn't forgive her for it. He wouldn't.

"Good-bye, Thack." The door clicked, and he stood in the middle of his dark, silent living room.

Alone.

Chapter 25

SUMMER WAS SO EXHAUSTED SHE COULDN'T EVEN CRY any longer. All she wanted to do was sleep. All she wanted to do was go back to her caravan and curl up on her bed and give up and tell Mom to do whatever she wanted.

But giving up wasn't an option. She'd ruined the thing she'd worked so hard to forge. She'd given up the thing she'd hoped for desperately for so long. Love. A future.

But she didn't care how angry Thack was. He was wrong. He didn't understand. She had no doubt—not one iota of doubt—that if it came down to saving Kate, he'd do exactly what she was doing.

Rally the people she loved? For what? So they could all be hurt? So they could all feel used and dirty and wonder how they had come from this woman? How they could love someone who had pieces of this woman in her?

She shook her head, surprised to find that she had more tears to shed. It didn't matter. She had things to do. It would be too late to talk to Dan without Mel around, but that didn't mean she couldn't get everything set up.

She would put her good-byes in motion and make sure everything was in order before she managed to get Mom away.

She parked her car at the bottom of the hill that Shaw house was planted into. She didn't want the engine or the lights to wake anyone up. It was late, and the house was dark. She had to pray they were all asleep and would stay that way.

She wasn't sure how long she had to do what she needed to.

Pushed by purpose and determination and *love*, no matter what Thack thought, Summer made it up the hill and into the house quietly. Instead of pocketing the key, she placed it on the kitchen counter. She'd love to keep it, to remember she'd had somewhere to belong…

But anything on her could end up in Mom's possession, and she wouldn't give Mom easy tools of destruction. It might not stop her, but Summer could put some roadblocks in her way. One way or another, Summer *would* fix this in the end.

A squeaking sound made her whirl toward the entrance between the kitchen and the living room. Even in the dark, she knew exactly who was there.

"It's late." Her father's voice was low and gruff, and there was just a hint of something else in it. Fear? Hope? She'd never know.

She'd never, ever know what made him tick. Why he'd let her go. Why she couldn't find a way to get over all the walls he'd built.

She stared at him, this man who had barely given her a second thought. All she'd ever had from him were a few kind words scattered over a year. Every little event she thought might be momentum had turned out to be just him backed into a corner.

Well, now *she* was backed into a corner. And part of it was his own damn fault.

"I need your help," she said, surprised at how strong her voice sounded. No hint of the way she'd sobbed at

Thack's, none of the squeaking or wobbling. No, facing her father, she knew exactly what needed to be done.

He stiffened, then gestured down at his wheelchair. "Doubt I can offer you any kind of help."

"You can, and you will. If you care about your family."

He grunted, then started backing his wheelchair out of the room. Oh no, she would not let him off that easily.

"She's here."

He stopped, and she knew she had to say the words, but she also had a sneaking suspicion he knew exactly what she meant.

"Who?" he demanded gruffly.

"My mother."

He didn't move, but he didn't say anything either. A rage she hadn't known existed flashed up inside her so fast, so dark and hot, that she didn't know how to do anything but unleash it. "She's here and she's ready to hurt everyone I love, simply because she can. She is *here*, and she is going to ruin all of our lives."

Still nothing. Summer wished she could shake him. Hit him. She could all but feel the satisfaction from cracking her palm against his cheek. But what would that serve?

"I know you don't care about her ruining *my* life..." She swallowed the lump in her throat, focusing on the anger that was getting her somewhere. "But Mel and Lissa... Even if you're not all there for them, I know you won't turn your back on them. I know there's more inside you than a man who would let that woman hurt his children." The ones he loved, anyway.

"What do you expect me to do?" She was surprised

how strangled his voice seemed, almost anguished, as if he did actually feel some damn thing.

"I need you to make sure Caleb and Mel stay away until I can get her out of here. I need you to make sure Lissa is nowhere near Shaw, and that someone's always got an eye on her. Until I can get Mom away from Montana, I need you to step up and be the head of this family."

Silence settled between them, and it was full of a million things, all of them dark and ugly. He was going to say no. He was going to wheel away. He wasn't going to change. Why would she think he would help? He didn't *want* to help. He didn't even want to live.

But *why* was her father still here if he didn't want to live? There had to be something inside him. Something that felt. That needed. That cared.

"You owe it to Mel and to Caleb. Everything you've put them through. You owe them this."

"What about you? Don't you think I owe you something?"

"I've given up on collecting. Now, I need you to—"

"Bring her here."

"What?" She'd misunderstood. He was…not understanding. "No, I can't bring her here. Are you insane? No! Caleb could wake up. He… Things are already hard for him. He's at his limit. He doesn't need her too. We cannot let her get anywhere near this house."

"None of us need her, but she is here. I can't go much of anywhere like this, at least not with only your help, so bring her here. You want me to be the head of the family? Listen, girl, bring her here. We're going to settle this."

"She can't be here. She can't. You don't know…"

"What is it you're so afraid of?"

Mom, she wanted to scream. How could he of all people not know the danger Mom posed? He'd traded one daughter's safety for his unborn child's. It didn't matter though. He must have forgotten the kind of damage Linda could inflict.

Summer hadn't. She had believed so much of what that woman had told her for twenty years, and she was so afraid…so afraid Mom could make her believe it again. So afraid Mom could step in and crush all the relationships and love Summer had built.

She'd leave before she let that happen. She'd… run away.

"Trust me, I can handle Linda. Bring her here. I'll settle it."

"How?"

She could feel his gaze more than she could see his eyes. Everything was so dark. Everything was so mixed up. She was so damn tired, and she wanted him to have an answer. She needed him to.

Then she smelled it. Perfume. She whirled around to find Mom standing behind her in the entrance Summer had walked through not ten minutes before.

She was sandwiched by her parents. The two people who were supposed to love her and didn't. The people who were supposed to protect her, guide her, nurture her, and hadn't. It took everything inside her not to cry—everything Caleb and Delia, Mel and Dan, little Lissa, Thack and Kate had given her. Hope and love and worth. So, no, she wouldn't cry, because she had more than she'd ever need from the people who really loved her.

That was *not* Mom, and Summer wouldn't ever…*ever* allow herself to believe it again. She would not be manipulated. She'd *escaped*. She was strong. Strong enough to fight, to sacrifice herself for the people she loved.

She would not cry over doing so. Not now. Not over that. "How did you get in here?" Summer demanded harshly.

Mom shrugged. "Old habits die hard, and I lived here a lot longer than you ever did. I know all the little secrets of this house. All of them. Why, hello, Cal. You're looking terrible."

"Linda."

Mom's eyes glittered in a beam of moonlight that shone through the window over the kitchen sink. It was that look, the one Summer had ignored over and over for years, the look that said Mom would do anything, *anything* to get what she wanted: Because what she wanted was all that mattered.

"I wonder if you'd feel a thing if I stabbed you in the leg," Mom said conversationally to Dad, and Summer tried to stand taller, tried to be bigger to stand between them. To protect him from Mom, even if he didn't deserve it.

"No need to stab me. You're here. That's pain enough," he replied as though completely bored by this turn of events. "Stand behind me, girl," he muttered, so quietly Summer barely made it out, so quietly she didn't think Mom heard at all.

Summer swallowed. He was going to protect her. Well, he was going to try. So, she closed her eyes and prayed that would be enough.

But when she heard Caleb's voice from behind them, demanding to know what the hell was going on, she had the terrible sinking suspicion it wouldn't be.

It was nearly one in the morning when Thack opened the door to his father. He'd lasted all of ten minutes wallowing in his own misery before he'd called Dad and asked him to come home.

It was stupid. It was potentially dangerous, but he couldn't let Summer do this. He couldn't let her sacrifice herself on the altar of her *mother*. The woman who'd showed up at his door with menace in her eyes, the one who had tried to turn Summer into a glorified prostitute.

No, he had to do something.

"I know you said it isn't an emergency, but demanding I come home sure scared the hell out of me, Son."

Mrs. Bart followed Dad inside on the heels of Dad's oxygen tank.

"I know you didn't invite me, but he's been having a bit of a rough hour," Mrs. Bart said apologetically. "That medication had really been helping too."

"I'm fine. It was that damn idiot burning his trash. My lungs can't handle smoke like that."

Dad and Mrs. Bart faced him like one entity, and for the first time it felt...good. Good that his father had someone.

"Summer's in trouble."

"Well, hell, boy. Don't stand around explaining. Get your ass out of here," Dad demanded in his wheezing voice.

"But you—"

"I'll take good care of him, and Kate, should she wake up, which she won't. Everything will be fine. You go help that nice girl."

It was amazing how that calm teacher voice could help steel his nerve, steel his determination. Yes, he needed to help, and he had the reserves to do that now.

Dad sank into his armchair, and though he was wearing the oxygen and looked tired, he certainly wasn't in the worst shape Thack had ever seen. His complexion wasn't gray and his lips weren't blue. All in all, this little episode was a mild one, especially since Dad been in such good health since the new medication.

"I don't know when I'll be back." Since he didn't have a clue what he thought he was doing.

"Got your phone?"

Thack nodded. "Phone. Keys." He glanced at the wall where the gun still sat. He'd barely taken his eyes off it since Summer had left.

"Wait one second," Dad said, for the first time noticing the rifle against the wall. "This is *carry your gun around* trouble?"

"I'm not sure. I just want to be safe."

Dad and Mrs. Bart exchanged a look. "Have you called the police?"

"Yes, and they didn't find anything. Look, I'm going to lock the rifle on the truck rack. I just want it on hand." For what, he couldn't say. It wasn't like he was going to shoot Summer's mother. It wasn't like Summer's mother was that kind of dangerous. Summer had called her poison, but hadn't said anything about her being... bodily harmful.

And yet, Thack couldn't get over the feeling that the woman who'd shown up at his doorstep trying to get invited into his home was capable of significant harm.

"I hope you won't forget you are all Kate has left,"

Dad said carefully, more carefully than he said just about anything.

"That's not the least bit true, but I'm not putting myself in any danger. I just don't want to be caught off guard." He wouldn't take a bullet for anyone. Because it wouldn't come to that. He was just going to let the Shaws know what was going on. He wouldn't let Summer do this alone, no matter how much she thought she had to.

"All right," Dad replied with a hint of reluctance. "Keep that phone on you at all times. Keep us up to date."

Thack nodded, grabbing the gun from the wall and marching outside. He did as he'd said, locked the gun into the gun rack on the back of the truck, just like when he went hunting.

He didn't know where Summer or her mother would be, and that didn't really matter. His mission was simple.

Tell the Shaws what Summer's plan was, and hope like hell they stepped up. Because if they wouldn't…

He was damn well going to.

Chapter 26

SUMMER HAD NO IDEA HOW LONG THEY STOOD THERE IN silence. When Caleb had first stepped into the kitchen, she'd thought she'd seen Delia behind him, but either Summer was losing it, or Delia had slipped back upstairs.

Oh, Summer hoped she stayed there. Stayed away from this. Caleb was bad enough. Poor overly sick Delia did not need to be dragged into this.

"Caleb, go back upstairs," their father said, his gaze never leaving Mom's.

"Oh, my darling little boy all grown up. Not in jail. Not dead. Impressive. But tell me something, Son. How many people have you hurt with that bad blood of yours?"

Caleb took a step toward Mom, but Mom let out a little screech, stopping everyone. Summer could only stare, wide-eyed, as her father rammed his wheelchair into her mother.

This was a dream. A hallucination. Things had not fallen apart like this.

"You little piece of shit," Mom all but spat, looking down at her legs where his chair had hit.

"I can't haul you out like I did then, but I sure as hell can make you bleed if you say another word about my children."

Summer had never heard her father talk like this, *emote* like this. But it was all wrong. Love and family were what was supposed to bring him out. Not...*her*. Not hate.

"You are the *cause* of all this. You. Montana. You don't get to hurt me. *I* am the victim here. You and your offspring are ev—"

Dad grasped her arm, and Mom jerked and writhed, but Dad's grip didn't loosen. "I told you once never to come back here, and I will repeat myself. But if you try it a third time, you will regret the very day you laid eyes on me."

"As if I already don't. I will end you. You have no idea what I'm capable of. You think you're so clever? You've turned them all against me now?" Mom laughed, low and horrible, like nothing Summer had ever heard.

Had her escape caused this panic in Mom? Because Summer didn't remember her being this unstable, this threatening, this...desperate.

It hadn't been like this before. It hadn't.

Or had it and she'd been too afraid to see it? To see it wasn't *normal* for your mother to use you to earn money from strange men?

"Stop," Summer said, so angry with herself when her voice came out weak. "Stop. Please. Just..." She tried to maintain her composure, to think clearly. She peeled Dad's thick fingers off Mom's arm, stepping between them, facing her mother, and turning her back on the Shaws. She had to fix this. It was her fault Mom was here, spewing her poison, being even more threatening than usual.

"Mom, we have to go."

"No. I'm not going anywhere. This man stole my home from me. My children." Mom's eyes filled with unexpected tears, and Summer's chest clenched. "You're not going to abandon me, baby, are you? You see what a monster he is. He kicked me out of here, knowing full well I was pregnant with you. I can't leave here without some retribution. Some repayment. He left us. He forced us out. You and me. He owes us."

"After you told me you fucked my best friend and said the baby was his. After you slapped our son and called him the devil. Threatened my girl. You left me no choice, Linda. And now Summer is grown and she has a choice, and it won't be you."

"I'm…not, am I? I'm not yours. That's why…" That *was* it. All of Summer's fears had been completely realized, all at once. Which was silly. What did it matter? He'd never welcomed her, accepted her, talked to her about much of anything. Caleb and Mel were why she'd stayed. Not him.

This shouldn't matter.

"You are. You're mine," he said gruffly. "I didn't know that at the time, but she tried to get money out of the other guy. He wanted a paternity test, and she wouldn't do it. You're mine."

"No, Summer, you're mine." Mom grabbed her arm and yanked. Hard. "You were mine. You have always been mine. You were supposed to be my ticket. You were going to make it all right. You failed me. This is all your fault."

She'd heard all of that from her mother before, but there was a kind of hysteria behind it Summer had never seen, a physical violence with very little restraint. Paired with the fact Mom had just blamed Dad for everything…

Maybe…maybe Summer wasn't at fault at all?

"Where…" Mel came to a skidding halt in the kitchen, and Summer couldn't even begin to decipher all the emotions that chased over her older sister's face. But why was she here? How had she come? This was getting worse and worse.

"What are you doing here?" Summer demanded.

"Delia called me. I didn't believe it. I really didn't…"

Mom's grip slowly gentled and slid down Summer's arm, and Summer felt nauseous. Terrified and reeling.

"Isn't this fun? A family reunion." Mom smiled, and it almost seemed genuine. "Just in time for Christmas. Can you believe it?" She seemed so close to being honest, but that gleam didn't leave her eyes, and the panic in Summer's gut didn't diminish. Someone took her arm—Delia, pulling her away from Mom and into the circle of her and Caleb, Mel and Dan. And there was their father sitting at the head of their little circle. Facing off with Mom.

Who only smiled. "Now, where's my granddaughter? I'd love to meet her."

All those emotions that had once been clear on Mel's face vanished into stone. "You'll set eyes on her over my dead body."

"Which will happen over mine," Dan added, stepping in front of his wife.

Everyone was here, gathered around each other, stepping in front of each other to protect one another, but… where was Lissa?

"Where…?" Summer whispered.

"Dan's parents are in town for Christmas. They've got her safe at home," Mel said under her breath before she muscled in front of Dan again.

"This is quite the welcome home," Mom said easily, trailing her hand over the counter beside her. "I guess I can't expect presents under the tree with my name on them, but—"

"I don't think you know what the word *welcome* means. No one wants you here. Go back to whatever rock you climbed out from under."

Mom's smile sharpened on Caleb. "I see you haven't changed." Mom's gaze drifted to Delia. "That your whore or your wife?"

Again, Caleb had to be restrained, and again Summer knew she'd lost all control, and this was all her fault. But before she could make a plan, find a step, before she could figure out a way to manipulate Mom into leaving, Dad shouted.

"Enough. You will leave my home. You will leave my property. Or I will call the police and have you arrested for trespassing. I think you know me well enough to know the strings I can pull will keep you sitting in jail for a while."

Mom sighed like someone who'd just been tasked with a tedious but ultimately meaningless job. "I really didn't want it to come to this," she said, reaching behind her. She pulled a gun out from behind her back, and Summer thought for a brief second she would faint.

But she had to be strong. She'd brought this evil on the people she loved. She had to be the one to fight it. To win. She had to.

Or is it time to rally with *the people you love and fight this together?*

"Now, I don't *want* to kill anyone." Mom's gaze drifted to Dad. "Except maybe you." The gun was trained on his head, and Summer tried not to whimper.

"But either I'm leaving with a heavy purse, or I'm leaving in a bloodbath. So take your choice."

"She's fucking insane," Delia muttered.

"Yeah, I think I know why she was so worried about me being bad blood," Caleb returned. "Came straight from her."

"Stop talking. Start paying up." She turned the gun toward Caleb, but he didn't flinch or falter. He simply made himself bigger to protect Delia.

Mom smiled again, that sharp, dangerous smile that said she would do anything—anything—to get what she thought she deserved. "It's in you too, my darling son."

"Guess I chose love and sanity over being a hateful bitch."

Something cracked, loud, and Summer screamed, but it wasn't a gunshot. Mom hadn't pulled the trigger, and no one was falling over or bleeding. It had sounded like a door slamming. But…they were all here. Who was left to come?

"Who's there?" Mom yelled, the gun glinting in the random filters of light from the Christmas tree. She turned toward the sound, still pointing the gun at the circle of her family. She whirled on them. "Who else would be here?" she demanded, waving the gun.

Everyone looked at one another, incapable of coming up with an answer. Who was left? No one. There wasn't anyone else who would be here at one in the morning.

"Maybe it's the wind," Delia offered. "Or a ghost."

"All right. Who's coming with me while I check this out, huh?" Mom demanded, still waving the gun.

Summer had to put a stop to this. Get Mom out and then she could think. "Me. I am."

She took a step forward, but Mom laughed. "No, I'm not holding a gun to my insurance policy's head." She pointed the gun at Dad. "You're completely useless in that thing. So…who's it going to be? My darling daughter. My darling son. Or the people they *love*." The word *love* dripped off her tongue like poison. "Yes. Love. You." She pointed the gun at Delia. "The whore."

Everyone stepped in front of Delia. Even Dad wheeled in tighter to block her. "You touch my wife, and you won't walk out of here," Caleb growled.

"Wife, is it? Oh, and don't think I didn't notice all the stomach touching. Let me guess…another little grandchild on the way. Well, I *am* lucky. Now, don't get any ideas about them calling me grandma. I'm far too young to be a grandma. Far too young to be tossed out on my ear by some man for some young slut who couldn't be half the woman I am. Not half." She slammed the gun against the wall, and everyone winced.

"I'll go," Dan said. So calm, so controlled.

Mom let out a heavy sigh. "You'll do. But don't think I won't shoot you if you even make a move to touch me. Got it? Actually, that's a good idea. We can talk about what you think your life is worth."

"Let go of me, Mel," Dan said evenly, prying his wife's hands off his arm with the help of Caleb. "I'll be right back."

"Do not go out there," Mel ordered, the emotion leaking out in her voice, in the tears filling her eyes.

"It will be fine," Dan said firmly, disentangling himself and walking toward Mom. "Let's go check things out, Linda."

Mel reached after him, the tears now streaming down

her cheeks, but Caleb held her back, shielding her from Mom's satisfied smile.

Dan disappeared out the door with Mom, and Summer had never felt more helpless, more useless, more at fault.

"I'm so sorry, Mel," Summer said, fighting tears of her own.

Mel brushed the tears away with angry fists. "No, none of us are sorry. This is on her. *She* is the one who is doing this, and she will regret it."

Summer didn't voice it, but all she could wonder was *how*.

Thack had no idea how any of this had happened. One minute he was going to warn the Shaws, and the next minute he was standing on the Shaw porch listening as Summer's mother threatened them with a gun.

He'd flung open the porch door and run in the opposite direction, trying to hide and dial his phone at the same time. He'd managed, breathlessly explaining what he'd witnessed to the dispatcher, hoping like hell she didn't think this was another false alarm.

"We've had another call from this residence as well. There's a deputy already dispatched, but it'll be ten to twenty minutes yet."

Thack swore and shoved the phone into his pocket. How could he possibly find twenty minutes to spare when someone was waving a gun at people? He had to pray for ten or less.

He couldn't risk himself, but he couldn't…not. Not knowing the Shaw house well, he searched the back side, looking for a way in, keeping an eye and ear out.

He found a back door. It was locked, but he couldn't say the frame or the lock looked particularly sturdy. He shoved his shoulder against it, and the door gave a little, some of the rotted wood splintering.

It took about ten more good shoulder knocks with his full weight to break through, and he stumbled into a little unfinished room. It was some kind of unused cellar, full of crap, but it was connected to the house and that's all that mattered. As long as that door wasn't locked—because he wouldn't be able to break that one open without fear of being heard. He picked his way through the boxes and old tools and parts, tried the knob, and held his breath when it gave.

He couldn't risk himself. Not when he had a daughter sleeping at home who needed him, but there were other people at stake here, other children. No matter how much Kate meant to him, he didn't know how he'd live with himself, even *for* her, if he didn't try to save Summer and her family.

He pushed the door open just enough to peer out. He saw an empty living room with a glowing Christmas tree, such a cheery antithesis to this night. He took a deep, steadying breath and stepped fully into the room. He could hear voices not too far away and he crept toward them.

"I heard something. I know I heard—" Caleb stopped short, as did all the people following him. Delia. Mel, tear-stained. His heart almost stopped that Summer wasn't with them, but he heard her voice.

"Why are we stopping?"

"What the hell?" Caleb muttered.

"I…may have broken in a door," Thack supplied lamely.

"Who gives a shit? Why are you here?" Caleb demanded.

Summer pushed to the front. "Thack. What... what... Why..."

"I knew you were in trouble," he managed, wishing he could cross to her. The fear kept him rooted—fear that he would lose sight of what he was trying to do. All he was here for was to let them know the police were coming and keep them out of shooting range.

But Summer crossed to him. He thought she might hug him or kiss him, but she only pushed him back toward the door.

"No. No, you can't be here. You have to get out of here. She has a gun. Kate... Where's Kate? You wouldn't have left her and—"

He stood firm. "I called Dad. He's home with her. Besides, it's too late. Your mother already knows I'm here. Well, that *someone* is, anyway. Listen, I called the cops. You just have to...keep her from shooting anyone for..."

"Ten to twenty minutes while county gets their shit together," Delia finished. "I texted Rose a while ago. She called for me while Linda was babbling on."

"You were texting... What the hell were you thinking?" Caleb demanded, whirling on his wife.

"Oh, maybe that I didn't want me or my husband or my family to get shot. Rose got hold of Garrett. They'd started looking into Linda after Thack's calls. She has warrants out of California. When they get here, they'll arrest her."

"So, we just have to keep her calm. With the gun down," Thack supplied, trying to believe that would be easy. He had to believe it was possible.

"You have to let me talk to her," Summer said, facing her family, though her hand remained on his shoulder, a connection. A lifeline. "I'm the only one she trusts."

"No." The word shot emphatically out of everyone's mouths.

"Well, I think your only other option is to shoot her," Summer replied as if that wasn't an option at all.

Thack had his doubts. It might come down to that.

Caleb took a step toward Thack and pointed to the rifle he carried. "I'll do it."

"You will not," Mel and Delia said in unison.

"No, I will."

"Oh, fuck that, Summer," Caleb replied.

"No one is shooting her." Mr. Shaw appeared, wheeling toward Thack and the gun. "Not a single one of you is going to ruin your lives over her. Listen to me… I got her to leave for over twenty years. I can do it again, if you all stay back and safe."

"What we need is to do the same thing you did back then," Summer said, her voice brittle. "Sacrifice me to save the rest of you."

Thack felt so out of his depth, his nerves strung taut, and he couldn't stop himself from reaching out for Summer's hand, from linking her fingers with his. Somehow he had to offer her…something when she was facing so much. It wasn't just about the danger either. There were past hurts here, deep lifelong ones.

She looked up at him with tears in her eyes, but there wasn't time to talk. There was barely time to think. They had to keep safe for ten minutes at least.

And then things could still go wrong.

"We're not sacrificing *anything*." Mel's voice was

edged with fury. "She has my husband. I will shoot her, and I won't suffer a second over worrying if it will ruin my life."

"What about your daughter's?" Mr. Shaw demanded.

"She won't hurt him. She knows how much money he has," Summer said, her fingers still laced with Thack's. She squeezed, as though she was taking strength from him.

"Where are you? Do I have to shoot you all to make you stay put?" Mom's voice shouted from the kitchen.

Dad quickly wheeled around so he could return to the kitchen. Mel ran, and Delia and Caleb followed. But Summer gave him another push.

"Go. Run. Please. For Kate. You can't go in there with us and put yourself at risk."

"I love you, Summer, but I'm not going in there with you," he said, squeezing her hand.

She let out a breath, a tear escaping. "Thank you. Thank—"

"But I'm not leaving."

"Th—"

"No time to argue." He slipped back behind the door to the cellar. The only advantage they had was the element of surprise, and he'd use it. He'd use it however necessary to keep Summer safe.

Chapter 27

SUMMER TOOK A DEEP BREATH AS SHE RETURNED TO THE kitchen. Absolutely everyone was here. In danger. Because of her.

She could keep letting them protect her. She could keep trying to fight them. Or…

Or they could all work together. They could all trust one another to find a way out of this. She couldn't fight Mom alone, not if she wanted to win. She'd only failed in that department before. And she couldn't keep trying to find a way around the people who were trying to protect her. She certainly couldn't be angry with them for trying to protect her, when that's what she was doing for them.

The thing of it was…she'd come here searching for family and love, and she had found both. It wasn't perfect love. It was complex and shrouded in secrets and past hurts, but here they were facing the seeds of that…

Together. Hand in hand. Dan stepping out with Mom, allowing a gun to be pushed into his ribs for the sake of his daughter and his wife. Caleb standing in front of Delia, and Delia having the good sense not to fight him over it.

Thack breaking in and being ready to help them… for her. At huge risk to himself when he shouldn't be risking anything.

But when you loved someone…

You risked the things you never thought you could.

Mom and Dan were standing in the kitchen. Mom didn't have the gun trained on him anymore, so he moved to Mel.

"All right. Much as I love a good reunion, we need to move this along. Montana sure is getting to me." Mom let out a little breathless laugh. "Something about that big sky, you know? I just feel the need to…put holes in things."

The circle around Delia tightened, as she seemed like the weakest link.

"I've already told you I'll give you whatever you're asking," Dan said, his voice still even, his arm linked with Mel's. Mel linked arms with Summer, so Summer reached back and took Delia's hand, the one that wasn't grasping Caleb's. They were a circle.

With Dad at the front.

With Thack somewhere in the back, a secret weapon.

He'd been so right. She should have come to them first. She should have asked for help. She should have realized that love was always stronger than fear, than hurt. It was stronger than her mother's words.

Love had given her everything, and she'd let fear and her mother almost ruin that. Again.

But from here on out…never again.

"Put the gun down, Mom. We know what you need. You just need some money, right? Get you all set up in a nice place?"

Mom's expression twitched a little, her lackadaisical grip on the gun tightening. "For good, this time. No more assholes running out on me, blowing up my life like they have the right."

"Well, you've come to the right place."

"Because the daughter I left behind did what I'd always tried to get this girl to do." Mom waved the gun in Summer's direction. "How does that make you feel, Summer? I bred you for this, gave you every opportunity, and she…this…*ranch woman* outdoes you."

"She loves him," Summer said quietly, bolstered when Mel's arm tightened its link.

Mom snorted. "Well, who wouldn't, sweetheart? You could have had a decent-looking guy with one hell of a bank account, and you failed. You ruined it all, and then you ran *here*."

Mom slammed the gun against the wall just as she'd done before she'd gone searching for the source of the noise.

Summer turned to Mel. "You have to let me go. Please. You have to let me go. I can handle this. Trust me. Please. I'll talk to her. Grab Delia. Keep your circle. Let me stand by…Dad."

It was the first time she'd called him *Dad*. Not my father or ours or yours. But Dad, as though this changed things between them. It didn't really. But she wondered if it could. They had to survive first.

"Trust me," Summer murmured again to Mel. "Like Delia trusted you to come." She looked around to all of them. "Give me a few steps, and then you can come in and back me up however you want."

Teamwork. Trust. Love.

Caleb and Dan nodded, then Delia, then most reluctantly, Mel. She loosened her grip, and Summer was free to move closer. She took a deep breath, looked into her mother's eyes—eyes she'd looked into year in and year out trying to earn her love, her acceptance, her understanding.

It had never come. It never would. But love could win tonight. It could. "Mom, you don't really want to hurt us."

"Don't I? Isn't that exactly what I want? To put an end to all of you... Every last one of you ruined my life. All of you." She spun the gun to Dad. "And it started with *you*."

But Summer stepped in between the gun's aim and her father, lifting her chin. "You don't want to hurt us."

"Summer," Dad said in a low, gravelly voice. "I'm not worth it."

She didn't look back at him, was afraid to lose the eye contact with her mother, but she spoke to him, because something good was going to come of this. One way or another. "You could be."

"Touching and all but—"

Again an unexpected bang, and again it wasn't a gunshot. Summer flinched anyway, but it was the door flinging open.

And Thack walking through. Summer felt her knees nearly give out, but her father's hand gripped hers, and it was surprising how that force could give her strength.

Mom didn't even flinch at the sight of Thack training a rifle on her.

"Summer, step forward," Mom said, that same voice she'd used on Summer her whole life. A deadly order, wrapped up in cheerful coldness. Summer found herself obeying, an old habit, but Dad's grip held her.

"Summer," Thack said evenly, his gaze never leaving Mom. "Stay exactly where you are."

"This is an interesting turn of events," Mom said, tapping her chin with her free hand. The gun she held in the other was aimed somewhere in Summer and Dad's vicinity, though Summer was shaking too hard to figure out who the bullet might hit. "Who's at home watching your little girl?"

Thack's jaw hardened, but he didn't otherwise react. In fact, the change was so infinitesimal that Summer wondered if she was the only one who noticed it.

"Pretty little thing." Mom's gaze moved to Summer, cold and calculating. "You'd sacrifice so much for..." Mom sneered. "So very little."

"I'd sacrifice a lot for love," Thack returned, his voice tense but not scared.

"You really think she loves you?" Mom's voice dripped with disdain, and Summer made a sound, tried to argue, but Thack shook his head, his mouth curving in the closest approximation of a smile a person could manage in this situation.

"I know she does." His gaze held hers, and Summer relaxed, as much as someone could relax with two guns being held up ready to shoot.

Mom's manipulations couldn't work here. Not with all this love. Not with her family working together.

"Put the gun down," Thack said coolly. "Everyone can walk out of here without anyone getting hurt."

Mom's gaze narrowed, and Summer watched in horror as Mom's arm twitched a little, the gun's aim coming to rest more clearly on Summer herself rather than Dad.

But Thack made a quick movement, and Mom swung the gun toward him. But she didn't get a shot off before two sheriff's deputies ran through the space Thack had vacated and tackled Mom to the ground.

The gun was wrestled from Mom's grasp and the handcuffs were slipped onto her wrists. She fought at first, but then went limp. "You ruined everything. Everything," she repeated over and over, as one deputy led her out and the other started taking statements.

Thack appeared in the front door, and Summer knew she shouldn't, after everything she'd messed up and said, but she crossed to him and collapsed into him. Her choices had been wrong, made in a panic, and she had no doubt those choices had hurt him, but that didn't erase how much she loved him.

He was here. That had to mean they could heal from this day. That they all could heal.

——— ⌁ ———

Thack held on to Summer, exhaustion seeping into his bones. Based on the way she could barely hold herself up, he supposed she was exhausted too.

But he didn't let her go, and she didn't let him go. Even while the police officers questioned them, going through the events of the evening, they held on to each other.

They weren't the only ones. Mel and Dan, Caleb and Delia—the only person not intertwined with someone else was Mr. Shaw. It struck Thack as sad, but he knew enough about complicated family dynamics to know there was more to what was going on here than he'd ever truly understand.

Once the police left, everyone seemed incapable of following suit. They huddled in the living room in the glow of the twinkling tree lights, feeling an odd peace and hush after the craziness of the evening.

Caleb eventually insisted that Delia get into bed, while Summer fussed over making her something to eat. Thack knew he should get back home. He didn't want Kate to wake up with him not there, and he had so much to do.

Technically, it was Christmas Eve.

But he couldn't get himself to go. Not without talking to Summer. She was fluttering around, taking care of everyone, and he noted how much the Shaws were depending on her warmth and strength to slowly move on from this moment.

Thack didn't belong here, that much was true, but he'd helped. He'd stepped in and kept Linda from taking a shot at anyone, kept her talking long enough for the police to arrive.

It wasn't as heroic as Summer standing completely defenseless between the father who hadn't given her much and the mother who'd failed her immeasurably, but he was never surprised that his Summer was a hell of a lot stronger than he was.

So, thank God for police and decent enough timing. Because everyone was okay, and he could go home to his daughter. He *and* Summer could go home to Kate and find a way to start something free of all this baggage and ugliness.

No, not free of it. You couldn't erase the past. He'd never erase his, but it could become a foundation instead of a rift.

Summer wouldn't be going home with him tonight—well, this morning. She had family issues to work through, but damn, he wanted her with him. Even if he was still angry with her, he was angry with himself too.

He'd been harsh and unfeeling, even knowing she was trying to help people, save people.

But, damn it, at the sake of everything.

He took a breath. That was not for tonight. Tonight she had a family to take care of, and so did he.

Thack touched Summer's arm lightly, and she looked away from the water she was foisting on her father. She didn't smile. She didn't frown. There was only hope and fear in her expression.

And then, her determination. Her determination never failed to impress him. Even here and now when all he wanted to do was hold her and make promises he couldn't keep.

He wanted to tell her that everything would be perfect from here on out.

Except that nothing would be *perfect*. He couldn't promise that. But they could make it right. They could make it good. "I need to head home."

"Oh, right." She glanced back at her father, who was studying Thack with an unreadable expression.

Thack ignored Mr. Shaw for now. There would be time later to maneuver the complicated family situation he'd waded into. After all, she'd waded into his without a qualm.

"Stay here. Take care of your family. For the love of God, rest, and when you've done all that, come…" He wanted to say home. *Come home to us*, but there were things to discuss and now wasn't the time. So he touched her cheek and did his best to offer some approximation of a smile. "Come over and we'll talk."

Her attempt at a smile was possibly worse than his. "It's…Christmas Eve. I don't want to…get in the way."

"Summer." That she could think, at this point, she'd be in the way about broke his heart. So, even with her father looking on, he drew Summer into the circle of his arms, holding on tight. "You're never in the way. Not ever."

She made a little sound, and he thought maybe she was crying, though she'd buried her head in his shoulder so he wasn't sure. He held on, rubbing a hand up and down her back, trying to comfort her the way she always seemed to comfort him.

"You need to go," she croaked into his shirt.

He only hugged her tighter. "I can hold on to you for a little while longer."

A broken sob escaped her, muffled in the fabric of his shirt, followed by another. He wasn't sure how long she cried into his shoulder, but it didn't matter. She needed this, a release from trying to be so brave.

Eventually her breathing evened out, and she slowly pulled herself from his embrace. She wiped at her face and smiled at him sheepishly. "Sorry about that, I—"

"No apologies or explanations." He reached out and wiped a tear on her jaw she'd missed. "Not for that."

Her lips wavered, but she pressed them together and gave a little nod. "Thank you. Now, go. Go home and rest, and I'll come by tomorrow."

"Promise me it'll be after *you* get some rest."

She blew out a breath. "Okay, I promise."

He tipped his hat and turned to leave, but her not-quite-steady voice stopped him. "Thack?"

He looked back at her. At some point when he hadn't been paying attention, Mr. Shaw had wheeled himself to a different corner of the room.

"Yeah?"

"I love you." No hurried words over a phone call. No desperation tinging her voice. Instead, she was giving him her heart.

"I love you," he replied, certain and sure and not at all wavering, because she'd had his love for probably a lot longer than even he realized.

Chapter 28

EVERYONE HAD GONE TO SLEEP, EVEN DAN AND MEL who'd decided to rest before heading back to Lissa and Dan's parents.

It was so late that the sun would be rising soon. Summer should have slept, but she found she couldn't.

She stood at the window in the living room, staring out into the darkness. Someone had turned the tree lights off, and it was just as dark inside the house as out. Summer didn't know what she felt except a disconcerting kind of numbness.

But she heard the telltale squeak and whir of her father's wheelchair, and it sent a skitter of nerves down her spine. Not the same kind of nerves her mother produced, but wasn't it sadly telling that neither of her parents afforded her much comfort or ease?

"You should be sleeping, girl."

Summer sighed. In the past twenty-four hours he'd said as much to her as he'd said in years, and here he was, telling her what to do. She was too exhausted and anxiously strung out to know how to feel about that.

"I can't."

"Come here."

She looked at the man who was, with no doubts any longer, her father. A man she barely knew, and one who over the last year had mostly treated her as though she didn't exist.

Still, she went, because there had to be some hope. Who would she be if she didn't hope for better? Who would they all be if tonight didn't change things?

The Christmas tree lights blinked on, and she realized he of all people had leaned over and flicked the timer switch to on.

In the white shining light of the Christmas tree Summer had helped Caleb pick out and dutifully decorated as Delia looked on, her father held out a small, wrapped gift.

She could only stare at it.

"Take it," he said with a grunt, jutting his arm toward her.

Summer had to swallow and *force* her legs to move close enough that she could take the outstretched gift.

A present. The wrapping paper was a plain, solid green. There weren't any ribbons or bows, but her name was written in black marker across the top.

"Open it," her father instructed, irritation and something she was afraid to name in his voice. Something like nerves.

With shaking hands, Summer slowly opened the package, lifting the tape carefully and trying not to rip the paper.

"What on earth are you doing, girl? Open the damn thing."

"It's the first gift you've ever given me," she managed to say through her too-tight throat. She glanced up at him as she carefully pulled the box out of the wrapping paper.

He looked pained, haunted by a million things she'd probably never fully understand. She opened the lid of a little white box and pulled out a necklace.

She swallowed at the painful, fizzling lump in her throat and held the necklace up to the light. At the end of a little chain was a golden sun.

"I don't think you have any idea how things have changed since you showed up," her father said, his voice low and gritty and...emotional. *Her* father. Emotional. "The warmth we were sorely lacking that you brought into our lives. I could never begin to explain to you how sorry I am, how...I'll never be able to make up for it."

"Do you remember what I said when you apologized to me this summer?"

He nodded carefully, and if Summer wasn't totally losing it from exhaustion, she thought the lights of the tree shone on a glimmer of tears in his dark-blue eyes. "That it was a start."

Summer nodded, not sure she could say anything more through the ache in her heart, happy and hurt, bittersweet all in all.

He cleared his throat. "Um, it's actually a Shaw family heirloom. That belonged to my mother, whose nickname was Sunny. You remind me of her."

Summer could only cry at this point. It wasn't just a thoughtful gift, it was a *family* heirloom.

"I've known all along I should've done everything differently, and I always figured this was my punishment for that," he said, pointing to his wheelchair, his voice more gravelly with every word.

"I don't believe that's how the world works," Summer said, her voice certain despite how the tears fell. She didn't and wouldn't believe that life's cruelties were punishment. They simply were.

"I don't really know what I believe anymore. I

certainly don't believe I have anything to give you kids, but you all seem to think I do."

"You should probably listen to us."

Dad was quiet for a long time, his eyes on the tree. Summer held the necklace he'd given her—such a thoughtful, amazing gift—in the tight grip of her palm, fisted at her heart.

"Maybe I'll try," he finally acknowledged.

"You should do more than try." It was Caleb's voice, and when Summer turned to look behind her, both Mel and Caleb were standing in the entryway to the living room.

"Come here, boy," Dad said, his voice gruff. "Will you find the ones for Mel and Caleb under there? They look just like yours," he asked, pointing to under the tree.

Summer did as her father asked, finding two identical green packages under the tree. One with Mel's name written on it, and one with Caleb's.

She handed the boxes to her siblings, and they all arranged themselves on the floor around their father.

"Open them," he ordered, the usual gruffness back in his voice.

Summer placed her hand on Mel's leg, and then Caleb's. They both tore through the wrapping, so different from how Summer had opened hers just moments before. Seeing how different they could all be made her smile and made her hurt.

Mel's box was bigger, and when she opened it, she saw an old and tattered-looking Bible sitting in tissue paper.

"It's the Shaw family Bible," Dad explained. "Since you're the oldest, I should have given it to you on your wedding day, but I should have done a lot of things. It's up to date. I put Summer and Lissa in it last night before I wrapped everything."

Mel stared down at the book, and for a moment the only sound was her sharp inhale, then exhale of breath. "Thank you," she managed to croak, looking up at their father. "Thank you."

"And yours," he said, moving his gaze to Caleb. "Those are your grandfather and grandmother's wedding rings. I should have given them to you when you married Delia, and I'm extremely sorry that I didn't."

Caleb scratched a hand through his hair. "I don't... know what to say."

"Nobody needs to say anything. These were things that needed to be done. Your mother showing up... Everything that happened tonight proved that I needed to step up. I need to step up."

They were silent for a few moments, each looking at their gifts, maybe trying to get a handle on their wayward emotions.

"Wait..." Summer looked up at him. "You said you did these last night. You had this all done before Mom showed up."

Dad blinked and scratched his hand through his hair, just like Caleb had done only minutes before. "Yeah. I've been...trying. Failing, mostly, but it's hard to keep failing when you all keep poking at me."

Mel got to her feet and wrapped her arms around their father. She didn't say anything, but Summer was starting to think none of them had to *say* anything. They just had to do. To act.

So she got to her feet and hugged him and Mel too. She glanced back at Caleb, and he gave a hearty sigh.

"Fine," he grumbled, joining the hug.

For the first time in Summer's entire life, she felt one hundred percent like a Shaw. Like a *part* of this family, this *whole* family.

———

Thack prayed to every available Christmas deity for the patience to get through Kate's hyper, Christmas Eve shenanigans.

"Oh, I forgot—"

Thack intercepted his daughter as she tried to dart out of the bedroom for the third time. He happily flung her over his shoulder, and she squealed in delight. He dumped her on the bed and tried to muster his sternest expression.

"Santa doesn't come until you're asleep."

Kate pouted, but she finally crawled under her covers and settled into her pillow. "Maybe we should put more cookies out. I don't think ten are enough."

Thack settled in next to Kate and smoothed down her hair. "Ten is more than enough, Katie Pie. But he'll never get to eat them if you do not *go to sleep*."

Kate sighed, but she'd been amped all day. Just sitting still was *finally* allowing exhaustion to catch up with her.

Thack rested his head against her headboard, warning himself against falling asleep. He was exhausted, and it would be so nice. Just a few minutes.

Kate murmured something about when Grandma and Grandpa would arrive, which reminded Thack of how much he had to do. Stan had called earlier to say they'd landed in Helena and would be driving up tomorrow. They'd be here in time for lunch.

Thack jerked awake he wasn't sure how many minutes later. Kate was fast asleep, breathing evenly in the glow of her pink lights.

Tiptoeing out of the room, Thack checked the time. Only ten thirty, so he hadn't dozed for too, too long. He'd managed to do most of Kate's Santa wrapping here and there over the course of the week, but he still had to fill her stocking and set the presents out and eat ten cookies, apparently.

He picked his way down the stairs, then stopped short at the woman crouching by the Christmas tree.

Summer slowly stood. "Hi," she offered, a tremulously hopeful smile curving her lips.

"Hi." He glanced around, but all he saw was Summer. "Where did Dad and Mrs. Bart go?"

"Well, after they let me in…" She opened her mouth, then made a little face and shook her head.

"I don't want to know, do I?"

"Let's just say, I think you'll have an extra person for Christmas breakfast."

An extra… Oh, yeah, he really didn't want to know that. But it made him think. Tomorrow. Breakfast. Summer. "How about…two? Two extra people for breakfast tomorrow."

She blinked a few times, obviously trying to hold back tears as he stepped toward her.

"You mean…me sleeping here?"

He nodded.

"I could…arrange that. I…" She shook her head, tears spilling over. "I think I just got everything I ever wanted for Christmas. Sleeping here, waking up here… it's everything I've wanted." She rubbed a finger over a necklace. Instead of her usual bands of crystals and gold, there was only one chain around her neck tonight.

"This is new," he said, reaching out and touching it, very purposefully grazing his index fingers against her hand.

"It was…Dad's Christmas gift to me. It was his mother's. My grandmother." She curled her fingers around it, clearly moved, and Thack was moved for her. He pressed his forehead to hers.

Her hazel eyes met his, filled to the brim with tears, but still she smiled. A warm, hopeful Summer kind of smile. "We have a *lot* of work to do before morning."

We. He liked the sound of that, more and more. "We do, but…maybe we should talk first."

She exhaled, then inhaled slowly. "Okay. Okay, we can do that."

He opened his mouth to speak, but she pressed her fingers to his mouth. "Me first. I just wanted to tell you…" Her hand dropped from his mouth, and she took a tiny step away from him, but she stood tall, like she was getting ready to deliver a speech. She straightened her shoulders, her gaze met his, and colorful Christmas lights gleamed in her hair.

He knew he should feel some sort of anger or worry, something related to what had happened yesterday. But standing here, he knew how angry he was would never matter. He loved this woman, and they would always find a way to straighten their shoulders, look each other in the eye, and love each other.

"You were right." She took a breath that caught halfway through, then let it out on a shaky exhale. "Yesterday. You were right. I shouldn't have tried to take everything on myself. I should have believed…that working together would always be better than trying to do it all myself. Sometimes you start to believe running away is the only answer." She gave a little nod, like that was her speech and that was all she had to say.

"And sometimes you're wrong."

She let out something that sounded almost like a laugh. "I guess I can be now and again. But mostly, I'm sorry. Sorry I couldn't listen or see." She managed a smile, her heart so clear in her eyes that it hurt to meet her gaze. The smile was small and wobbly, but it was a smile, and he couldn't resist pressing a kiss to it.

She looked up at him, hope so bright in her eyes that it physically hurt. "Is that forgiveness?"

"That's love. Which, I believe, goes hand in hand with forgiveness."

Her eyes searched his, shiny with tears. "As long as we don't always need a weapon-wielding family member on a break with reality to get it through our heads."

"I'll put that in my…" He stopped himself from saying what he'd meant to say. He knew he wanted to propose to Summer, and the past forty-eight hours had driven that certainty home. But he didn't have a ring, and he most certainly didn't have a plan.

"You'll put that in your what?" she asked, and the way her eyes got big for a second made him think she'd figured it out.

He thought about how she'd said she'd loved him on the phone when he'd called to warn her, because she'd thought it was her last chance. Which should make him mad that she hadn't unloaded the truth then, but he couldn't hold on to the anger. Not after yesterday.

No matter how inadvisably she'd done it, she'd acted out of fear and love. He knew that the combination could eradicate sense. Hell, they'd eradicated *his* sense when he'd let her walk out that door.

But even at her weakest, at her most wrong, she'd said she loved him. She'd grabbed the moment, because she'd feared it would be gone.

Then she'd said it again when the crisis with Linda was over, certain and sure, not caring who was in the room to hear.

He thought of all the moments he'd been so careful with. He'd been waiting for the right time all of his life, always thwarted by the world not waiting for him. "I was going to say *vows*. I was going to say I'll put that in my vows."

"Like…" She paused but her gaze didn't falter. "Wedding vows."

"Yes."

"You haven't asked me to marry you."

"No, I haven't." He wouldn't do it tonight, but that didn't mean she shouldn't know he would. And soon.

"But you were…going to?"

"I was thinking about it."

She pressed her lips together, but the grin must have been too strong because she smiled big and wide, a few more tears slipping over her cheeks. "All right," she said in a choked whisper. "Good to know. When did you start thinking about that?"

He touched a thumb to a tear on her cheek and swept it away. "Every night when you go, there's a hole in my heart. When you're sleeping less than a mile away and it isn't with me. I thought I'd plan it out. The right number of months. The right number of words, but the hole is there, and it only gets wider the more I know you and love you."

"Thack…"

"And I do love you. I've wasted a lot of moments by trying to plan them out right and control my life. I've kept everyone and everything safe and secreted away, and I've missed things because of it. That attitude hasn't done much more than allow me to survive. I don't want to wait. You've become a part of our family. There's no point in not making that official as soon as possible… unless you don't want to."

"Do you honestly think there's even a one percent chance I'd say I didn't want to?"

It was his turn to grin. "No, that's why I said it."

She took a step toward him, placing her hand over his heart as she'd done so many times. Soothing, supportive, romantic. She could put her hand over his heart a million different ways, and this was one he would never forget.

"I love you too. I came here for love and to find my future, although a part of me didn't think I'd ever get it or deserve it. But how you love and take care of Kate showed me otherwise."

"Sum—"

"No, you made your grand declaration, so you don't get to stop mine. I think you're the strongest, sturdiest… *best* man I know. I'll ever know. However we cobble our lives together, our weaknesses and strengths, our vulnerabilities, I will always come to you instead of running away."

He couldn't speak beyond the lump in his throat, so he drew her into his arms instead. He held on, because as much as he got something out of holding her, she got something out of being held. Most surprising of all, it worked the other way around as well.

He'd given her his words, his heart, and she'd returned them. There would be days that the fear of losing that, losing the family he'd thought he'd already had and lost, would be powerful. Overwhelming even.

But there would always be this, and so he would always remember.

He wasn't sure how long they held on to each other in the glow of the Christmas tree she'd helped decorate, but eventually they let each other go. Eventually, they put out Santa's gifts and filled Kate's stocking. They ate the cookies, and Summer made sure to leave crumbs on the plate and wrote a special letter from Santa.

And when Thack went to bed, he went to bed with the woman he loved, and that was definitely the best Christmas present he'd ever received.

Epilogue

"You're making me dizzy," Delia groaned as Summer fluttered around the dining room table, making sure they had enough plates and glasses.

"Then go sit down," Summer retorted, giving Delia's still-flat belly a little love pat.

Delia glared at her. "I'm only letting you get away with that because it's Christmas."

Summer beamed at her sister-in-law. "Okay, I think we have enough dishes. Now, hopefully there's enough food."

"Summer, you made enough for fifty people. Adding six more isn't going to make a dent."

Mel popped her head into the dining room. "I think the Lanes are here."

Summer made a little squeak that both Mel and Delia rolled their eyes at, but they also smiled as Summer hurried to the front door. She flung it open and grinned—possibly a little giddily—as Thack and Kate, Mr. Lane and Mrs. Bart, and Kate's grandparents piled out of two cars.

Summer had met Kate's grandparents on their arrival this morning. Though the meeting had been slightly awkward, Stan and Marjorie had been too happy spending time with Kate to dwell on it. And, without too much discussion, they had agreed to come to the Shaws for Christmas dinner.

Summer had escaped at lunchtime to put her dinner plans into place, though Mel and Delia and Delia's legion of sisters had already started things for her.

She ushered everyone inside, taking coats and accepting a hug from Kate, a kiss on the cheek from Thack.

Never in a million years—even last Christmas when she'd been here with the Shaws, and Mel and Dan had been married—had Summer dreamed her life would be *so* full even a year later. Even her most fantastical dreams couldn't match up to this reality.

She made introductions where introductions needed to be made, and soon everyone had found someone to chat with. Summer snuck away to the dining room to make sure everything had been laid out properly.

"You know it's all going to be amazing, right?"

She glanced up at Thack, who had apparently followed her.

"I just wanted to make sure it was…perfect." She grinned. "But it already is, isn't it?"

Thack nodded. He was wearing a green button-down shirt that made the green of his eyes that much brighter. He was so handsome, and he was hers. *Hers*. This moment truly *was* perfect, no matter what challenges lay ahead of them. "Let's get everyone seated then." She walked over to him, ready to walk out to the living room, but his hand grasped her arm.

"Wait." He nodded toward the ceiling. "Mistletoe."

Summer looked up, but all she saw was the plain white ceiling of the dining room. "What are you talking about? There isn't anything—"

But his mouth closed over hers, and she smiled and leaned into the kiss. A perfect moment she would always,

always cherish. When he pulled away, she grinned up at him. "Sneaky, sneaky. You probably don't need to be sneaky to get a kiss from me."

He grinned right back, that levity she loved seeing in him all over his face. "I'll have to remember that."

Arm in arm, they went back to the living room and guided everyone to their seats around the large, heirloom table. The room was packed to the gills with people, but that somehow made it all the more perfect.

How often Summer had spent lonely holidays with only her mother, or only strangers, or even occasionally all by herself. This was certainly her Christmas miracle.

"I'd like to make a toast." Dad's voice rumbled through the room, garnering curious looks from his children and their spouses.

Though Summer had been moved by Dad's words and gifts, both to her and to Mel and Caleb, she hadn't expected him to engage quite so much. She could see the strain of it in the lines around his mouth, in the bags under his eyes.

But he was doing it anyway, and that made her heart fill more—if that was even possible.

Dad lifted his glass. "To family," he said simply.

It was all that needed to be said. Because here they all were, surrounded by family. Shaws, Sharpes, Rogers, and Lanes. Three generations of strong-willed, flawed, *loved* people.

"To family," Summer repeated with everyone else. She clinked her glass with everyone she could reach, and underneath the table she linked hands with Thack.

She looked around at the smiling faces, her siblings and their spouses, her niece dozing in Mel's lap, Kate all but bouncing in her seat next to the grandparents she so deserved to get to know. Mrs. Bart and Mr. Lane smiling happily at each other.

Family. Love. Hope. *Happiness*.

A Christmas miracle, indeed.

About the Author

Nicole Helm writes down-to-earth contemporary romance specializing in people who don't live close enough to neighbors for them to be a problem. When she's not writing or taking care of her two rambunctious boys, she spends her time dreaming about someday owning a barn. Visit her at www.nicolehelm.wordpress.com.

Rebel Cowboy

Book 1 in the Big Sky Cowboys Series

by Nicole Helm

***

Under a big sky

For hotshot NHL star Dan Sharpe, hockey isn't just his job—it's his everything. But when claims of cheating get him bounced from the ice, he finds himself feeling lost. Everyone thinks he's crazy for taking on his grandfather's ramshackle Montana ranch, but, hey, he's Dan Sharpe: How hard can it be?

As it turns out? Plenty hard.

Mel Shaw has been fighting tooth and nail to keep her family from falling apart. The last thing she needs is a distraction, but taking a job as some city slicker's consultant may be her only chance to save the land she loves. She never expected someone like Dan to come roaring into her life, and it doesn't take long for Mel to realize this hockey star turned cowboy has the power to upend her carefully ordered world—and heart—for good.

***

"Full of emotion, a little heat, and some great banter."
—*Long and Short Reviews* on *Flight Risk*

For more Nicole Helm, visit:

www.sourcebooks.com

Outlaw Cowboy

Big Sky Cowboys

by Nicole Helm

—⁓—

BIG SKY TROUBLE

Ever since his father's accident, Caleb Shaw vowed he'd mend his wild ways, and he means to keep his word. He's a changed man. A better man. And he knows he should want absolutely nothing to do with his crazy old life…or the maddening temptation that is Delia Rogers.

Delia's been stealing her sisters away from their violent father ever since she was old enough to fight back. But now, with the police on her trail and all her bridges burned, there's nowhere left to run but back into the arms of the one man she knows she shouldn't need. Caleb has always been too good for her, no matter how bad he claimed to be. Yet when close quarters turn into something more, Delia and Caleb are forced to decide what really matters: mending their reputations or healing their wary hearts…

—⁓—

Praise for *Rebel Cowboy*:

"Plenty of sexual tension and scintillating love scenes… A true page-turner." —*Publishers Weekly*

"A beautifully crafted romance."
—*USA Today Happy Ever After*

For more Nicole Helm, visit:
www.sourcebooks.com

How to Wrangle a Cowboy

Cowboys of Decker Ranch

by Joanne Kennedy

—◊◊◊—

A city girl whose love for her inherited ranch won't pay off a mountain of debt...

A rugged ranch foreman raising his little boy all by himself...

Amid the exhilarating scent of hay and sagebrush under the wide-open sky, these two tenderhearted, stubbornly idealistic people face conditions they can't control. Going toe-to-toe against each other won't get the job done. At the end of the day, Lindsey Ward and Shane Lockhart can only make the right choices if they make them together...

—◊◊◊—

Praise for *Joanne Kennedy*:

"When it comes to capturing the appeal and feel of the west, nobody does it better." —*Booklist*

"Absolutely perfect." —*Fresh Fiction* for *Cowboy Fever*

"Kennedy's characters are sexy, smart, troubled, flawed—real. If you are a fan of Western romances, Joanne Kennedy should be at the top of your list of favorites." —*Fresh Fiction*

For more Joanne Kennedy, visit:
www.sourcebooks.com

Reckless in Texas

Texas Rodeo

by Kari Lynn Dell

———

Texas Homecoming

Violet Jacobs is fearless. At least, that's what the cowboys trusting her to snatch them from under the hooves of bucking bulls think. Outside the ring, she's got plenty of worries rattling her bones: her young son, her mess of a love life, and lately, her family's struggling rodeo. When she takes business into her own hands and hires on a hotshot bullfighter, she expects to start a ruckus, but she never expected Joe Cassidy. Rough-and-tumble, cocky and charming, Joe's everything a superstar should be—and it doesn't take a genius to figure out he's way out of Violet's league.

Joe came to Texas to escape a life spiraling out of control. He never planned on sticking around, and he certainly never expected to call this dry and dusty backwater *home*. But Violet is everything he never realized he was missing, and the deeper he's pulled into her beautiful mess of a family, the more he realizes this fierce rodeo girl may be offering him the one thing he could never find on his own…

———

Praise for Kari Lynn Dell:

"An extraordinarily gifted writer." —Karen Templeton, three-time RITA award-winning author

For more Kari Lynn Dell, visit:

www.sourcebooks.com